PRAISE FOR *THE FANDOM*

'[A] glorious epic ode to fan culture . . . For fans of
Fangirl and *Caraval*.'
BUZZFEED

'Compulsive, intricate and genre-busting: I devoured
The Fandom in one sitting. I am most definitely a fan.'
KIRAN MILLWOOD HARGRAVE

'I couldn't put it down, and honestly, I can't wait to pick it back up.
Utterly compulsive, relentlessly paced, and cleverly plotted.'
MELINDA SALISBURY

'Pacy writing and a really compelling, twisty plot . . .
One to watch out for.'
THE BOOKSELLER

'The power of *The Fandom* is real.'
MAGGIE HARCOURT

'Gripping, witty and full of plot twists, this book is a love
letter to the strength and heart of fandom.'
LUCY SAXON

'Hugely enjoyed this fantastic book full of adventure,
friendship, family, and of course . . . fandoms!'
KATHERINE WEBBER

'*The Fandom*, which feels particularly fresh, combines adventure,
humour and heart to create a story that pushes you to the
edge of your seat and keeps you there as it hurtles towards
its epic conclusion. It's already one of my all-time favourite
YA reads, and a definite recommendation for anyone
in search of something a little bit different.'
CATHERINE DOYLE

'With a startli̶̶̶ ̶̶̶ ̶̶ ̶̶ ̶̶ ̶̶ ̶̶ ̶̶tive, and a
li̶̶ ̶̶̶ ̶̶ ̶ ̶̶ms

A MESSAGE FROM CHICKEN HOUSE

Violet, Alice, Katie and Nate face the very real consequences of fan fiction in this dramatic and pacy sequel. They left a burgeoning utopia – but now, the story is continued by a mysterious writer online . . . and it's turning dark. Alice is the only one able to find the rogue writer and save the lives of her friends, trapped in a story that's trying to kill them. Hold on tight: this is a heart-pounding roller coaster of a thriller from Anna Day – and watch out for a TV series in the making!

BARRY CUNNINGHAM
Publisher
Chicken House

THE FANDOM RISING

ANNA DAY

Chicken House

2 Palmer Street, Frome, Somerset BA11 1DS
www.chickenhousebooks.com

Text © Anna Day 2019
From an original idea by Angela McCann
© The Big Idea Competition Limited

First published in Great Britain in 2019
Chicken House
2 Palmer Street
Frome, Somerset BA11 1DS
United Kingdom
www.chickenhousebooks.com

Anna Day has asserted her right under the Copyright, Designs and
Patents Act 1988 to be identified as the author of this work.

Cover design and interior design by Helen Crawford-White
Barbed wire image © Karina Vegas/Arcangel
Typeset by Dorchester Typesetting Group Ltd
Printed and bound in Great Britain by CPI Group (UK) Ltd, Croydon CR0 4YY

The paper used in this Chicken House book is made
from wood grown in sustainable forests.

1 3 5 7 9 10 8 6 4 2

British Library Cataloguing in Publication data available.

ISBN 978-1-911490-08-1
eISBN 978-1-911490-76-0

For Mum and Dad

PROLOGUE

In less than a week, my brother will die. I've said these words to myself over and over, yet somehow they don't seem real. Because while Nate lies in that hospital bed, laced up with tubes, chest rising and falling, there's still hope I can save him. Even if it means doing the thing I fear the most: returning to that God-awful place.

1

VIOLET

Alice looks at the list on my desk. 'I can't believe you wrote a list, it's ages until uni. You're such a planner.'

I swipe the sheet of paper from beneath her nose, annoyed at myself for leaving it in plain sight, especially with the words 'Jumbo tampons' scrawled at the bottom. 'Lists stop me worrying so much, you know that.' I'm starting university in September and I'm bricking it. This is the twenty-fifth list I've made, and it's only July.

'What's there to worry about?' Alice says. 'We'll know each other and we're totally going to hit freshers' week.' Her mouth slides into a half-smile. 'Especially armed with those jumbo tampons.'

But I can tell she's bricking it too. The skin around her eyes tightens and she fiddles with her hair.

Katie lounges on my bed, clutching her iPad and scrolling through *NME*. 'I hope it's more than jumbo tampons you'll be introducing to your vagina this year, Violet.'

'Will you stop with all this virgin crap,' I say. 'It's like being back at school.' I tug the curtains shut, hiding the remnants of dusk, hoping my friends will take the hint and leave so I can go to bed. Since the weird dreams stopped – the ones featuring the strange old woman with apple-green eyes – I've been binge

3

sleeping. It's been so good, not feeling tired all the time.

Katie laughs, the freckles on her nose widening with her smile. 'I'm only teasing. I know you're saving yourself.'

'*Some day my prince will come*,' Alice sings in a high-pitched Snow White warble.

'I don't want a prince,' I say. 'I want the exact opposite, an anti-prince, someone real and honest . . .' I tail off before those familiar images worm their way into my brain again, images which confuse the hell out of me, stirring up my insides with a muddle of excitement, fear and longing. Images of feathers bursting into the air, eyes the colour of winter, black hair against translucent skin.

Alice spins in my swivel chair, clearly bored now *Queer Eye* has finished. 'Well, freshers' fair will be awash with teenage boys lacking in personal hygiene and social graces. You'll find your anti-prince there.' Her phone pings. She pulls it from her pocket and starts tapping and swiping, her nails clacking against the screen.

'Do you think it will be weird?' Katie asks. 'What with us being a year older than everyone else.'

'Nah.' I perch on the foot of my bed. 'There'll be loads of students who took gap years.'

'Can we call it a gap year?' Katie asks.

'We can call it what we want,' I reply.

'Fred,' she says. 'Can we call it Fred?'

I laugh. 'You're bonkers. No wonder you're in therapy.' It jumps out of my mouth before my brain can stop it. But fortunately, Katie doesn't take offence. I would hate her to think I'm mocking her for seeing a therapist. She has nightmares and flashbacks, that's all she's told us. Though we all know why, we just try not to talk about the super-sized elephant slumbering in the corner.

All three of us sat our A levels late, somehow passed, and took a year out. Alice and I were approached by a publisher right after we woke from our comas – the combination of her fan-fiction popularity and the media attention surrounding the incident at Comic-Con, I suppose. We co-wrote and published *The Gallows Song*, sequel to *The Gallows Dance*, in record time. It gave us the excuse we needed to hide in our rooms and dream about Nate, alive and well.

I glance at our novel's jacket, framed and hanging on the wall behind a frowning Alice so that it looks like a rectangular thought bubble sprouting from her head. The book's cover always reminds me of Nate, or more precisely, the *loss* of Nate. Not that he's dead. But it sometimes feels like he's in some halfway house, stopped at the motorway services between destinations. Life . . . over-priced refreshment break . . . death. And it reminds me how stupid I was, actually believing that creating a character in his likeness would somehow breathe life into his waxy, half-dead body. So every time I look at that jacket, I get a double whammy. Nate's loss. My stupidity. I only leave it up because it was a gift from my parents.

'Do you think people will know who we are?' I ask Katie.

'Of course they will,' she says. 'You both wrote a bestseller, and Anime Alice here has shagged Russell Jones.'

'I bloody wish,' Alice mutters, still scowling at her phone.

Katie laughs, sweeping her red hair over a shoulder. She's grown her bob out and it really suits her. '*We* know that. But the rest of the world doesn't.'

5

Alice looks up, fixing us with her inky-blue eyes. 'I stood next to him at Comic-Con. Once. Unless he has a super-stealthy, bendy knob, I can't quite see how that would work.' She returns to her screen.

'Now there's a headline,' I say. *'His knob was so stealthy, it didn't even rustle.'*

'Ha!' Katie says. 'Good one. You're going to walk this creative writing degree, both of you. I don't know why you're bothering, you've already written a best-seller.'

'To feel normal, I guess,' I say.

We fall quiet. My words nudge a little too close to the strangeness we went through last year.

Alice sighs, shoving her phone in her back pocket. She looks like she'd quite happily punch someone.

'What was that about?' I ask her.

She forces a smile. 'Nothing.'

I immediately know it's a bad review. She always tries to hide them from me, ever since I burst into tears at our first one-star rating. But I've grown immune to them now. 'It's OK, I can cope.'

'It kind of sucks,' Alice says. 'I mean, they tagged me in it, who even does that?'

I hold out my hand, determined to show how strong I am now.

She stands her ground. 'Seriously, Violet, I don't think you should read this one. It's kind of . . . personal.'

I keep my hand where it is, hovering before her, demonstrating my grit.

She sighs, reluctance weighing down her move-ments as she unlocks her phone and finds the page for me.

My eyes scan the screen. 'Daily Dystopian,' I mutter. 'They reviewed *The Gallows Song* when it was first released.' They're one of these big fan-based websites. They have followers in the six figures, and their shining review really helped our sequel fly.

Alice shrugs. 'I told you it sucked. They've changed us from five stars to one star.'

'Can they do that?' Katie asks, standing beside me so she can read the screen.

'They can do what they want,' Alice replies.

I scan the lines; the grit I so clearly felt rapidly dissolves, turning my insides to slush.

> As you know, we adored Sally King's novel, *The Gallows Dance*, a book in which genetically-enhanced man (the Gems) subjugate non-genetically-enhanced people like you and me (the Imperfects, or the Imps.) We reviewed the sequel, *The Gallows Song* by Alice Childs and Violet Miller, when it was first released and, if you remember, we gave it a big thumbs up. Well, we've since had a reshuffle here at the Daily Dystopia and wanted to update our review. Sadly, it isn't good, folks. *The Gallows Song* is completely off-key and out of tune.

'Oh, you leave music out of this, you two-faced nipple-ache,' Katie says, reading over my shoulder.

> Following the tragic death of Rose, Willow joins forces with some of the other characters from Sally King's much adored novel: Ash, Baba and, of course, Thorn. Well, the tensions within this group run high, resulting in what can only be compared to chain-watching Jeremy Kyle episodes. But some-how, they manage to lead a revolution and overthrow the dastardly Gem President, imprison-ing him somewhere hi-tech and Gem-like. The government is reformed with new players, such as

Willow's dad, and each major city is given an alliance to oversee Imp emancipation. The London alliance is formed by Ash, Willow, Baba and Thorn, which I can only assume paves the way for more Jeremy Kyle magic.

The only breath of fresh air is a new character, Nate. A young Imp with exceptional wit and intelligence, who becomes part of the London alliance. His lack of family is a bit of a well-worn trope, but we loved his fresh take on everything. Sadly, even Nate couldn't save this sequel. And frankly, Miller's attempt to milk her brother's long-term condition left a bad taste in our mouths.

A hurt little noise catches in the back of my throat. Katie squeezes my shoulder, obviously reaching the same bit.

The book ends on a strange open note, a failed attempt at developing a utopia. The sole concrete change is the removal of the Gallows Dance, which was probably the most entertaining part of King's original novel.
In summary, Childs and Miller got rid of all the good bits of dystopia. They essentially took the diss out of dystopia, and left us with soggy nothing. I bet Sally King is turning in her grave right now.

I feel sick, really sick. Alice and I put everything into *The Gallows Song*, we built ourselves back up from our comas word by word. This review feels like I'm standing naked in a huge room and everyone is pointing and laughing. And what they said about Nate, about milking his accident, it makes this black anger rise inside me. 'How could they say that about Nate?' I manage to say, tears brimming in my eyes.

Alice takes the phone from my hand and hugs me. 'Oh balls, I knew this would upset you. Ignore them, Vi. They're just trying to generate conversation, up their views, it'll be someone else they're bashing tomorrow.'

Katie hands me a tissue, and I feel a flush of embarrassment that I'm crying over a crappy review *again*. But Alice was right, this one felt personal.

'It's OK to feel upset,' Katie says. 'Sit with the emotion, go through it, not round it.'

This makes me smile, I love how she comes out with her therapist's lines sometimes. It's like I'm getting second-hand counselling.

'I better get home,' Katie says, gathering up her things and shrugging on her cardigan. 'I'll see you after my cello lesson tomorrow though, yeah?' She pulls me into a hug. 'Review is another word for opinion, you remember that.' An extra squeeze and she's gone, leaving Alice and I alone with the hateful words hanging between us.

Alice's phone pings again. I'd forgotten I was still holding it. I hand it back to her with sweaty, trembling hands.

'Text from Timothy,' she says.

Timothy's our editor. Alice holds up the screen so I can read it too.

Meet me at my office tomorrow,
2 p.m. Very important. I will provide
biscuits.   T x

I check my phone, even though I already know he hasn't texted me too. I briefly wonder if he means for me to go as well, but Alice and I come as a pair, so if he's trying to squeeze me out, he can sod right off. 'Do you think he read the review?'

'Maybe,' she replies.

'Does he really think biscuits will sway us? I swear sometimes he thinks we're five-year-olds.'

She laughs. 'Are you in or out?' Her finger hovers over the screen, itching to tap out a reply.

I can't help noticing that she didn't say, *Are* we *in or out?* which makes me think she's going regardless, so I say, 'In.'

She flashes her beautiful smile. 'It was the biscuits that did it, wasn't it?'

'Every time.'

Her nails frantically click out a sentence.

Agreed. But only if they're bourbons.

A x

'Shall I just meet you there?' she asks. The publisher's office is near the Natural History Museum, and she knows I like the excuse to drift around it, sipping on a latte and pretending I'm with Nate. It was his favourite outing when we were little. He'd stuff his sandy head full of random facts, hoarding them carefully away, only to spout them off at inopportune moments, like when Aunt Maud came for tea and learnt all about the mating rituals of Pigmy hippos. *Pigmy hippos.* Funny how the airy ceilings and cool walls of that museum fill me with warmth, yet my own book, *The Gallows Song*, leaves me hollow on the inside and cold all over. One day I'll figure it out.

I nod. 'Yeah, I'll meet you outside. Don't go up without me though, the receptionist hates me.'

'Don't sweat it, that bitch hates everyone.' She blows me a kiss and says, 'Sleep tight, and promise me you won't read that poisonous gobshite again.'

I blow her one back. 'I promise.'

2

ALICE

I'm hogging the only full-length mirror in Karen Millen, pressing a lavender dress against me. It's Mum's birthday in a few weeks and I want to buy her something she'll love, something that will make her fling her arms around my neck, exclaiming, 'Oh Alice, you're the best daughter in the whole wide world!' The birds will sing, rainbows will fill the sky . . . you get the idea. We're about the same build and we've got the same colouring; she actually calls me her 'Mini-me'. If it looks OK on me, it'll look OK on Mum. Problem is, it doesn't look OK on me. It drains my skin and emphasizes my veins.

I catch the shop assistant's eye and she smiles. I look away. I can tell she's thinking I'm a vain cow. That I'm so narcissistic, I may as well gaze into a river until I die. Well, maybe Narcissus was insecure. Maybe Narcissus was thinking how badly his eyebrows needed waxing. Maybe he died longing not for himself, but for a pair of tweezers.

I wander to the till, feeling a little lost. This is the fourth shop I've tried, and I'm yet to find that perfect rainbow-summoning dress. Defeated, I slop it on the counter and offer the assistant my card and a half-arsed smile.

While I'm paying, my phone rings. It's Violet. *'Alice, where are you? Timothy is expecting us in ten minutes.'*

I glance at my watch. 'Shit. Sorry, I'll be there in a sec. Tell him I've got my period or something, you know, make him blush so bad he can't get pissed. Hang on a mo.' I grab the shopping bag and mumble my thanks to the shop assistant. 'OK, I'm just leaving the shops.' I weave my way around the autumn collection and step into the air-conditioned dome of the shopping centre.

'You're *shopping*?' Violet hisses.

'Maybe. Just a bit. But I'm literally minutes away. See you soon, love you.' I slip my phone into my bag.

I pass a group of lads on the escalator. They're practically drooling, but thankfully, they don't say anything. I'm so over the whole man thing. Something about Comaville changed me. Since puberty, I've been defined by my relationship with boys. If I slept with them, I was a slag. If I didn't, I was a prick tease. If I was single, I was fair game. If I was in a couple, I was Alice and *insert name*.

I think I forgot how to be just Alice.

As promised, I arrive at Timothy's office ten minutes later, bang on time. I've already rammed the lavender dress into my handbag so Violet doesn't give me *that* look. She's my bestie and I love her, but sometimes she can sit on the judgey side of sanctimonious.

She sees me and grins, visibly relieved at not having to see Timothy alone. I suddenly feel way less bothered about my inability to find a mother-pleasing dress.

'Good morning,' I say to the sour-faced receptionist.

She offers me a stiff smile. 'Good morning. Timothy is ready to see you.'

Timothy's oak-panelled office always reminds me of the inside of a coffin. A grand, luxurious coffin, but a coffin all the same. A shiver creeps up my spine even though it's so hot I could fry an egg on his desk.

He sees us and beams. 'Darlings,' he says, embracing us each in turn. He pretends he's late twenties, but me and Violet reckon he's closer to forty. There's a full-on dad bod hidden beneath that designer shirt, and Violet said she once made out the beginnings of a comb-over.

'It's so wonderful to see you both, please, do sit.' He gestures to a cluster of leather chairs in the corner of his office, right next to the ceiling-tall bookshelves. One of the shelves is a reconditioned grand piano, tipped on to its side, strings and hammers replaced with rows upon rows of books. It looks like the kind of pretentious crap my parents would buy.

A tray of coffee and bourbons has been laid out in anticipation of our visit. I sit beside Violet, recline in my chair and push my sunglasses on to my head. The key with Timothy is to act cool, to never show your weaknesses. Masks matter, that's what Dad always says. The impression you give the world defines you, and once you let that mask slip, there's no going back.

Timothy sits opposite us. 'Alice, you look amazing.' His smile is so bleached I consider replacing my shades. 'When *The Gallows Song* is turned into a film we must see that you're an extra, a Gem, obviously. It will drum up some lovely publicity for you.'

I smile politely. We all know the offer is futile; Violet and I have barely left the house in a year and now we're starting university degrees.

He looks at Violet. 'And Violet, my sweet Parma Violet, how's that brother of yours?'

'No change,' she says.

I squeeze her hand. Mostly for her benefit, but also for mine. I miss Nate so much, it makes my stomach ache.

Timothy's smile melts into an expression of sympathy. 'I'm sorry to hear that, really, I am.'

The puppy-dog eyes vanish and he switches to business mode so seamlessly it's a little unnerving. 'So . . . I asked you here to discuss something very important, something I didn't want to put in an email.' He picks up the coffee pot, ready to pour, but stops just at the crucial moment. 'Your next book,' he says.

Excitement fizzes in my stomach. 'Oh yes. Violet and I have had a few ideas. One of our mates plays the cello and we thought an orchestra might be a good backdrop—'

He laughs. 'No, no. The next book in *The Gallows Dance* trilogy.'

Violet and I stare at each other. An expression crosses her features which I can't quite place. Book three is a sore point for her. I've never worked out why, but with Nate in a coma and her parents close to a meltdown, I haven't pushed it.

I wait for her response, aware that this is her battle, but when she freezes, I step in. 'It isn't a trilogy.'

He hands me a cup of coffee. It's really bloody hot, but I'll be damned if I let him see how bad it burns.

He watches me. 'Come now, Alice. This is dystopia. Bad things happen in threes.'

Violet finds her voice, even though it shakes slightly. 'There isn't going to be a third book. It was written as the last part of a duology, you know that. It's why we called it *The Gallows Song*, because it sounded a bit like swansong. Alice and I left the characters in a world they'd want to live in. A world *Nate* would want to live in. I know it sounds crazy.'

Timothy widens his eyes like he's dying to shout: *Hell yes, crazy lady.*

'There's nothing crazy about wanting a happy ending,' I say.

Violet throws me a grateful smile.

'At least hear me out,' Timothy says, clapping his hands together. '*The Gallows Song* has only been out a couple of months, but it's already an international success. You turned a dystopia into a utopia. But there's one small problem.' He sips his coffee, giving him the excuse to leave a dramatic pause. 'Utopias suck.'

'I beg your pardon,' Violet says. She sometimes does that when she's taken aback, ages fifty years and sounds like my gran.

'It's a fact,' he says. 'I take it you saw that review yesterday. I mean, the Daily Dystopia is one of our biggest platforms, we need to take heed.'

'Review is just another word for opinion,' Violet says, channelling Katie's fight.

He raises an eyebrow. 'But they've got a point. The world is a scary place, our futures are full of uncertainty. Sales of *1984* and *The Handmaid's Tale* are through the roof for a reason. Readers don't want an unattainable, fairy-tale ending which can never be achieved, they want a book which explores their fears, reflects their concerns, captures the current milieu.' He picks up a plate and shoves it in front of Violet's face. 'Biscuit?'

'Uh, no thanks,' she says.

I take the plate from his hand and place it back on the table. Nobody force-feeds my bestie. 'Did you rehearse that speech in front of the mirror, Timothy?' I ask, my tone clipped.

'Several times. Was it that obvious, my darlings?' He always does this. Wraps up bad news in charm, like little shit parcels. You undo the big red bow, carefully fold back the tissue paper, only to discover a turd. 'Our researchers have been tracking your Fandom carefully online, trawling through chatrooms, fanfic, bloggers and vloggers and so on. Everything points to the exact same thing.' He stands and walks to the piano-shelf. I can make out the dark hairs shaved close against his chin. 'The Fandom is hungry. And when something is hungry, what's the obvious thing to do?'

'Feed it,' I say.

He nods. 'And this Fandom seems to want a healthy portion of conflict.'

Violet speaks out. 'OK, so the world's scary, but surely that means the readers want something good to hold on to. That's why fairy tales were so popular in difficult times, they promised a better life filled with love and friendship and comfort. They gave people hope.'

He begins to pull books from the shelf. 'You're talking about stories written for infants, Violet. Your Fandom is predominantly young adult.' He places the books on the table, fanning them out with one smooth motion so I can read the covers. *Divergent. A Clockwork Orange. The Handmaid's Tale. 1984. The Hunger Games.* 'Young adults want paranoia, because Big Brother *is* watching them. They want violence and retribution, because that's what they see in the media every day. They want sex, because their bodies are overflowing with urges and hormones.' Finally, he pulls out *The Gallows Dance* by Sally King and places it on the top of the pile, triumphant. 'They want *this*. Tragedy, passion, loss . . . that's why the Daily Dystopian changed their rating, my darlings; they were feeding the beast. And *you* need to do the same.'

'But we told you,' Violet says, her voice a little shrill. 'We told you right from the start we would only write one book. You promised us that would be it.' All of the colour has drained from her face. *Why does this matter to her so much?* I need to find out, but now is not the time; she looks like she's about to puke.

16

Timothy breathes out, long and slow. 'Look, why don't you come to Comic-Con on Saturday. I'm doing a panel with Russell Jones, the actor who plays Willow.'

'We know who Russell Jones is,' I snap.

Timothy ignores me. 'Come and meet your Fandom, sign some books . . . think about what that third book would mean to your readers. Comic-Con is, well . . . it's where the Fandom is at its strongest.'

Just the thought of going back to Comic-Con makes my heart race and my head spin. It makes me think of earth tremors and waking up in hospital one week later. It makes me think of Nate still sleeping. And it makes me think of . . . of . . . things I can't even begin to make sense of. Things which gnaw at the edges of my dreams and bring tears to my eyes from the sheer effort of NOT thinking about them.

No. I can never go back to Comic-Con.

I put my shades back on, just in case I'm tearing up, and stand from my chair. Then, pushing back my shoulders and summoning my best 'screw-you' voice, I say, 'Look, Timothy, Comic-Con is absolutely out of the question. And if you need to ask either of us why, then frankly, you are not entitled to call yourself a human being.' I'd planned a dramatic exit, head held high, Violet beside me mentally giving him the finger. But the desk blocks my way.

He takes the opportunity to clasp my palm in his dry, steady hands. 'Please do think about it, my darlings.' And just before we leave, he drops a final, parting shit-bomb on us from a great height. 'You're both so talented and I would hate to have to ask another of my authors to write it.'

3
ALICE

Violet and I walk back to the tube station in silence. My body feels heavy and my brain aches. Even the hum of central London doesn't cheer me up.

Finally, Violet speaks. 'Surely he can't let someone else write the third book. I mean, we invented new characters for God's sake, a whole new plot line. He can't just give it to someone else to build on. Wouldn't it be theft?'

'You'd think so.'

'What did the contract say?' she asks.

I remember the contract well. Violet was so cut up about Nate, she left all the legal stuff to me. I had Olivia, our agent, look over it. She said it was fair, that someone else could write the sequel if the publishers and Sally King's estate wanted. The concept wasn't ours.

I swallow down an unfamiliar bitter taste. 'Dunno. Bloody agents, hey? They're worse than editors.'

'Maybe we should talk to Olivia,' she says.

Panic flickers in my chest. 'Does it matter now? It is what it is.'

'But there must never be a third book, Alice. It doesn't matter who writes it. I can't explain it, but I feel like the world of the Gallows Dance should be left alone. We wrote them a lovely ending, regardless of what that bastard review said. It was an ending filled with hope

18

and possibilities, and now they're free to live their lives.'

The passion in her voice unsettles me. *Why does this matter to her so much?* She said she can't explain it. And truth is, I'm afraid to ask. Afraid to pick at those unanswered questions. Afraid to pick at that scab. I up my pace, the concrete reassuringly hard beneath my heels. 'Violet, I know you get pissy when I say this, but they're just characters. Even Nate. Sure, we based him on your little brother, but that was because we knew how chuffed he'd be when he woke up.'

'Yes, well, in case you hadn't noticed, he hasn't woken up yet.'

It feels like she's punched me. 'Of course I've noticed.' I drop my voice. 'I love him too.'

We turn a corner and the tube sign comes into view.

'I know you do.' She touches my hand, her voice softening. 'Sorry.'

I sling an arm around her narrow shoulders and hug her against me. 'It's OK. We both miss him, it makes everything a bit . . . raw.' My eyes struggle to adjust to the lack of light as we drop down the steps into the tube station. I leave my shades on all the same.

'I still think we should ring Olivia,' she says. 'Just to make sure Timothy isn't bluffing.'

Oh crap, oh crap. That bitter taste is back. Maybe it's my conscience, repeating on me like a bitch. *I should have told her about the contract.* We reach the bottom of the steps and I catch her by the hands so we face each other. I take a deep breath and force myself to speak. 'He isn't bluffing, Violet.'

Her face drops. 'You knew about this? You knew someone else could write the sequel if we refused?' She looks like she did when she was four years old, getting knocked into the prickly hedge outside nursery again and again by Gary Walsh. Too hurt to even cry. Back then, it was me who saved her, me who scared away the bad guys. This time, I'm Gary Walsh. Worse, I'm the pigging hedge.

'Olivia said there wasn't much we could do about it.' My voice sounds cold, which is strange because my chest burns red hot with the effort of holding back the tears.

'Well, you could have told me,' she says.

'And what would you have done?'

'I don't know. But I would have at least *tried* to get the contract changed.' She begins to walk again. I don't think she's freezing me out, she just can't bear to look at me.

'I didn't think it was a big deal,' I say, catching her up.

'You knew it was a big deal to me.' She suddenly stops, as though a terrible thought has smacked her round the head. 'Did you plan this?'

'What do you mean?'

'You knew the threat of someone else writing the third book would make me agree to write it.' She slaps her bank card on to the reader.

Wow. Another punch in the gut. 'Jeez, Violet. I'm not some evil mastermind.'

We reach the platform. The grumble of an approaching train creeps through the soles of my Jimmy Choos.

She gazes at the open mouth of the tunnel. 'I don't believe you,' she whispers.

The air begins to stir, lifting my hair from my neck. And suddenly, Violet doesn't look like Violet any more. She looks like every other girl who judges me on the height of my heels. Anger swirls in my stomach. I grab her arm, forcing her to look at me. 'Why are you even my friend? You clearly think I'm a cow.'

She's looks as mad as I feel. Her jaw bone sticks out and her nostrils flare. The train approaches and the wind chucks her hair around her face. She's in full-on Carrie mode. Thank God there's no crucifix nearby. She shouts over the din, 'So if I refuse, will you write another sequel without me?'

The carriage windows ripple past as the train pulls alongside us. I see my own face gazing back at me from the windows. Mascara-stained tears run from beneath my sunglasses. Dad would not approve, but I'm past caring. 'Of course not, how could you even think that?'

'Because you've betrayed me before,' she screams.

Her words stun us both. We stand still, jostled by the tourists getting on and off the train.

'When?' I say. 'What are you on about?'

She shakes her head quickly. Carrie has officially left the building and Violet looks completely lost. Bewildered. I'm about to ask her again, but she wriggles from my grip and steps into the tide of passengers, allowing herself to get swept through the carriage doors.

I don't follow her. 'When?' I mouth at her through the window.

She stands close to the door, gripping the yellow pole like it's the only thing real in her life.

'Violet, when?' I mouth.

But the train pulls away and she doesn't even look at me.

VIOLET

That night, I dream of the strange old lady again.

I stand in an orchard. It's filled with leaves and gold light and the thick scent of summer. The branches

21

waver above me and a changing web of lights and darks crosses my skin. I'm just starting to think how familiar this place is, when I see the old lady again. She has her back to me, and when she turns, I see just how green her eyes are.

She blinks slowly. *'Violet, my child. It's so good to see you again.'*

'Where have you been?' I ask. When I first woke from the coma, she visited me most nights, talking in gentle tones, calming my nightmares. But it's been months since I've seen her.

She smiles. *'You haven't needed me for a while, my child.'*

Without warning, the sky darkens, clouds gelling together to form a grey, dense canopy which sucks any warmth from the air. She moves far quicker than her old body should allow, grabbing my wrists and squeezing hard. The strength in her fingers surprises me.

I suppress a yelp. *'You're hurting me.'*

But she doesn't stop. *'There must never be a third book, Violet. You and Alice excelled yourselves, you gave us back our freedom, in more ways than one. You broke the loop, and finally we're happy.'*

'It's just a book,' I say, trying to wrench myself free.

'Do you really think that?' Rain spots her face.

My wrists crack. I twist my arms, pumping them back and forth, trying to shake her off, but she's too strong, and eventually, I fall still.

I trace her line of sight and find myself looking up, through leaves and twigs and fruit towards the angry sky. What is it about this place? I've been here before. I get the feeling I'm reaching deep into my memories, leaning as far as I dare over a pool of confusing sounds and smells and images, and yet still, there's something just beyond my grasp – something of vital importance, some missing puzzle piece. *Is it just a book?* I shake my head. *'No. It's more than that.'*

Her mouth yawns open – I can just make out the shape of her teeth under her gums. *'It feels like things have already started to turn, like the winds have changed and there's nothing I can do about it.'* The breeze lifts her hair and shakes her skirt, carrying on it the scent of lilies and woodsmoke.

'What do you mean?' I ask. The clouds collapse beneath their own weight, releasing a torrent of water. My clothes stick to my skin within seconds.

'My powers are not what they were,' she shouts, her voice struggling to overpower the thwack of rain against earth. *'Nate's safe, at least for now. But I sense trouble ahead, trouble in both worlds.'*

And just before my head reels, just before the colours of the orchard melt into the quiet hues of my bedroom, she lays her hands on my sodden temples and says: *'It's time for you to remember, Little Flower.'*

I wake with a start, covered in sweat, heart thrumming, ears ringing, one singular thought clear in my brain: *The old woman is Baba.*

Not book-Baba or film-Baba. Not some fictitious character. Actual, real-life, air-breathing, thought-sucking, riddle-talking Baba.

I sit bolt upright, heaving in mouthfuls of air.

Baba's real.

Of course she is. It seems so obvious now. I remember her soft, doughy skin, her gummy smile, the ache of her palms as they rested on my temples.

Baba's real.

Then it hits me.

'The Gallows Dance is real,' I whisper. It sounds ridiculous, so I say it again, this time louder. *'The*

23

Gallows Dance is real.' I fling back my duvet, my sweat-drenched pyjamas transforming from cotton to cling film. 'I was there.' And for the first time since I woke from that coma, thinking doesn't feel like swimming through porridge. That patchwork of disjointed pictures, sounds and aromas begins to knit into something meaningful and seamless.

A map.

No. More than that.

A story.

My story – with climaxes and twists, loss and joy, terror and betrayal.

I remember *everything*.

Rose died. I took her place. I fell for the boy with eyes the colour of winter. *Ash is real*, I think to myself. *Ash is real.*

I try to stand, but instead sink into my carpet.

'I ate a rat,' I tell my bedside rug.

I see the Duplicates, so clear in my mind's eye, the space where almost-Willow's legs should have been. I see a scythe, raised high and glinting in the sun. *Nate nearly lost his hands.* I rotate my own wrists, seeing my veins as if for the first time. I feel the scratch of the twigs on my skin as I climbed that bastard tree, see bronzed limbs wrapped together – Alice slept with Willow. *I knew she'd betrayed me.* I see the cerise light of the Meat House, inhale the scent of roasting flesh, caught in the blaze of a Gem helicopter. And I hear the unforgiving bleat of the flatline, Nate bleeding out on my lap, his taupe eyes gazing at the stars. *The bullet wound. I always said there was something special about that scar.* I touch my stomach, the place where Nate was shot, and tears spill down my face. Suddenly, I can feel those twisting metal tentacles wrenching me from the river. I met President Stoneback. He told me about the infinite loop. The Fandom.

'Sweet Jesus,' I whisper. 'The Fandom. The collective conscious. They made it *real*.'

I stood on the gallows with a noose around my neck.

'I love you too,' I whisper to my bedroom walls, my fingers grazing my split-heart necklace. Alice sacrificed everything for me.

And then I fell.

I died.

My eyes fall upon the framed cover of *The Gallows Song*. It all makes perfect sense. Baba brought me into their universe so I would return to ours and write a pro-Imp sequel, breaking the loop and allowing the Imps to prevail. I start to laugh, only vaguely aware of how unhinged I must look, kneeling on my carpet, snot pouring from my nose, chuckling to myself.

But I don't care. Because if the Fandom created an alternate universe, if *The Gallows Dance* is real, then everything Alice and I wrote in *The Gallows Song* is real too.

I wrap my arms around myself, afraid to let myself believe in case I'm wrong.

Somewhere far, far away, my little brother is awake and well.

4
ALICE

All the way home, her words play in my head. *You've betrayed me before.* What did she mean? We've both done some shit in the past, when we were younger and figuring stuff out, but nothing which left a scar. Nothing I expected to be thrown at me years later. And I've never *betrayed* her. I've never sold her out, tweeted her biggest secret or stolen her boyfriend.

I walk up the drive. My house always manages to look hard and blockish in the sun. It looks way better in the winter, maybe because it's used to cold temperatures. Speaking of which, Mum lounges in the kitchen, magazine propped open against a bottle of fizz. It's early to be drinking, even for her. She's wearing a Calvin Klein shirt-dress and she's curled her hair. She looks lovely. And suddenly, I'm so proud of being her Mini-me, it makes my chest sting.

'Hey,' she says, not looking up.

'Hey,' I reply.

'Your father's working late so I've ordered in sushi.'

'Thanks,' I say, grabbing a juice from the fridge.

She scowls at the glass in my hand. I'm about to get another lecture about sugar, or maybe it's fruit acids this time, but the lavender material poking out of my handbag saves me. She has a sixth sense when it comes to shopping.

'Buy anything nice?' she asks.

26

I shrug, pretending to be all casual. 'Only your birthday present.'

'Please tell me it isn't clothes. You always get my size wrong.'

A fake smile erupts across my face. 'No, no. Course not.' I down my juice. Then pour a second glass and down that too, but I still can't shift that bitter taste.

'Alice? Are you OK?' Mum asks.

'I'm fine.'

'You don't look fine.'

'I'm fine, really.'

I've discovered if I say it enough, I start to believe it. And I think, because I look fine, people just accept it. *Well, of course she's fine. She's wearing Gucci and she's clearly exfoliated.*

Well, I'm not fine. Not today. Today, I feel like I've been turned inside out.

First Violet, then *this*.

I run upstairs and stuff the dress in the bin.

I wake to the ping of my phone. Violet's name lights up the screen. My head thrums with relief. I open up her message, still blinking the sleep from my eyes.

Emergency meeting, 9 a.m., Frank's
cafe x

There's a kiss. Praise the Lord, there's a kiss. I message back immediately.

If I haul my ass out of bed, will you
forgive me for being such a dick
about the contract? x

My nail taps impatiently against the screen, counting the milliseconds before she replies with two messages seconds apart.

No, but I'll buy you a coffee x

Though I can't promise not to spit in it

Katie is next to jump on the group chat in her own inimitable style:

You've just woken me up, dick
cheese!

I bite my lip, typing out the words: *When did I betray you?* My finger hovers over the send button. But I'm too scared to start picking. That scab is holding back a flood of something terrifying, I just know it. I delete the message, suddenly feeling very fragile.

I pull on a pair of jeans and apply my favourite red lipstick, praying it will awaken the warrior inside. It doesn't, so I creep downstairs. The fear of waking my parents stops me using the bathroom; I can't face them this early. I grab my bag, not even pausing for a quick juice. I'm about to pull on my heels when Mum appears at the top of the stairs, wrapped in her silk kimono. Dammit.

'Where you off to so early?' she asks.

'I'm meeting Violet and Katie for breakfast.' I fiddle with my shoes, which have no laces or buckles, so it's a fairly obvious avoidance tactic.

She pads down the stairs towards me, her pedicured feet coming into view. 'I thought you girls only did brunch?'

I look up and fix a smile on my face. 'We're practising for uni. We can't lie in for ever.'

'Nude face and red lipstick?' she says.

I reply with a grunt.

'Do you want a quick cappuccino before you go?' she asks. 'I can fire up the machine.'

Mum rarely fixes coffee. Maybe she found the

lavender dress stuffed in the bathroom bin like I hoped she would. The temptation to accept coffee and have her actually mother me is overwhelming, but after the bizarre row with Violet, her accusation of betrayal, I want to be on time for a change. 'No thanks, Mum, I'll get one there.'

She shrugs, and heads back to her room without so much as a goodbye.

I arrive at Frank's place at nine. We often come here before visiting Nate, pooling our courage and filling up on coffee. Violet stands at the counter ordering our drinks. She looks wired, like she's already had several hits of caffeine. She's wearing her split-heart necklace though, so she must have forgiven me.

I stand beside her, too scared to touch her shoulder like I normally would. 'Hey,' I say.

She sees me and smiles. 'Hey.' Her hair is wild and she obviously hasn't showered either, but I haven't seen her looking this full of life in an age. I really want to hug her, but I'm afraid she'll push away.

'Sorry about the contract,' I say. 'I should have told you, I know. It's just you were so bummed about Nate not waking up.' My eyes flick to the café floor as the thought of Nate lying in hospital simmers in my head. 'We all were.'

'Yeah, I'm sorry too. I know you would never write that book without me, I was just . . . really mad.'

I grin. 'You totally hulked out on me.'

She makes a silly growling noise – her best Hulk impression. It makes me laugh. She looks less Carrie and more angry cockapoo. I want to ask her about the betrayal thing, but things are going well and I don't want to rock the boat.

'What's so important?' I ask as we settle into a corner booth.

She sits opposite, straight-backed and concerned. I can tell she's bursting with it, but somehow manages to restrain herself. She swirls the froth of her cappuccino with a wooden stirrer, watching as the sprinkles turn to streaks. 'I want to wait for Katie first.'

'Don't be a tit, you know I hate surprises.'

'Katie first.'

I can't help the irritation as it buzzes through my veins. Before Katie arrived on the scene, Violet would never have made me wait. Right on cue, Katie walks through the door, her easy smile reaching across her face.

She slides into the booth beside me. 'What the Donald Duck, Vi? It's nine in the morning. It's like being back at school.'

'Good morning to you too,' Violet says, sliding a latte over to her.

She sees it and sighs. 'Thanks.' She wriggles out of her cardigan and I notice two dark sweat patches under her arms. She's obviously rushed to get here, braving the early commuters and dashing across London at silly o'clock. One thing we've always had in common; we both love Violet.

'Now can you tell us?' I ask.

'Yeah, what's the big emergency?' Katie says. 'We're still going to visit Nate, yeah?'

Violet nods. 'I just have to tell you something first. Something big.' She takes a deep breath and opens her mouth, then just sits there, frozen and silent.

'Violet? Have you had a stroke?' I say, clicking my fingers in front of her face.

Katie slurps her latte. 'Yeah, stop stalling, woman. Alice is the designated drama queen in our trio.' She winks at me and I can't help but giggle.

Violet shakes her head. 'OK. But do you promise you

won't think I'm mad? Do you swear you'll hear me out?'

'Seriously, you're killing us,' I reply. *What on earth could be so important?* Is she about to pick the scab? I feel like the kid from *The Shining*, watching the lift doors . . . just waiting for the tsunami of blood.

She takes a deep breath. 'So it's been over a year since we woke from our comas . . .'

The word *coma* sounds in my head like an alarm. 'We don't talk about that,' I snap.

'It's the secret rule,' Katie says. 'Don't break the secret rule, Vi, or me and Alice will dump your ass and find another bestie.' Her mouth smiles, but her eyes fill with panic.

'But why don't we talk about it?' Violet pleads.

The coffee turns into something acidic which I can't swallow down. 'Because it's terrifying,' I say. 'We fell unconscious for a week for no medical reason.' I drop my voice, the words painful in my throat. 'What if it happens again?'

Katie cradles her cup with both hands like she's trying to comfort it. 'And Nate, he's still sleeping. It's hardcore.'

Violet leans forwards, an urgent look on her face. 'It's more than that though, isn't it? I mean, yes it's terrifying, but not just because we fell into comas, but because . . . because . . .' She stares into her froth like the right words will suddenly appear, scrawled in chocolate sprinkles. ' . . . We weren't really in comas.'

Katie grabs her hand as if trying to silence her, causing her latte to tip and slop on to the table. She doesn't seem to care. 'Stop it, Violet, please.'

I can't hear this. My head is going to explode.

But Violet doesn't stop. 'Do either of you ever have crazy dreams, or images which flash into your brain? I don't just mean normal everyday stuff, I mean *crazy* stuff. Do you ever remember being . . . *there*.' She whispers the last word.

No, no, no. I can't think about Comic-Con. I can't think about those memories that gnaw at my dreams.

'It's a trauma response,' Katie says, suddenly noticing the spillage. She bundles some napkins into the coffee pool. 'My therapist told me. It's normal after trauma to have strange dreams and flashbacks. Knowing you were in a coma can threaten your sense of safety. It can bring your mortality into sharp focus.' She sounds like she's quoting her therapist word for word, and she continues to mop, even though the table is now completely dry. 'And we were at Comic-Con, filled with *Gallows Dance* stuff, we *met* Russell Jones and Julia Starling, of course *The Gallows Dance* was on our mind.'

Violet slams her hand on the table. 'So you dream of *The Gallows Dance* too?'

Katie stops mopping but continues to stare at the table. 'All the time.'

Violet looks at me. 'Alice?'

I can't hear this.

'Alice?' she repeats.

'Yes,' I croak. 'I have strange dreams too. But Katie's right. It's a trauma response or something.'

'No,' Violet says, her face determined. 'We were *there*. We were in *The Gallows Dance*.'

Katie laughs – a hectic warble. 'Don't be such a twat-puffin.'

I try and sound sure of myself. It takes everything I have. 'Violet, *The Gallows Dance* is *not* real.'

Violet leans forwards in her chair. 'The old lady came to me last night in my dreams, she's visited me before but I didn't know who she was, well, maybe part of me did, but I was in denial like you. It was Baba, Baba from *The Gallows Dance*. She unlocked my

32

memories. Seriously, it was like all those weird images suddenly made sense. When we were unconscious, we were in *The Gallows Dance* for *a week*, trying to put the story right so we could get home.'

There's a long pause. It's like my body has shut down. My brain doesn't work. *I can't hear this. I can't think this.* I glance at Katie, but she looks as freaked as me.

It's the strangest thing to do considering the situation, but my hands take over, rummaging through my handbag and finding my lipstick. I click open my favourite compact, the one with the dragonfly on the back, and slowly reapply. By the time I've finished, my hands are steady and my face feels like it belongs to me again. I slip my things back into my bag and manage a sip of my drink. 'Jesus, Violet,' I eventually say. 'Exactly how much coffee did you drink before we got here?'

Katie forces a laugh. 'It's not the coffee I'm worried about. It's what's in the sugar bowl.'

Violet slumps back in her chair, tears welling in her eyes. 'You know I'm right, you just don't want to sound crazy, or think about how close we came to getting stuck there. But I remember it all. Everything. Katie, you befriended Thorn; at first we thought he fancied you because you look like Ruth, but then you figured out that Ruth was pregnant when she died, and you reminded Thorn of their unborn child. You saved my life, you were so brave.' Tears begin to roll down her face. 'And Alice, you shagged Willow and nearly threw the whole canon off track. That's what I meant when I said you betrayed me, I just didn't know it at the time.'

That's the betrayal? That's what she meant? My stomach flips and my ears start to ring. If I had a safety word, I would be screaming it right about now. But instead I laugh, muttering, 'I think I might remember if I shagged Willow.'

Violet ignores me. 'I was so mad at you, I started to think you'd gone to the dark side completely. But in the end, when Willow chickened out of saying his lines, you said them instead. It was such a beautiful moment, you were awesome.'

Katie looks transfixed. 'And what about you?'

'I took Rose's place,' Violet says. 'I *became* her. But I didn't fall for Willow, I fell for Ash, the anti-prince.'

'You hanged,' Katie whispers, covering her mouth with her hand. 'I saw it. I was standing in a giant cage with some other Imps and you were on a stage with a rope around your neck. The hangman pulled the lever, and . . .' She clasps Violet by the hand. 'I watched you die.'

Violet laughs with relief, that weird laugh people do when they're still crying so they kind of blow tears everywhere. 'Yes. That's right. I had to complete the story so we could travel home.'

Katie starts crying too, and I think we're attracting some attention, laughing and crying and spilling our drinks. And suddenly, I'm not terrified, I'm angry. Not only is Violet talking about the thing we never talk about, Katie is encouraging her. They're not picking at the scab any more, they're ripping open my flesh.

I slam my hands on the table, my body sizzling with rage. 'For Christ's sake, that is enough. What you're saying is simply ludicrous.'

Katie wipes her eyes. 'I don't know, Alice. I sometimes dream about Thorn, and it just feels so real. We were in this strange, orange room together and—'

'Yes, and I sometimes dream about Willow,' I snap. 'But it doesn't mean anything.'

'Stop being so dismissive,' Violet says, my anger clearly infecting her. 'We fell into medically unexplained comas at exactly the same time, stayed unconscious for exactly the same length of time, and nobody knows why we woke up. That in itself sounds crazy, what I'm suggesting is only one step further.'

'It's more than a step. It's a whopping great moon-leap,' I reply.

Katie studies her hands. 'Yeah, Violet. And what about Nate. Why is he still asleep?'

Violet falls quite for a moment, all the fight draining from her face. Eventually, she says, 'You remember the scar on his abdomen?'

We nod.

'It's a bullet wound.'

It's too much. I'm the kid from *The Shining* again, but this time, the lift doors have already opened and the wall of blood is gushing towards me. I rise to my feet, knocking the drinks and trying not to scream. 'I can't listen to any more of this shit.' I dart through the tables, clumsy with anger, knocking into furniture and elbows.

'Alice, please,' Violet calls after me.

I shove through the door. The air feels cool and fresh on my face. I suddenly wish I wasn't wearing heels so I could just run and run and never hear those words again. The Gallows Dance *is real*.

'Alice, wait,' Violet blunders up behind me. 'I'm telling you this for a reason. Baba told me we mustn't write another sequel.' She catches me up and grabs my arm, spinning me so I face her. 'The Fandom in our world created their world. The power of the collective conscious. We created that utopia for a reason, what we wrote in *The Gallows Song* has happened for real. We freed the Imps. If we write another book, a dystopia the way Timothy wants, it'll balls everything up for them. Don't you get it?'

I blink, confused. 'Is that what this about? You're

trying to convince me I'm losing the plot just so you don't have to write another book?'

'Christ, Alice. This really *matters*. These people are real, and you're forgetting something very important.'

'What?'

'We wrote in a new character when we wrote *The Gallows Song*.'

Her words smack me in the face. *I can't hear this. I can't hear this.* I swallow hard. 'Nate,' I manage to whisper.

She looks at me with her big brown eyes. With Nate's big brown eyes. 'Please, Alice. I need your help.'

But because I'm terrified, because I'm in denial, because I don't want to drown in a wave of blood, I walk away.

5

VIOLET

'Let her go,' Katie says from behind me.

I watch Alice walk away. 'You believe me, don't you?' I ask Katie.

'I don't know, Vi. It does sound far-fetched.'

I turn to face her. 'But you saw me on the gallows, you saw me hang.'

'Yeah, I know, and I *do* have a faint memory of Alice jumping on the stage and shouting out . . .'

'"I love you, Violet",' I finish for her.

She studies my face, I mean really studies it. 'I'll talk to Carol about it, see what she says.'

'Carol?'

'My therapist.'

'She'll ask you to pass on her number.'

'Maybe that wouldn't be such a bad idea.'

Instinctively, we begin to walk towards the hospital.

'I'm not having an episode, Katie, I swear it. We were really there. You, me, Alice and Nate, we were in *The Gallows Dance*. Please say you believe me.'

'I don't know what to believe.'

We walk the rest of the way in silence.

There's always this moment before I walk into Nate's ward when I expect his bed to be empty, the sheets pulled taut across the mattress, the machines beside him abandoned and quiet. And next to that smooth, unused bed, I expect to see him. Standing tall, eyes open, smiling. He never is, of course. Maybe it's wishful thinking, but whatever it is, it's a form of self-torture, because as soon as my eyes fall upon his waxy skin and slack face, I can't help but feel the slap of disappointment.

But today, for the first time in over a year, I don't feel disappointed. I feel bloody livid. Because I now know why Nate didn't wake up when Alice, Katie and I did. He died when we were stuck in *The Gallows Dance*. Obviously, I don't know the ins and outs, the scientific explanation. It would probably make my monkey brain explode, as President Stoneback once told me, condescending bastard. But I have a sense of it. When Nate died in *The Gallows Dance*, he died in the real world. The medics brought him back, but they couldn't bring him all the way.

I perch on Nate's bed, my body shaking with emotion. If Nate really is awake and well in an alternate universe, what does that mean for *this* Nate, for the waxy, still boy lying beside me? Could this Nate somehow be linked to the Nate who Alice and I wrote? I study his face, and can't help wondering what's going on in his head; is he dreaming of broken cities and beautiful, symmetrical faces, or is it just a blank nothingness?

I try and match the rhythm of my breath to the rasp of his ventilator – it makes me feel connected to him somehow. He looks older than he did when he got shot, even though his muscles are wasting. His face is perhaps more angular, his cheekbones more pronounced. He was fourteen when he fell into a coma, though he looked about twelve. I remember his fifteenth birthday, only a couple of months after I woke. I baked his favourite chocolate cake, same as every year, and held it beneath his nose in case he could smell it. Then me and my parents, Alice and Katie all sang 'Happy Birthday' in tear-pinched voices. Maybe he really could hear us.

He'll be sixteen soon, so it's hardly surprising he's finally starting to look more like a young man and less like a child. It's just such a shame he isn't awake to see it; he always hated the fact he looked so young. I know the kids at school used to call him 'titch', or if they were feeling mean, 'the pubeless wonder'. I touch his cheek. It's only a bit fuzzy, but he definitely needs a shave. I'll ask the nurse if I can do it later.

I'd hoped that seeing Nate would bring clarity, would allow me to see how the whole alternate universe thing would affect him. But I'm still clueless. Disappointment and frustration combine to form a heavy, leaden feeling throughout my body.

'Are you OK?' Katie asks. Her hand on my shoulder pulls me from my thoughts.

I can't figure this out on my own, I need her to remember too. I quickly check the nurse has gone – she has – so I pull back the sheets and lift up Nate's pyjama top.

'What are you doing?' Katie asks.

'You know what I'm doing.'

The once-red circle has faded to a pearly scar, slightly raised and crinkled.

'It could be anything,' she says.

'It's a bullet wound.' I tuck the blankets back around him. 'He died in *The Gallows Dance*, that's why he can't wake up.'

She frowns. 'I remember a lot of weird shit, but I don't remember Nate dying.'

'You weren't there when it happened, that's why.'

'Is that why you wrote him into *The Gallows Song*?'

Katie asks. 'To give him life in another universe?'

'Maybe. Although I didn't know it at the time.'

She slides her hand from my shoulder and I suddenly feel very cold. I stroke Nate's arm, just wishing I didn't feel so alone. 'They tried to chop off his hands when we were there,' I say, tracing the line of his knuckles with my fingers. 'Just because he wasn't wearing his regulation gloves.'

'Violet, I really think you should talk to someone, a professional I mean. I know these memories seem real, but they *can't* be.'

I ignore her and lift his hand from the bed, pointing to his wrist. 'They put tourniquets right here, I remember how scared he looked, kneeling on the ground with his arms stretched out in front of him.' The image of the glinting scythe bursts into my head, causing my stomach to contract. I begin to sketch an invisible line around his wrist, the place the scythe would have cut had Alice not appeared. I slowly rotate his hand so I can see the underbelly of his wrist, so pale and smooth, the blue veins resting just beneath the surface like faint rivers on a map.

And that's when I see it.

Several inches above his wrist. A small, dark mark. A mole perhaps. But the centre is missing so it looks more like a tiny, black polo tattooed on to his skin.

I know that mark, I've seen it before. I squeeze my eyes shut, sifting through memories as fast as I can. *Where have I seen that mark?*

'Violet? What is it?' Katie asks.

'This mark, it's new.'

'Are you sure?' She leans in to get a better look.

'Yes, I'm sure.'

'It's just a mole, surely?'

I run my finger over it. Completely smooth. 'No, it

has a slightly blue tinge, more like ink, and the middle is missing.'

'Oh yeah, that is weird. Do you think one of the nurses did it?'

I shake my head. 'Why on earth would they do that?'

She shrugs.

'I've seen it before. I just can't think where.' I move closer, so my nose almost touches his arm. It isn't a perfect hoop. Its edges are irregular and it thins right down before thickening up again. It's too small to make any sense of. I sit up, frustrated. 'What do you think it is?'

'It's just a bit of ink.' Katie says. 'One of the nurses probably splattered him with their fountain pen when they were writing notes.' But I can tell from the way her voice wavers she isn't convinced.

'Seriously, take a look. It's some sort of symbol.'

'I don't want to.' She sounds afraid, not defiant.

'Katie, don't be wet. I need you right now.'

She blinks a few times. For a second, I think she's going to walk away, but my words must do the trick, because she tucks her hair behind her ears, matter-of-factly, and bends down. 'Yeah, it's weird. What is it? A wreath, maybe?'

'No, it thins out too much, just here.' I point. It makes my fingertip look so fat. 'It's too bloody small, I need a magnifying glass.'

'OK, Sherlock, I've got one in my pocket, right next to my pipe.'

I grab my phone. It's a really good one, I bought it with part of my advance, telling myself I would use it to write, but in all honesty, I just wanted a good phone. I zoom in on the mark, as close as I can without blurring the detail. *Snap.*

'Genius,' Katie says. She sits beside me on the bed

and I can feel her thigh trembling against mine.

I blow up the mark so it fills the screen. It's a rat, curled in a circle.

Katie tips her head to one side. 'Is that a sleeping mouse?'

I shake my head. 'It isn't sleeping.'

'It looks pretty cosy to me.'

'It's eating its tail.' I point to the open mouth, sure enough, swallowing down half of its tail.

'Ew,' Katie says.

'Still think it's a bit of fountain pen leakage?'

She shakes her head, and I notice she's gone white. I feel a jolt of guilt, thinking of how freaked out she must be. But I wasn't lying, I do need her right now.

'How did it get there?' Katie asks. 'Someone must have crept into his ward and tattooed him without anybody noticing, that's totally bizarre.'

I gaze into her pea-green eyes. 'What if the someone wasn't from this world?'

Her skin fades again. I didn't realize anyone could turn so pale, her freckles – usually fair – stand out dark russet against her cheeks. 'What do you mean?'

I try to talk slowly, for her sake, but the words pour out of me all the same. 'What if this happened to the other Nate, the Nate in the alternate universe, and it's crossed over on to *this* Nate's body.'

'What?'

I begin to laugh, excitement pulsing through my veins. 'They're linked, Katie.'

'Who's linked?'

'This Nate and the *other* Nate, the Nate who Alice and I created, Nate from *The Gallows Song*. They're linked.'

Katie covers her eyes with her hands. 'Violet, this isn't funny. I've had a year of therapy, a whole year.'

I gently prise her hands from her eyes, as though I can help her see more clearly. 'If Nate is really over there, then maybe I can bring him home. Maybe *this* Nate, the *real* Nate, will wake up.'

I get home just before tea, exhausted from all the excitement and lack of sleep. The scent of roast chicken fills the hall and my stomach growls accordingly. I enter the kitchen-diner, and the checkerboard tiles and shiny surfaces make me feel calm, if only for a moment.

Mum glances up from her saucepan. 'I made your favourite, sweetie. Roast chicken with all the trimmings.'

Today's Friday. Mum only makes a non-Sunday roast when she's trying to pull the family together over something – a poor test result, an argument between me and Nate, that sort of thing. Nate and I always used to joke that she thought she could glue things back together with bread sauce and gravy. She's wearing jeans and a sweater instead of her work clothes, and the dark crescents beneath her eyes look painted on. Something isn't quite right.

'Didn't you go to work today?' I ask.

She shakes her head, avoiding eye contact.

Dad walks through the door, dressed in a Nirvana T-shirt which must date back to the last century. They've both taken the day off, and they both look knackered. A feeling of unease spreads through me.

'Hey, pudding.' He touches the top of my head. 'What you been up to?'

I shrug. 'Just visiting Nate.'

They glance at each other, their faces tight.

'What?' I say.

Mum starts dishing up, moving around the pots and pans with the grace of a woman used to juggling kids and work and household chores. Dad starts setting the table, getting the knives and forks the wrong way around, same as always.

'What?' I say again, swapping the cutlery over so it makes sense.

Mum sets food on the plates – carrots, chicken, roast potatoes – her cooking looks even better now I can recall my diet of dried bread at the Harper estate in *The Gallows Dance*.

'Why don't we eat first?' Mum says, looking pointedly at Dad. I hate the way parents think they're so subtle, like they've got this magic parent code that their kids can't decipher, when in reality they're just rolling their eyes, grimacing or winking in plain sight and it's bloody obvious.

'Tell me now,' I say, irritated.

We take our usual seats. Nate's empty chair always seems bigger than the rest.

Dad begins to cut up his chicken. 'It's about Jonathan.'

'Yeah, I guessed that. You went all creepy-still when I mentioned his name. Have the doctors said something? Because I was there earlier and I didn't see you guys, and nobody mentioned anything.'

Mum takes a little too long tipping salt on her dinner, I can see the crystals shining from her carrots and melting into the gravy.

'I think that's enough salt, Mum,' I say, reaching across the table and taking it from her hand.

She laughs, stiff and brittle like she's trying not to cry. I've come to know it as her 'glass jar laugh'. This fragile, transparent container, unable to hide the sadness inside.

'Has his GCS score deteriorated?' I ask. The Glasgow Coma Scale is a measurement the doctors use; deterioration would be very bad. My stomach churns and the scent of chicken seems to transform into something vinegary and unpleasant in my nostrils.

Dad stares at his plate. 'It isn't that, Violet.' He takes a deep breath. 'Your mum and I had a really long chat today.' He glances at her and tries to smile. 'We made a really hard decision, a big decision, and I hope you'll support us.'

I don't like the sound of this. I begin to feel full-on sick. 'What?'

He stares at his chicken. 'We're withdrawing Nate's care.'

My first reaction is to laugh, but it's fuelled by shock and growing terror. 'Withdrawing care? What does that mean?'

He finally looks at me, tears glazing his eyes. 'We're turning off his respirator.'

6
VIOLET

My fork clatters against the table, sending a streak of gravy across the table. 'You're *what*?'

Dad's face doesn't belong to him any more; it belongs to a much older man, a sadder man. All of the sparkle stripped away. 'I'm sorry, darling. But it's been well over a year and there's no improvement.'

'Mum?' The word leaves my lips like I'm five again.

She stands and moves around the table so she can clasp me to her chest. It's warm and smells of star anise and jasmine. I can feel her heart beating really fast. 'We need to let him go, Violet. We need to mourn our son.'

I push her away. 'But he isn't dead.'

Mum tries to hold me again, so I stand from my chair and take a step back. 'He's just sleeping.'

She holds my gaze with those big, watery Mum eyes. Her hands begin to twitch and I can tell she's aching to hold me. 'He isn't going to wake up. The doctors told us, we've been holding on for, I don't know what . . .'

'For a miracle,' Dad says.

'But miracles can happen,' I say. 'Alice, Katie and me, we all woke up suddenly, within minutes of each other. That was a miracle.'

'Please, Violet,' Mum says, her face pleading. 'This is going to be hard enough without you fighting us on it. We need your support on this.'

'I will never support you killing my brother.'

'We're not killing him,' she says. 'We're setting him free.'

'Bollocks,' I shout. 'Absolute bollocks.' I swipe my hands through the air, the shock crystallizing into something hard and angry. 'How could you even consider this? Murdering your own son, my brother. And what? You came up with this in a day? You both took the day off work and just decided *this*? Like you're planning a holiday or a house move or something?'

They both get this stunned look, like I've just reached out and smacked them. There's a long pause, and I think maybe Dad's about to change his mind – his hands playing anxiously around his face – but he doesn't. 'Please try to understand,' he says.

'You can't kill him now,' I say, my voice collapsing into a breathy rasp. 'Not now. There's something you wouldn't understand, something I don't really understand, but I'm figuring it out . . . I found this mark on his wrist, I don't know what it means yet, but I think it means they're linked.' The words taste sharp and hot as they leave my mouth.

'What are you talking about?' Dad asks.

'I think I can bring him back,' I say.

'Don't say that,' Mum says. 'Just don't say that.' She starts to cry. And not that delicate, feminine crying you see on the television; we're talking snot and tears and a strange rattling noise like she can't quite breathe, like that glass jar finally shattered, blocking her throat with tiny shards. 'I can't even bear to think it,' she manages to gasp.

I understand where she's coming from, really I do – false hope can sting more than a straight, honest loss. And even though I'm still mad, still desperate, I love my mum and I can't bear to see her so upset. I wrap my arms around her and she folds into me, like I'm the mother and she's the daughter. Suddenly, Dad is behind us. I never even noticed him stand. He holds us both in a massive bear hug and rests his head on mine. His body sways as he takes great, jerky breaths of air.

I take a second to order my thoughts: I can't tell them about *The Gallows Dance*. They'll never understand. They'll probably have me committed, and then what use will I be to Nate? I have to buy some time. *Think, Violet, think.* And suddenly, sandwiched between my parents, held safe in a pocket of hot breath and tears, I have an idea.

'It's his birthday in a few days. He turns sixteen.' Mum starts to cry even harder, which wasn't the desired effect, but I carry on talking all the same. 'Just let me make his favourite cake, same as always. Let me make his favourite chocolate cake and sing him "Happy Birthday". Just let me have that, then I'll say goodbye.'

My parents slowly untangle themselves so we become three separate entities again. They glance at each other with swollen eyes. They think they're doing that secret parent code thing again, but I know what they're going to say before they say it.

'OK,' Mum says.

In less than a week, my brother will die. I've said these words to myself over and over, yet somehow, they don't seem real. Because while Nate lies in that hospital bed, laced up with tubes, chest rising and falling, there's still hope I can save him. Even if it means doing the thing I fear the most: returning to that God-awful place.

It's nearly midnight, but I can't sleep. I lie on my bed and stare at the crack on my ceiling, my body feeling like a giant bruise. I have to go back to the world of *The Gallows Dance*. You see, I think I've always known this – from the moment Baba figuratively opened up my scalp and poured in those memories, I've always known at some level that I would have to return and try and bring him home. What did Baba say last night? *Nate's safe, at least for now.* Which Nate did she mean? Sleeping Nate – *my* Nate – or the Nate in her universe? Perhaps they're one and the same. The mark certainly suggests that.

The mark. It sits uneasily in my stomach. Alice and I didn't write anything about a mark in *The Gallows Song*, but then I guess their universe has a habit of embellishing the story, adding details and twists which weren't in canon. Baba's words return to me. *It feels like things have already started to turn, like the winds have changed and there's nothing I can do about it.* Are bad things starting to happen over there?

The crack on my ceiling begins to blur as my focus slips – another, identical crack appears alongside it so it looks like a fuzzy train line. I blink firmly so the cracks become one again. How could bad things happen over there? *The Gallows Song* left them with hope for a utopia, it even broke the cycle. I know this because Baba told me. Perhaps someone in this world has started to write that third novel. Timothy *did* say there were other authors.

I roll on to my side, frustrated, staring at the cold cup of tea Mum brought me several hours ago. I need to cross into the world of *The Gallows Dance*. Last time, we were at Comic-Con. There was some freak accident, although we were later told there was no accident – no light came loose, no scaffold fell. There was just a minor earth tremor and the four of us keeled over for no apparent reason. So I'll rephrase . . . we *thought* there was a freak accident. President Stoneback told me he used Gem technology to bring Alice over, accidentally transporting me, Katie and Nate too. Of course, I then learnt that even this was no accident. Baba piggybacked on the President's idea, making sure I crossed over too.

Simple.

I start to laugh.

I squeeze my eyes shut. Last time, over a year ago, we were at Comic-Con. Why Comic-Con? My eyes flick open as I remember Timothy's words: *It's where the Fandom is at its strongest.* Maybe the Fandom was amplified, maybe that's why we crossed at Comic-Con. And then it clicks into place. Today's Friday, which means there's another Comic-Con tomorrow.

Could it really be a coincidence? Comic-Con falling the day after we discover Nate's mark and my parents decide to turn off his life support? Somehow, I doubt it. Baba's always had a master plan.

Frantically, I text Katie and Alice, my fingers slipping over the screen and leaving a maze of sweat lines. I don't tell them about Nate's life support. I just can't bear to see it typed out on my screen – the letters so clear and final. Instead, I type:

> I'm going to Comic-Con tomorrow.
> Who's in?

Katie doesn't ask why. She doesn't even remind me of all the therapy it will cock up. She just texts back:

> Ok, but I'm not dressing up this
> time x

Alice is more circumspect, though:

> Why do you want to go to
> Comic-Con?

Such a short question requiring such a long response. I settle with:

50

You know why!!!!

So tell me then!

TO GET NATE!!!!!

I'm worried about you, I'm going
to ring your mum!

No you're not ☺ So are you
coming or not?

I'm sorry, I can't.

A L I C E

I stare at my phone for what seems like hours.
I'm sorry, I can't.
That text really gets to me. Sitting on my screen like
that, it looks like a right tool sent it. The text doesn't
show how scared I feel, or how confused it all makes
me. No amount of emojis would come close! I try to
swallow but my mouth is too dry. Violet said she was
going to get Nate. Does she honestly believe Nate is
trapped in the world of *The Gallows Dance* and somehow she can rescue him? Jesus, this is all kinds of crazy.
Scabs aside, terrifying gnawing things aside, she clearly
needs me. And this little voice at the back of my mind
just won't be silenced: *what if she's right?*
I wash my face, apply my lipstick, and dash down the
stairs. I'm going to Comic-Con. That way, whatever
happens, we'll be together.
I'm going to Comic-Con.
Crapbags.

7

VIOLET

The Olympia centre looks exactly how I remember. Two semi-circles of glass suspended at either end of a giant tunnel; dark pillars stretching towards white metal lacework, like the entire structure's been decorated with fragments of the Eiffel Tower. And that smell – hot dogs and sweat and perfume – makes my heart jump into my throat. I take in the giant posters fluttering from the balconies, the huge balloons hovering in the space above us, the colourful mass of cosplayers.

'It's exactly how I remember,' Katie says, as if reading my mind.

'Yet I feel completely different.'

She nods. 'Completely.'

We watch Gandalf play-fight Harry Potter, and I briefly wonder if Katie feels jealous too. We should be dressed up and having fun, pointing our wands at each other, swishing our cloaks, not clutching each other's hands, our heads bursting with horrific memories, our cheeks wet with tears. A group of stormtroopers march past, hiding the wizards from view. Their replica guns look scarily real and I get a twisting sensation in my gut.

'So now what?' Katie asks.

Her words spur me into action and I begin weaving between the partitions, clocking the various stalls. 'We go where the Fandom's at its strongest.' My eyes settle on

The Gallows Dance stall and I make a beeline towards it, accidentally knocking Wonder Woman out of my way.

'What do you mean?' Katie asks, catching me up. 'Why does the Fandom need to be strong?'

'Because it's the Fandom that made their world real. The power of the collective conscious. And I think we crossed over last time we were here because Comic-Con somehow magnified it – the Fandom, I mean.'

She pauses for a moment, and I drop my pace to match hers.

'What do you mean when you say the Fandom made their world?' she asks.

'I don't know, it's complicated . . . it's like, so many people believe in *The Gallows Dance*, they've actually brought it to life.'

She blinks a few times in disbelief and we begin to move towards the stall again. Suddenly, she grabs me. Even through the laughter and the theme tunes and the whir of the vending trucks, I hear her gasp. She must have seen him before I did. Thorn. At least, a beautiful young man dressed as Thorn.

'Shitbags, shitbags, shitbags,' she mutters. I can see why she's losing it. He's a pretty convincing cosplayer – dark skin, perfect smile, eyepatch breaking up his even face. But his physique is obviously Imp; he's just shy of six foot and has narrow shoulders, unlike the taller, broader and genetically enhanced rebel leader. And, of course, he looks way too friendly to be Thorn.

'Ladies.' He pushes a couple of flyers into our hands.

'What the funk?' Katie whispers.

'So you're a *Gallows Dance* fan, huh?' he asks, obviously clocking Katie's strange response. 'It's OK. It's just a costume.'

I pull her away, forcing a laugh. 'Yeah. She knows. She's just got a thing for eyepatches.'

I continue to march towards the *Gallows Dance* stall, and as we draw nearer, Katie drags her heels. She's gone that whiter-than-white colour again, and I can feel the muscles in her arms are all knotted up. I have a sudden rush of guilt, dragging her into this. If this doesn't work, I've just retraumatized her for no reason. And if this does work, I'm pulling her into a dangerous, unpredictable, violent universe, with no guarantee of ever returning home. I stop in my tracks. Rapunzel and Steampunk Cinderella walk into us. They mutter their apologies, even though it was clearly my fault, and I manage a casual wave of my hand.

I turn to Katie. 'Look, I shouldn't have asked you to come. I don't mind if you want to leave. Maybe this is something I need to do on my own.'

Her hair looks even redder in the mid-morning sun, making her washed-out complexion all the more alarming. She narrows her pea-green eyes. 'Don't be a jizzmonger. I've just bumped into a man whose throat I watched get slit. I'm not about to leave you here on your tod.'

A smile creeps up my body and into my mouth. 'So you believe me now? *The Gallows Dance* is real.'

'Maybe. Sometimes. Blah.' She sticks out her tongue and feigns vomiting. 'Anyway, even if it *is* real, that doesn't mean we're going to cross over again.' But she doesn't sound convinced, and we walk the last few metres to the stall really slowly because I'm worried she may vom for real.

Several Rose lookalikes surround me and that top-to-toe bruised feeling returns. Somewhere in the distance, a camera flashes. Then another, and another. It's this shimmer of light far away – the twinkle of a Christmas tree in my peripheral vision. I get an irrational sense that it's happening already, that we're beginning to cross. I squeeze my eyes shut. Order my stomach not to empty its contents. But nothing happens. The cameras stop and the sense of some impending drama slips away.

'So this is the Fandom at its strongest?' Katie asks.

I scan the T-shirts, the mugs, see my own name emblazoned across the front cover of *The Gallows Song*; I skim Russell Jones's face, which looks all wrong now I've met the real Willow.

'I guess,' I say.

'It's not working.'

'Yeah. I noticed.' I'm not sure if fear or disappointment turns my voice into something sharp and irritable.

'So are you going?' someone asks. He's dressed as Ash. At least I think that's who he's supposed to be. He wears Imp overalls and has black hair. I get a tugging sensation in my chest.

'Are you going?' he repeats.

At first, I think he's asking if I'm crossing over, so my mouth just hangs open. But then he gestures to the flyer in my hand. I look for the first time at what fake-Thorn handed me.

'Katie, look,' I say.

She reads the purple letters in a nipped voice. '*The Gallows Dance*. Russell Jones and Timothy O'Hara in conversation. Comic-Con. Saturday, 11 a.m.'

'This is where the Fandom will be at its strongest,' I say.

'We've got five minutes,' Katie replies.

ALICE

I grab a black cab. It costs a fortune and I can smell the driver through the Perspex screen, but the traffic is light and it wins me some time back. We stop outside Olympia and I perform my public duty for the day – tipping the cabby enough for a can of deodorant. I glance at the queue and groan. I haven't got time for this. I need to find Violet ASAP. I have to be the friend she clearly needs right now. So I suck in my stomach, stick out my tits, and own the stretch of concrete which separates me from the main gates. Nobody challenges my shameless queue jump, at least, not until I reach the door.

'Ticket?' the woman at the door says.

'I'm Alice Childs, author of *The Gallows Song*, I'm here to meet my editor.' Thank God my voice isn't shaking as much as my hands.

I thought she'd be difficult, but she just smiles. 'One second, Alice.' She shuffles through the name tags. 'Hmmm, Alice Childs. I can't seem to find you, are you on a panel?'

'I'm doing a signing. It was very last-minute.' It's a barefaced lie. But sometimes lies can be a good thing.

She locates a lanyard with the word 'Guest' hanging from it. 'This should do the trick. Sorry about that.'

'It's fine,' I reply, slightly embarrassed that she's apologizing when I'm the one lying my tits off.

I hook the lanyard over my head and hurry as quickly as I can towards the main hall. I glance at my watch. It's just before eleven. I've no idea where Violet and Katie will be, though the *Gallows Dance* stall is a sensible place to start. Then I'll check out the dystopian panels and the green room.

I step into the main hall. The smell makes my head buzz. Not that it's particularly unpleasant (though a pop-up Lynx stall wouldn't go amiss), it just brings back those terrifying memories. I don't have time to figure it out, or to marvel at the beauty of the hall. Christ, I don't

56

even have time to check out the hot cosplayers. I've got to find Violet and stop her holding some batshit crazy séance for Nate's lost soul.

I stride through the crowds towards the humungous Russell Jones banner, but I'm walking faster than my heels think is reasonable, and before I know it, I'm hurtling into Deadpool and face-planting on the tiles. The pain is completely eclipsed by the humiliation, and I just pray that if there is a God, he isn't stood beside me with a camera phone, logged on to YouTube. I try and summon the strength to leap up like it never happened, but I just lie there looking at the costumed feet around me, feeling dazed, stupid and utterly alone.

'Alice?' I roll over and expect to see Deadpool, but it's Gandalf who stares down at me. I blink a few times. How does Gandalf know my name? Beneath the grey beard and pointed hat, there's heavily lashed brown eyes and a concerned half-smile. He helps me into a sitting position. 'Are you OK?'

'Yeah. Just embarrassed.'

'Don't be,' he says. 'Deadpool came off worse.'

I raise an eyebrow and Gandalf laughs, revealing teeth a little too big for his mouth. 'Don't worry, I hear he has remarkable self-healing powers.' He removes his beard and hat. He has dark brown skin, wide-set eyes, and black curls which skim his ears. 'You don't recognize me, do you?'

Even though I'm shaking my head, I recognize him all right. My ego's bruised from my epic tumble, and there's no quicker way to build yourself back up than making someone else feel small. I hate how much I'm like my dad sometimes.

'It's Danny,' he says in a matter-of-fact tone, like he never expected me to know. 'Danny Bradshaw from sixth form.'

I always liked Danny. He was a complete geek at school, really into IT and boring crap like that. But he never once gawped at me, and he loaned me his spare calculator on several occasions. You see what I mean? He had a spare calculator: #nerdfest.

'Oh yeah,' I say. 'Course it is. Sorry, the costume threw me.'

'I knew I should have rocked this look at school, my bad.'

I can't help but smile. He helps me stand and I dust off my jeans. My eyes return to scanning the hall.

'Looking for someone?' he asks.

'Violet and Katie. Remember them?'

'Yeah, course I do.'

'Don't suppose you've seen them?' I say, aware that it's a long shot.

'No, but they may be going to see that Russell Jones idiot; he's doing some sort of *Gallows Dance* talk with a book editor dude. I suppose you might know them, actually.' His cheeks flush. 'Sorry.'

I wave a hand, showing my lack of offence. 'When?'

Danny glances at his watch. 'I think it started a few minutes ago. I can take you there if you want, protect you with my massive staff.' He slaps the palm of his hand to his forehead. 'Jesus, stop talking, Danny.'

'That would be great,' I say, stifling a giggle.

Together, we head deep into the throng of cosplayers.

8

VIOLET

The room is brimming with *Gallows Dance* fans. Thorns, Roses, Willows, even a Daisy lookalike. Shit. Daisy. I'd completely forgotten about Daisy. I wrote Ash a girlfriend in *The Gallows Song*. A *Gem* girlfriend. Tall, beautiful, caramel-skinned. I essentially wrote him the me I long to be. I even called her Daisy. Another little flower. I begin to laugh. I'm jealous of the girl I made up, and angry at a boy who doesn't know who I am. It's a complete head-screw.

We file into rows of flimsy chairs, facing a small platform at the front. I can smell dust and aftershave and the tang of old beer. A painted backdrop of the Coliseum – well, the film-set version – hangs at the back. My ribcage seems to shrink, barely able to contain my heart.

'For Nate,' I whisper to myself. 'I'm doing this for Nate.'

'You were right, the Fandom's really strong here,' Katie says. She looks at the group of Thorns, the whites of her eyes swallowing up the green. 'Because this is like the worst bloody flashback ever.'

'If this works, if we cross over, it will be worse than any flashback. You know that?'

She nods. 'Which is exactly why I can't let you do it on your own.'

I squeeze her trembling knee. She's starting to

believe that this will work, that we'll cross over. Her faith plants a strange emotion inside me. Fear and hope and a sense of removal – like we're not really here and we're already stretched out in a hospital bed.

'It won't be as bad as last time,' I tell her. 'Not since Alice and I wrote *The Gallows Song*. The Imps aren't hanged any more for a start.'

She nods. 'I know. Christ, I'm glad I've read the books this time.'

'It will still suck though.' I feel like it's my responsibility to tell her this, so she knows what she's letting herself in for. 'There's still violence and poverty and disease. And Baba seemed to think bad things were starting to happen.'

'What do you mean, bad things?'

'I don't know, she didn't say. But I think it may be related to the mark we found on Nate's body. I think someone in this universe may have started writing the third book.'

'OMG. Who?'

I shake my head. 'I don't know. Timothy said he had other authors. Maybe one of them has started drafting something, maybe a few people have started to read it, a kind of mini-Fandom, and the changes are manifesting in the world of *The Gallows Dance*.'

I close my eyes and try not to think about all the terrifying things which await us if this works. The brutality, the hatred, the stench of rotting bird. Instead, I focus on the feathers, the palest blue eyes I've ever seen and, of course, my brother's face.

The theme tune to *The Gallows Dance* begins to play. Violins, cellos and bass drums fill the room. For obvious reasons, I haven't watched the film since I woke from my coma, and hearing it now is like hearing the voice of an ex-lover, not that I'd know. A combination of nostalgia and anger wells inside.

The theme tune ramps up a notch and the crowd begins to clap. Katie and I are sitting in the middle of a row. I feel kind of trapped, and panic builds on panic, layering inside in my stomach. Timothy climbs on to the platform, his suit shiny and blue beneath the glare of the emerald stage lights. He sits beside a small table, a glass of water waiting for him. Russell Jones follows. He's as handsome and smug-looking as the first time we met him. The crowd begin to whoop and cheer, and he does a little bow as he makes his way to his chair at the front.

The theme music dips but doesn't die completely. Timothy waits for the clapping to fade – grin plastered across his tanned face. 'Hi there.' His voice sounds like it comes from behind us. He must be wearing a mic. 'Thanks for coming today everyone. It's my absolute pleasure to welcome Russell Jones, otherwise known as Willow Harper.'

Russell begins to wave and the room erupts into applause again. A couple of people cheer, and the Nate lookalike behind me begins to whistle. It hits my ear like the discordant call of a steam train.

Timothy again waits for the applause to die down. 'We wanted to talk about what's next for the Gallows Dance franchise, both in terms of books and films. Unfortunately, the authors Alice Childs and Violet Miller couldn't make it,' he says.

The crowd groans, and I feel a flush of something pleasurable. A room full of people want me. Maybe I should stand up and shout 'Surprise!' But I never was great at public speaking, and I want to see where this is going.

Timothy looks serious. 'They avoid Comic-Con like the plague, understandably. It's nothing personal, you understand.'

The light above him must be on the blink; his cheeks oscillate between tan and green. And those bloody violins have really started to grate – they begin to sound like they haven't been tuned in a while.

Timothy doesn't seem to notice. 'But first, I have an exciting announcement to make . . .'

This doesn't sound good.

The pause lengthens and the crowd collectively holds its breath. Timothy clearly loves the power. The flickering of the bulbs increases, like they're impatient too.

He sits forward in his chair. 'There's going to be another instalment.'

The room begins to cheer and clap. A couple of Thorns are bashing their feet against the floor so it feels like a stampede. I begin to feel sick again. Sick with anger, sick with confusion, sick because that bastard light won't quit.

I turn to Katie, my voice frantic. 'Alice and I haven't agreed this, he *must* have another author.'

But Katie doesn't even look at me. She's studying the ceiling, a faraway look in her eyes. 'Something isn't right,' she says. 'I feel kind of giddy.'

That's when I remember. The flickering lights – the same as the first crossover. The scent of medicine and burning fabric fills my nostrils.

I try and focus on Katie, but her face seems to shift suddenly to the left.

'It's happening,' I say.

And through the droning violins, the clap of the crowd, the thud of boots, I hear Timothy. Loud and clear and smug. 'There will be another instalment, my dear Fandom. And rest assured, there will be betrayal, death . . . There will be *conflict.*'

The crowd erupts into a loud applause. I open my

mouth to shout: *There must never be a third book.* But the words lodge somewhere in my throat.

Somehow I manage to stand, steadying myself on the chair in front. The cosplayers are starting to look at me now, but I don't care. I have to reach Timothy before I cross over. I have to make him understand that there must never be a third book. Not ever.

I begin to edge my way towards the aisle, my body coated in sweat. The room begins to spin and I think that gasping noise is coming from me, yet still I keep moving. I step on a Thorn lookalike's toes, lunge over a couple of wannabe Gems, and end up ploughing into another Nate lookalike. My heart aches at the sight of him, and I'm so confused, I begin to think maybe I've already crossed over, that maybe this *is* Nate. But before the excitement can take hold, I hear Timothy's voice, merging into the screech of the violins.

'Violet? Violet? Is that you, my darling?'

I can hear the crowd now, murmuring to each other, the applause fading to a mere smattering. I don't think they quite know how to respond – I must look an absolute sight.

There must never be a third book. The words rise up my throat, but it's like they're stuck on my tongue and I can't for the life of me spit them out. I'm about to enter the world of *The Gallows Dance*, *Katie* is about to enter the world of *The Gallows Dance*, and Timothy's talking about death and betrayal and conflict like it's nothing more than a book or a film. I *have* to make him understand.

I reach the aisle, tripping over my own feet. A security guard appears from nowhere and places two firm hands under my armpits. I think it might be a gentle restraint, but I'm hugely grateful to those hands, because they've just saved me from an almighty face-plant.

Timothy chuckles. Over the sound system, through the fug of my brain, he sounds really sinister, and I'm momentarily reminded of the villain from a pantomime. 'Are you OK?' he asks.

I force my eyes to his face. Green, tan, green, tan.

I watch as his mouth opens into a huge yawn, the white of his teeth cast in an emerald glow. 'Let's hear it for Violet Miller, the co-author of *The Gallows Song*.'

The sporadic applause strengthens and the ground thunders beneath my shoes. The security guard guides me to the front of the stage, and the stench of medicine makes me want to gag. I'm so close to Timothy now. Maybe I can manage the faintest of whispers. *There must never be a third book.* Maybe I can tell him before I cross over. But my head is about to explode and a series of images unfold before my eyes: the palest blue eyes I've ever seen; a scythe raised high and glinting in the sun; Nate bleeding out on my lap; a noose closing around my neck; my feet dancing, searching for solid ground.

The room fills with feathers and bubbles and thistle-down. If I wasn't so confused, so seasick, I would enjoy the beauty of it all – the air alive and swirling like I'm caught in the strangest of snowstorms. But my heart is slamming into my chest, my mouth filling with bile, and it doesn't help that President Stoneback is staring at me, his face distorted by a passing bubble. *Has it happened? Have I already crossed?* No. It's just another cosplayer. I can still hear the theme tune, the rumble of the crowd. I'm still in the real world, and I can still reach Timothy in time.

I smell his aftershave – honey and spice – and he's leaning from the stage, his grin shining at me through more feathers and thistledown. But beneath the grin lies desperation. He knows he's busted. He reaches towards me and the security guard hoists me on to the platform.

'Violet, darling, come and meet the Fandom,' he says.

And just before I hear Katie scream my name, just before I tumble forward, snatching at the backdrop and dragging it from its mount, the words finally emerge. Loud and clear as they catch in Timothy's mic.

'There must never be a third book.'

And then there's only black.

ALICE

Danny leads me up some stairs, towards a door. There's a poster announcing the *Gallows Dance* panel and a massive photo of Russell Jones looking like a fairy-tale prince, the kind of prince that would slay the dragon and kiss the princess with blood still warm on his cheeks.

I feel the ground move just as I reach towards the door handle.

'Whoa,' Danny says, 'did you feel that?'

I nod, fear building in my chest.

'Probably nothing to worry about,' Danny says. 'Not like last year.'

Nothing to worry about. Sure. Suddenly, my legs take over and I'm racing through the door. I know exactly what I will see: darkness and smoke, the flicker of a smashed-up light, fallen scaffolding, my friends, sprawled and bleeding.

I enter the room, my heart hammering like crazy inside my chest.

It looks completely unscathed. There's no smoke, no smashed-up light. It's just a regular room, filled with chairs and cosplayers. But something isn't quite right. A crowd gathers, and between the collection of legs and shoes, I can just make out two people lying on the ground.

'Alice?' Danny says. 'Are you OK? You look like you've seen a ghost.'

I *wish* I'd seen a pigging ghost. A ghost I could cope with. Somehow I manage to push my way through the crowd, even though my legs feel like they're about to give way and I can't catch my breath. In the centre of the crowd are Violet and Katie. Someone has already put them in the recovery position so that they look like they're taking an afternoon nap in a rather inconvenient place.

Oh my God. Violet was right, it was real. *How could it be real? It's a book, a film. It simply can't be real.* But I remember last year's accident at Comic-Con like it was yesterday. I remember waking up in the Coliseum.

The guilt comes quickly, filling me with self-loathing and regret. I release a loud sob, my mask ready to finally slip.

I was too late.

9
VIOLET

I hear a strange, animalistic noise – halfway between a rasp and a cry. Hot breath fills my ear. I try and open my eyes, try to move my hands, but it's like my brain has been cut off from my body. I wonder if I'm dreaming; trapped in that moment between sleep and waking up. The scent of medicine hangs in my nostrils, thick as smoke . . . maybe it *is* smoke. *Am I dreaming of fire?* I hear the strange, animalistic noise again. It's someone coughing.

The cough becomes a series of words. 'Please, Vi, you need to walk.'

I recognize the voice. *Katie?* I try to say, but I can't move my tongue.

'You're too heavy,' she says. She's pleading with me – pleading and dragging. I can feel her hands, knife-sharp under my armpits. My foot hits something jagged. Pain shoots up my calf.

'Bollocks,' she says, followed by another cough.

I manage to open my eyes. My eyeballs itch from the smoke and I can see only black. I hear this whirring noise, the repetitive clack of something spinning loose, the clang of metal against metal: noises pulled directly from my nightmares. A light flickers high above – a green strobe – and I begin to pick out a tangle of chair legs, the fallen backdrop, and the twinkle of broken glass against the dark boards, like a night sky.

The chairs, the backdrop, the glass . . . I'm at Comic-Con. The room was full of cosplayers, of the Fandom, but now there's only Katie and me. This strikes me as odd, even in my confused state. I think this happened the first time we crossed over. Russell Jones and Julia Starling just vanished . . . or rather, *we* vanished.

It dawns on me. *Holy shit, we've done it – we've crossed over again.* I get intense palpitations, driven by excitement or terror, or maybe both.

'For Christ's sake, Vi. What have you been eating?' Katie lugs me over another bump. The jolt and the blast of adrenalin shocks my body into action; my feet suddenly respond, aligning under my bulk so they can take my weight. I turn so Katie can wrap an arm around my waist and we flounder towards the fire door, coughing and stumbling, trying not to fall.

Katie leans against the doorframe and catches my eye. Even through the fuzz of smoke and panic, I can tell what she's thinking: *there's no going back.*

And together, we open the door.

ALICE

I feel numb. It's like I've become the mannequin everyone thinks I am. I stare at my two best friends and all I can think is: *I should be there too.*

A voice cuts over the buzz of the crowd. 'Alice? Alice? Is that you?'

I squint into the distance, my vision clouded with tears. Timothy strides towards me. I've never seen him look so rattled before. 'Oh Alice, thank goodness you're OK. I don't know what happened, really, I just don't know . . .' he tails off.

Russell appears beside me. He raises his voice and

speaks with sincerity, as though playing a role in a film. 'An ambulance is on the way. Please, clear the room and don't take any pictures.' He holds out his hand to a nearby Thorn wannabe, who hands his phone over with a sheepish grin. Russell deletes the image and hands it back.

The security guards begin shooing people away and the crowd thins. I kneel between my friends, touching them both on the hand. The guilt is crushing. I can barely breathe.

I was too late.

A pair of strong arms wrap around my shoulders. My first instinct is to sink into them, but my rational brain quickly kicks in. *Someone is touching me and I don't know who.* I spin to face the owner.

It's Russell.

He smiles sympathetically. 'Anime Alice, how on earth has this happened again? I mean, I thought the whole Comic-Con curse thing was a joke.'

My bottom lip begins to quiver.

'Sensitive,' I hear Danny mumble.

Russell catches himself. 'God, I'm so sorry, me and my big mouth.'

'It's fine,' I say, trying to stand with a little dignity. 'It *is* one hell of a coincidence.'

The paramedics arrive, a blur of green uniforms and precise movements.

Danny takes me by the arm and guides me to a nearby chair. 'Come and sit down before you faint.'

I let him usher me into a seat, and I clutch at my knees, trying to stop them shaking. Danny gives me a reassuring smile. I try to smile back, but my face isn't doing what I want at the moment. The paramedics tend to my besties, attaching oxygen masks and checking vitals. Within minutes, they're loaded on to stretchers and wheeled away. There's so much to think about, so much to figure out. But I press the pause button on my brain. I just need to get to hospital with them.

'Can I ride in the ambulance?' I ask a paramedic.

He shakes his head. 'Sorry, you'll have to get there under your own steam.'

I'm too shocked to even think about sticking out my lady lumps and working my magic. I turn to Danny. 'What should I do?' I sound like a child.

'We'll get a cab. I'll come with you.'

'Thanks.'

Russell steps in. 'It's OK. I'll ask my driver to take you to the hospital.'

'I'll come too,' Danny says.

Russell offers him a lazy smile. 'Sorry, buddy. What with Timothy coming along, car's full.'

Danny looks at me, determined, his Gandalf beard still gripped in his left hand. 'I'll meet you there, then.'

But Russell's already steering me in the direction of the door.

'It's OK,' I call over my shoulder. 'I'll text you later.'

It's only when I reach Russell's SUV I realize I don't have Danny's number.

The journey to the hospital is totally surreal. I ring Violet and Katie's parents and let them know what's happened. Somehow, I manage to sound calm; I don't even break when Violet's mum starts crying.

We follow the ambulance, so we make good progress even though the traffic has thickened. The siren and the flashing blue light are the only things that really get how I'm feeling right now, everything else looks so peaceful, like it's just another day and my world isn't falling apart, even though my eyes are aching from the effort of not crying and my throat is on fire.

Timothy looks anxiously at his phone as it lights up in his hand for the millionth time (I'm guessing the press have heard about the second bout of comas) and Russell is yabbering on about something Hollywood-related. I wish he would just shut up.

'Alice?' he says. 'Alice?'

'Sorry, what?' I say, gazing out of the window.

'What do you think then?'

'About what?'

'About when you're going to write the third book. Like I was saying, I could really do with a third film to look towards.'

Idiot! I can't believe I fancied him. 'Now's not really the time,' I snap.

He smiles. 'Of course, sorry, that was so selfish of me. I'm such a loser sometimes.'

'It's cool,' I say.

Timothy looks up from his phone. 'Do you want me to ring someone for you?'

'Who?' The three most important people in my life are unconscious.

'Your parents?'

'Ha!' I say.

'Your . . .' He falters. ' . . . sister? Or your brother?'

'I'm an only child.'

He puts an arm around me and squishes me against his man boobs. 'They woke up once, they'll wake up again. I promise.'

Timothy's being *nice*. This surprises me. Not that he's awful or anything, we've just always had a business relationship. I suddenly think maybe he's trying to get into my knickers. But he's never given me that feeling before. I kind of assumed he was gay. He's literally never stared at my rack. Not once.

The car pulls up behind the ambulance.

'I'll come into the hospital with you then,' Timothy says. He sounds a bit like a dad . . . not *my* dad, obviously. A normal dad. This makes me well up and I'm scared to reply in case I just snot everywhere.

'No . . . no . . . thank you. I'll be fine,' I manage to say.

'Well, somebody needs to come with you,' Russell says.

Christ, no. The last thing I need is Russell talking shit at me all afternoon. 'Thanks, but Violet's parents will be there, we're pretty close. I'll be fine.'

Russell helps me from the car and Timothy leans over the seat so he can look me in the eyes. 'Keep me updated, Alice. You can call me any time, I mean it. Any time.'

The car drives away and I stand outside the hospital all alone.

Finally, I burst into tears.

10
A L I C E

Violet and Katie lie next to each other. Only a partition curtain and a selection of monitoring equipment comes between them. I can't help feeling left out. Christ, I'm such a jealous cowbag. I sit on the edge of Violet's bed and let a lock of her beyond-soft hair slip through my fingers. I touch a finger to her split-heart necklace, and then press the same finger against my own half. Tears well in my eyes. At least now I understand why she was so desperate we never wrote a third book. She wanted Nate to keep his happy ending. I should have listened to her at the café. I shouldn't have been such a coward.

I duck beneath the curtain and sit beside Katie for a moment. She agreed to go to Comic-Con immediately, no questions asked. Saint Katie. That's why I'm a bit off with her sometimes; she makes me look bad. And the worst thing . . . I love that annoying ginger Scouser. Even though she gets on my nips, even though she's always sucking up to Violet, I still love her. I just wish she'd piss off back to Liverpool sometimes. I stroke her cheek and sigh. 'You better be looking after her, Weasley.'

Well, I may have been too late to go with them, but there's still one thing I can do to help. I can make sure nobody writes that third book. The last thing Violet needs is someone putting the diss back into dystopia (I bloody hate that pun) while she's stuck in that world.

I ring Timothy's number, convinced I can persuade him not to get some other author on board. It goes straight to voicemail. So much for 'any time'. I suppress another wave of tears, because I actually thought he was being kind, then I switch off my phone in anger.

I swing by Nate's room. He looks so peaceful, stretched out in his bed like that. I sit beside him and take his hand. He really needs a shave, and with Violet in a coma, I wonder if the nurses will let me do it instead. Violet said in her text that she was going to get Nate. Just about the last thing she ever said to me as I left the café was: *We wrote in a new character*. Did we really write Nate into life in another universe? It sounds so ridiculous, and yet I remember arriving at the Coliseum so clearly . . . I swallow hard. I have to think about it, I have to let my mind return there. If not for me, for my friends. Because there may still be a way I can help them.

I close my eyes and let that strange, terrifying, beautiful week play out in my head almost like a film. I still can't believe I shagged Willow. I mean, firstly, *I shagged Willow*. But secondly, it was a totally sucky thing to do to my friends. Violet was right; it was a betrayal. It could easily have thrown canon off track and stopped us all going home. But I don't think I cared at that point – it was so good fitting in, not being silently resented for the size of my tits or the length of my skirt. It was so good to belong.

And Willow was so kind and warm.

I cover my face with my hands and begin to weep.

There are some things I'm just not ready to remember quite yet.

A voice makes me jump. 'Oh, I know, it's such a shame.' I look up and see a nurse. I didn't even hear him come into the ward. I wipe my eyes, embarrassed I've had yet another public display of tears, but the nurse doesn't seem to mind and watches me with compassionate eyes. 'Did you know him well?' he asks.

I nod.

'Are you going to be there?'

I don't know what he's talking about, but I play along. 'Yeah, course.'

'Ah, that's nice. Seeing as his sister can't be.'

'It's what Violet would want,' I say.

A smile of sad acceptance touches his lips. 'I thought they may postpone it, what with the older one being back in a coma now. But they're insistent.'

I nod as if I know what he's getting at.

He leans down and strokes Nate's hand. 'Breaks my heart, it does. But at least you'll all be free to grieve.'

I suddenly realize what he means, and it's like I've been kicked in the windpipe. They're turning off Nate's life support.

'When's it scheduled for again?' I ask.

'Wednesday.'

Violet's parents arrive.

Her dad, Adam, embraces me. 'Alice, love, thanks for coming.' He smells of gravy and old spice. I think that's how a real dad is supposed to smell.

Next, Violet's mum falls on me in an embrace that feels almost angry. She probably is pissed off. Why should her children lie in hospital beds while I stroll around unharmed?

'Mrs Miller, I'm so sorry,' I manage to say.

I haven't called her Mrs Miller since I was four. She likes me to call her Jane. But it's easy to slip back into child mode when a lovely, jersey-clad mum gives you a hug.

'Oh Alice, sweetheart, what happened?' she asks.

I swallow down my guilt. 'I don't know, I wasn't there.'

She stands by Violet's bed, tears coursing down her face.

'She text me and said she was going to Comic-Con,' I offer. 'I did go, but I was too late.'

'Why would she go to Comic-Con?' Jane asks me. 'After what happened last time, what was she thinking?'

I want to tell her about *The Gallows Dance* being real, about Nate being stuck over there, about the third book Timothy wants us to write. I think I'm about to, but a doctor enters the room. She speaks to Jane and Adam in a low voice and clearly doesn't want me to hear, so I head to the family room. It's empty except for me. I stick the kettle on and sit at the table.

The tick of the clock bounces off the hard surfaces until it sounds like a hammer. Alone is a dangerous place to be when you're terrified of your own thoughts. I close my eyes, and again let my time in *The Gallows Dance* play out in my head. Willow and I slept together and Violet found us. God knows how she climbed that tree; she pulled a muscle lifting her rucksack back in Year 7. But find us she did, and God was she upset.

And the next morning – my throat aches with the thought of it – the next morning, Willow sat me down and told me he didn't love me. He couldn't love me, because he was in love with someone else. I knew who he meant of course. Rose. Violet. My best friend. Even in a world where I fitted in, I was still just a pretty shell.

Jane walks in, her face all puffy and tear-stained. 'Katie's parents have arrived,' she says. 'They're in a right state, not surprising really. I said I'd make them a cuppa.'

I wipe my eyes. 'I'll do it.'

But she flaps me away with her hand. 'You've been through enough today. And besides, I need to be a mum right now.'

That's the thing Jane doesn't realize; she's always a mum, she couldn't stop being a mum even if she tried, it's sewn into the fabric of her being. Unlike my mum, who tries it on every so often, like one of her outfits.

Jane sticks on some toast. 'You're in luck, they've got granary.'

She knows it's my favourite. We listen to the hum of the toaster, the tick of the clock, and again, I consider telling her about *The Gallows Dance*, about Nate being alive and stuck over there. But the toast popping up breaks my flow.

Jane grabs the toast and starts buttering like a woman possessed. She stops buttering long enough to say, 'I just can't believe the same thing would happen again.' She looks a little wild. 'There's something crazy going on, Alice. Maybe there really is some kind of curse.'

She hands me the toast, and then pulls a note from her pocket. It's Violet's writing, and the sight of it makes me want to cry again.

Mum and Dad,
Whatever happens, please keep your promise to me. The cake recipe is in my silver folder in the cupboard above the kettle.

All my love, Violet.

Jane sits at the table opposite me and leans forwards, dropping her voice to a whisper. 'It's like she *knew* she was going to fall into a coma.' She straightens up and laughs a frantic laugh. 'But that's just mad, isn't it?'

I pause, not sure how to respond. Eventually, I say, 'What promise?'

'Oh, Alice. I can't bring myself to tell you. You'll think I'm awful.'

I reach across the table and squeeze her hand. 'You mean about Nate. They just told me now.'

She looks at me, her face crinkling around the edges with shame. 'And you're not mad?'

I begin to eat the toast. Because actually, I am mad. I'm fuming. How could they even think of turning off Nate's life support? But Jane looks so sad, and I can't bear to kick her when she's down.

'Why now?' is all I manage.

'We're setting him free.'

I don't know what to say so I keep eating toast. I suddenly wish it had jam or chocolate spread on it, just to get rid of that bitter taste.

'You're not mad?' she repeats.

I shake my head and she seems to relax a tiny bit.

'Violet was so mad,' she says. 'Devastated. I keep thinking maybe the shock of it put her back into a coma.' Her voice breaks up. 'But that doesn't explain about Katie, I suppose.'

'What did Violet say?' I ask.

'She started saying she could bring Nate back. She was begging us to give her more time. We agreed to give her a few days, because it's his birthday soon. She wanted to bake his favourite cake. That was the promise she meant in the note.'

'Are you going to give it more time now? You could wait until Violet wakes up?'

'I can't,' she says. 'I just can't. I don't expect you to understand, but we need to do this. Seeing him like that every day, it's killing me.'

'I'm sorry,' I say robotically.

She doesn't acknowledge my apology, perhaps because it sounded so flat. Instead, she slumps in the chair next to me. 'What did she mean, she could bring him back?'

'I don't know,' I reply.

She pulls out Violet's iPhone from her pocket. 'The doctors gave me this. Do you know the code?' she asks. 'Perhaps if I could read her messages . . .'

'Sorry, I don't.'

She exhales, long and slow. 'I'll let Katie's parents know there's tea and toast.'

She leaves the kitchen. More importantly, she leaves the phone.

I lied when I said I didn't know Violet's code. Like I said, sometimes lies are a good thing. She's my bestie. Of course I know her code. I quickly tap the number in: 050710. It's the date that Nate won his first science prize. Random to everyone else, but to Violet, it was one of her proudest moments. She said it was the first time she realized her little brother was a genius. She'd offered to help, and ended up just passing him the glue gun all night. I get a stab of something in my heart. Regret? Guilt? Jealousy? I don't know what it is, but it really sodding hurts.

I skim through her old texts. Boring. Her phone remembers her password, so I quickly check her emails. Boring. I move to her web history. Christ, she really *is* boring. Not a single dodgy site. I can hear steps coming down the corridor. I open up her photo albums. The last photo she took was a strange picture . . . I squint . . . a loop of some description. I can see sandy hairs and the texture of skin running beneath the ink, so I'm guessing it's a close-up of a tattoo. I bring the screen closer to my face. A rat eating its own tail. *Not quite so boring.*

I replace the phone on the table just before Jane and Adam appear.

Adam puts a cup of tea in front of me. It's gone a bit cold, but I drink it anyway. We pretty much repeat the same conversation again. Talking about Comic-Con, about Nate, about how they simply have to turn off his life support. I begin to feel numb again.

It's only as I'm leaving Adam says something of interest.

'Violet mentioned a mark on Nate's arm. We had a quick look and couldn't see anything out of the ordinary. Do you know what she was on about? I think she was just so upset.'

I shake my head. And this time, I'm not lying.

But I'm going to find out.

11

VIOLET

The fire door swings shut behind us. At first, I notice only the absence of things: noise, the scent of medicine, that crushing sensation. Then all at once the stench of rotting bird finds me, the cold air hits my skin, and an expanse of colourless sky hangs above, merging into the grey of stone and concrete.

We've arrived in Imp London.

'It worked,' I whisper.

I hear Katie in the background, high-pitched and disorientated, firing question after question as if I have the answers. I block her out and stumble forwards, trying to take it all in. Jagged rooflines, crumbling bricks peeking through a mass of thistles, concrete pushing through the soles of my shoes. But something isn't right. Above the sound of my own pulse, the ringing in my ears, I can hear cheering, braying – the sound of an angry crowd.

It makes my insides reel.

'Can you hear that?' I ask Katie.

She nods. 'But I can smell the river. Surely we're miles from the Coliseum.' She turns in a circle, then gasps, clutching my arm so hard it hurts. 'Look.'

I follow her line of sight. The church stands proud and tall, risen from the ashes like some bizarre, stone phoenix.

She strengthens her grip. 'I watched it burn to the

ground. How is it still standing?'

Not only is it standing, it's been restored, just like Alice and I wrote in *The Gallows Song*. The polythene in the windows has been replaced with glass and the holes in the roof have been tiled over; and the spire still reaches towards the sky, desperate to finally pierce the sun and release some colour. My mouth hangs open, the adrenalin of crossing over momentarily eclipsed by wonder. I knew *The Gallows Song* would change their world, but seeing it first-hand is astonishing.

'Violet?' Katie says.

'The infinite loop,' I finally reply.

'What loop?'

I force my lips to move, even though they feel numb. 'The Imps and Gems were stuck in a time loop, where the story of *The Gallows Dance* just circled from the end back to the beginning for ever and ever. Only a few Gems could remember it, the President, Baba. That's why they brought us over in the first place, so we would return to our Earth and write the sequel.'

'And break the infinite loop,' she says.

I nod. 'When we returned home, the loop reset. As far as everyone here is concerned, we never existed, Rose died on the gallows the way she was supposed to. And the church, *this* church –' I gesture to it with a trembling hand – 'never burnt to the ground.'

'What about *The Gallows Song*? Did that happen?'

'From what Baba said, it sounds like it did. So . . . this is afterwards. A new story.'

'Unknown territory,' Katie says, and we exchange a nervous glance.

Katie narrows her eyes, the way she does when she's concentrating. 'An infinite loop . . . Like the rat on Nate's arm. I didn't think of it before, I was too weirded out, but it's like a version of the ouroboros – a snake eating its own tail. We studied it in Classics last year. It means infinity, a constant loop.' She turns to me. 'Do you think there's a link?'

I'm about to respond, anxiety knotting up my chest, when the chaotic noise of the distant crowd converges into three, hard words. A chant which builds and builds, striking terror into my core. '*KILL THE TRAITORS . . . KILL THE TRAITORS . . . KILL THE TRAITORS . . .*'

Katie's features widen with fear. 'Sounds like there's an execution going on.'

Before I can answer, before I can even think, my legs are moving, pumping as fast as they can, hammering into the concrete and carrying me towards that terrible chant.

'Violet, wait,' Katie shrieks, her footsteps slapping behind me. 'We're supposed to run *away* from death.'

But I ignore her, sailing down the tarmac, hurdling stones and pieces of debris, the cold river air curdling in my lungs. *The infinite loop.* I suddenly know where I've seen that mark before, the one on Nate's arm. I recall President Stoneback's nasal voice: '*A never-ending cycle. A perpetual loop.*' The mark was on the President's arm.

'Violet, please,' Katie gasps. 'What's going on?'

'It's Nate,' I say, even as my throat aches and that ever-increasing chant fills my head. 'Nate's the traitor.'

ALICE

I'm leaning against the yellow tube pole. And this time, I really need it. I don't think I'd be able to stand otherwise. An older lady asks me if I'm OK. I smile and say, 'Yes, thank you. I'm fine.' And because I'm wearing

Gucci and I've clearly exfoliated, she believes me.

Mum's waiting for me when I get home. She must have heard the news from her friends at the gym. She's missed her spinning class for me, which makes me smile. Dad's nowhere to be seen. He must have heard the news too.

'Are you OK?' she asks.

I nod.

'I tried to ring, but your phone was off.'

'I didn't fancy speaking to the press,' I say.

She runs a chilly finger under my eyes. 'Your mascara's smudged. Go wash your face and we can have a late lunch.'

'I had toast.'

'Carbs!' She says the word like it's dirty. 'I'm making salmon with asparagus.'

I don't really feel like eating, but it's so rare Mum cooks, I'm kind of curious. 'OK. Thanks.'

I change my clothes and wash my face. The coldness of the water against my skin wakes me a little, and I suddenly get an urge to check my phone and see if Mum really did ring (Mum never rings). Turns out, she did, which makes me happy. *Really* happy. Orphan-Annie-gets-chosen-by-Daddy-Warbuck-happy. I reward her by pulling on a sundress. She loves it when I make an effort.

I return to my phone, hoping to hunt Danny down on social media. I want to tell him thank you, and in all honesty, I want to speak to him again. There's something about him that felt familiar, something that made me feel calm. But thoughts of Danny quickly vanish when I see just how many alerts I've got. There's a load of tweets and Facebook messages. Instagram has gone mad. The world has clearly heard about the curse of Comic-Con. I know I should probably read them when

I'm feeling stronger, but curiosity wins the day. I perch on the edge of my bed and submerge myself in the world of social media. It sometimes feels like jumping into a bottomless river, like I'll never surface if I'm not careful.

They're mostly condolences. Love and wishes to be passed on to Violet from fans of *The Gallows Song*. Some of the messages are checking if I'm OK. I think about quickly tweeting that (yep, you've guessed it) I'm fine. But a tweet from someone called *@eternalrose* catches my eye.

You've got some competition, @animealice ☺

#fandalism #fanboy #Gemuprising

Gem uprising. Two words which, when combined, make my heart stop.

I click on the fanboy hashtag. He's a *Gallows Dance* fanfic writer who calls himself simply 'Fanboy'. He's got a fan fiction website: Fandalism. Talk about puntastic. And it turns out, whoever *@eternalrose* is, they were right. I really have got some competition. The tweets about his new site seem to go on for ever. And according to the Fandom, Fanboy is not afraid to write a true dystopia.

I click on the heart-stopping link. Fandalism. It takes me to a fanfic site with some of the best graphics I've seen. Cartoons of Nate, Ash and Thorn, each with large eyes and pointed chins. And, wrapping the text in a sense of danger, is an angular frame of barbed wire. I haven't written any fanfic for a while, but when I did, it never looked like this. I'm a bit worried about reading it now. If the writing's anything like the graphics, then Anime Alice is about to look like a massive sack of shit. I swallow and remind myself that I'm the one with the international bestseller. Not him.

I scan the site. He's been posting for about two weeks. There seems to be a new post every day, so that he's matching real time to the passage of time in the world of *The Gallows Dance*. Clever. I scan the latest entry. It's written well, there's no arguing, but it isn't stunning like the graphics. Still, within minutes, I'm hooked. He certainly knows how to keep the tension going.

It's set after *The Gallows Song* took place. It's kind of like a fanfic sequel, told in daily instalments.

'Alice, lunch is ready,' Mum shouts up the stairs.

'It's OK, Mum, I'll warm it up,' I shout back. I'm going to have to read this from the beginning, because I have a horrible feeling it has something to do with Violet and Katie being in comas.

I click on the first post.

> Nate paused beside the group of rebels. They looked at him and laughed. 'What? Not doing maths in your head just to impress Thorn?' one of them sneered.
>
> Nate walked away.
>
> He'd show them, he thought to himself. One day, he'd show them all.

I scan through the next couple of weeks, transfixed by how seamlessly Fanboy shows Nate's steady spiral downwards. He starts out as our Nate, the Nate we wrote in *The Gallows Song*, the Nate we know and love, but gradually he transforms into a bitter, lonely shell. It's so skilful how Fanboy uses Nate's sense of isolation, of being different, to drive him to eventually contact Howard Stoneback – the old President's nephew – and betray his own. It makes me shiver, because I can really relate.

As I move through the posts, the likes and shares increase dramatically. They start off in the tens, quickly jump to the hundreds, and move into the tens of thousands. He's been busy, this Fanboy.

Then, a post a few days ago makes me gasp. Or, more precisely, the graphic makes me gasp. It's the rat from Violet's phone.

I read the text beside it:

> Howard removed the stamp from Nate's arm. The smallest of dots rested on his skin.
>
> 'This is the symbol of the Taleter, Nate,' Howard said, handing Nate a magnifying glass. 'It's a rat swallowing its own tail.'
>
> 'Why a rat?' Nate asked. 'A snake would make more sense. The ouroboros symbolizes infinity and growth.'
>
> Howard smiled. 'The President, my uncle, designed it himself. When he was a boy, he loved to catch vermin so he could torture them. He's always been fascinated by basic biology and the mechanisms of pain.'
>
> Nate resisted the urge to call the President a sadist.
>
> 'Anyway,' Howard continued, 'he liked them alive, as torturing corpses had little appeal. So he devised a trap which rocked shut when the rat walked inside, locking it away, unharmed. One day, Uncle went on holiday for a few weeks, and when he returned, the traps were filled with rats.' He paused. 'They'd all died, of course.'
>
> 'And they'd eaten their own tails,' Nate said. He

had an annoying habit of finishing off everyone else's stories, but Howard didn't seem to mind. Nate always noticed that Gems were less threatened by intelligence than Imps.

'Very good, Nate,' Howard said. 'Driven by hunger, panic, who knows. But every one of them died with their tail clamped between their teeth, or chewed clean away.'

'Let me guess, the Imps are the rats?'

'Absolutely. If you keep a rat alive, it will gnaw its own tail and die anyway. A swift kill is far kinder. And that is our ultimate aim, Nate. The swift elimination of vermin. For ever.'

'But they only eat their tails when they're trapped,' Nate said.

Howard smirked. 'I think you know as well as me, the Imps are not trapped by the Gems, they are not trapped by a city wall – they are trapped by their own flesh and blood.' He looked at Nate, long and hard. 'No offence.'

Nate smiled. It didn't offend him at all. 'So now that I'm a Taleter, am I one of you?'

Howard nodded. 'As close as you can be, genetics allowing.'

The mark Adam mentioned. The tattoo on Violet's phone. I bet it's on Nate's arm in the hospital. Balls. Balls. Balls. Big. Fat. Hairy ones. We need never have worried about a third book. It's fanfic which is the issue.

Fanboy is unknowingly changing the universe of *The Gallows Dance*.

12

VIOLET

The river comes into view, glinting like a thousand metal blades in the afternoon light. We slide down a hill and come to an outcrop of rock which shields a silty bank. Beneath us, a crowd of Imps stand in a circle, spitting out those three hateful words.

KILL THE TRAITORS.

And that's when I see the centrepiece of this sick show: three posts reaching towards the sky. Every muscle in my body solidifies and I turn to stone – heavy and cold and about to crack. I'd anticipated the gallows, of course I had. I'd pictured a rope slung from an overhead bridge or swaying from a lamp post like the pendulum of a grandfather clock, marking each second before death. But what meets my eye is even more horrific. The posts jut from a giant nest of wood; a blanket of kindling topped with bundles of sticks, logs and broken pieces of furniture.

I think I'm going to puke.

Because tied to those posts are people.

I see their feet first, three sets – dirty and completely bare, shards of wood digging into the flesh, puncturing the skin and drawing blood. *They'll be the first thing to burn*, I think. My eyes follow the path which I know the flames will take, sweeping up the bodies to the terrified faces.

Nate isn't there.

My whole body seems to shut down with relief. Sweet Jesus, my brother isn't about to burn.

But any reprieve is short-lived.

I know those faces. Saskia and Matthew. The rebels who helped us last time we were here.

And slightly elevated, displayed in the middle like a prize . . .

Baba.

A L I C E

I lie back on my bed, phone clamped in my hand. I'm barely aware of Mum's voice drifting up the stairs harping on about the bastard salmon.

I ignore her and read yesterday's post.

> Nate stopped dead in his tracks. He could hear a soft, metallic whir from behind a wall. It could have been the scratch of a cat, or a hungry mouse, but his brain was on high alert. Partly because he'd just returned from No-man's-land, quite literally the hinterland between the Imps and extinction, and partly because he'd just met with Howard Stoneback. If Thorn found out, he'd kill him without hesitation. Nate decided to peer around the brick wall.
>
> He was right to check. Because it wasn't a cat or a mouse. It was Baba, slumped in her hoverchair, her face unusually hard. 'Oh Nate, how could you?' she whispered.
>
> 'How did you know?' Nate asked. 'Howard said that your powers have been obsolete of late.'
>
> She smiled. 'I can no longer see the future, that is

true. But I can still hear you, Nate. We have a connection which cannot be severed.'

If my heart wasn't burning so hard in my chest, I would laugh. *Hinterland? Your powers have been obsolete of late?* Whoever this Fanboy is, he's clearly ancient. No self-respecting teenager would speak like that.

I reach the final blog post on Fandalism, posted this morning. My breath catches. If my theory's correct, if Fanboy really is influencing the world of *The Gallows Dance*, then Violet and Katie have landed right in the middle of this. I skim-read to the drama. And boy, is there drama.

'There is a traitor in the fold, and I will find them.' Thorn's voice was low and quiet. A warning perhaps.

Nate had begun to worry that Thorn had sent Ash and Willow away for a reason. Maybe Thorn wanted free rein.

Nate took some deep breaths. He has no way of linking it to me, he told himself. Just stay calm.

But Thorn stared at him with demons in his eyes. 'Water pipes don't just blow themselves up. Who knew? Who knew about the laying of the new water system in the city this morning, who could have leaked the information?'

'It could have come from the other side?' Baba replied. 'From the Gem side.'

Thorn ignored the old lady and smiled at Nate. 'You forget how keen a Gem's sense of smell is, Nate. You have dried your clothes well, but the stink of the river hangs on them like death. Which makes me wonder, why would you cross the river? What could possibly be at No-man's-land?'

Nate's mouth hung open, his heart beating faster than he ever thought possible.

'He was following me,' Baba said.

Thorn laughed. 'You expect me to believe you made it across the river in your chair, old woman?'

'Of course not,' Baba said. 'I paid a couple of Imps to row me across.'

'And why are you telling me this?' Thorn asked.

'Because I don't want Nate to die,' she replied. She knew he was guilty. And she was lying for him. 'I don't want him to die.'

And this was the only true thing she had said, and she said it without a moment's hesitation, a moment's doubt, even though it meant her execution.

VIOLET

My eyes hover on Baba's face longer than I can bear. She looks how I remember her. Her skin soft and doughy, her mouth kind. But something is very wrong. I can see her eyes. Apple green. Her eyelids are missing.

They've been sliced clean away.

My hands fly to my face in horror.

'Baba,' I whisper.

Saskia begins to scream, her words barely audible above the crowd. 'Please, we've done nothing wrong.' The wind changes direction, dragging her grey-streaked hair from her face. Her port wine stain looks

92

like a smudge of soot, as if the fire has already started.

'You have to believe us,' Matthew shouts, blood smeared across his kind features.

I feel a surge of love for them both, remembering how they saved me last time we were here. I'm about to move, about to slide down the bank, when I get a stabbing sensation in my eyes. I think I may have dropped to my knees; Katie's concerned hands flutter around my face. I blink. Push my fingers against my eyelids. The light seems to increase tenfold so that it blinds me.

Even through the agony, I know that it is Baba. I hear her voice in my head.

Little Flower, you came. Thank you.

The sound of her voice nearly breaks me. But I dry-swallow and wipe at my eyes, the pain receding to a dull ache. Shakily, I stand. I can hear Katie asking if I'm OK, but I zone her out. I need to focus on the mind blend. I fix my gaze on Baba, settle my breathing, and concentrate on forming silent words. *What's happening, Baba?*

I swear the corners of her mouth twitch into the faintest of smiles at the sound of my voice. *I fear my story ends here*, she says, *when yours, it seems, has just begun.*

Tears moisten my cheeks. *Why are the Imps about to kill you?*

It's Thorn. He doesn't trust anyone any more, especially an old precog who's technically a Gem.

I scan the crowd for the other members of the London Imp–Gem alliance. *Where's Ash? Where's Willow? They would never allow this to happen.*

Thorn made sure they were out of the way. She must sense my panic, because she quickly adds, *Don't worry, my child. They are safe.*

A loud gasp escapes Katie's lips, breaking my concentration and my link with Baba. Thorn appears from behind a line of Imps. He also looks just as I remembered him: dark, glossy skin, blacker than black hair. The eyepatch is long gone though. Alice and I wrote it out – there remained no reason to hide his genetic enhancement once the Imp–Gem treaty was signed in *The Gallows Song*.

The crowd falls quiet at the sight of him.

Thorn raises his voice so that it seems as though ten men speak instead of one. 'The precog Baba has been tried by a jury of her peers and found guilty of the crime of treason.'

'Bollocks!' Saskia screams. 'Baba would never betray the Imps and you know it.'

Thorn smiles, long and slow. 'She sold Imp secrets to the Gems. I have a confession . . . and a witness.'

I look to Baba. The green of her eyes causes my throat to constrict. *A confession?* I ask her.

It was me or Nate, she replies.

And with no warning or introduction, Nate appears, stepping from behind the other Imps. The bottom falls out of my stomach. He looks exactly the same as my little brother. Not my little brother from last time we were here. But Nate now. Nate as a young man on the brink of turning sixteen. And I realize that my internal representation of Nate is a boy frozen in time. It's strange seeing this older version. He has the same angular cheekbones, the same shaggy, dark-blond hair, and that same look around his eyes like he's either just stopped laughing, or he's about to start. But he's taller now, way taller than me; he looks less like a boy and more like a man. Joy surges up my throat, infecting my face and forcing my lips into a stupid grin.

'Nate!' I shriek. It's out my mouth before I can stop it, and I begin skidding down the bank, thinking only of reaching my little brother, not caring he stands beside a sociopath in the midst of an execution. 'Nate!' I shriek again.

Violet, STOP! Baba shouts in my head.

Her words bring me to my senses. I slide to a halt just as I reach the crowd.

But Nate must have heard. He looks at me for a second. Nothing. Not even a flicker. I am a stranger to him. The joy falters, though only for a moment. At least he is safe, at least I have a chance of bringing him home. I can't help glancing at his arm. It's pulled close to him so I can't see if the mark is there or not.

Baba looks at Thorn. 'I take responsibility for my actions, Thorn, I do. But Saskia and Matthew had nothing to do with this. Release them, I implore you.'

Thorn grins, a flash of pink as his tongue whips across his lip. 'Why would I believe anything you say, old woman?'

Nausea gathers in my stomach and sits there like a rock. I can barely catch my breath. *You're covering for Nate*, I say in my head. *You're covering for Nate, and now you're going to die.*

Baba doesn't look at me, but I hear her voice. *Yes.*

Thorn reaches into a nearby barrel and pulls out a long cane, the end of which has been wrapped in cloth and soaked in liquid. It leaves a trail of dots on the mud, iridescent in the sun. The scent of accelerant catches in my nostrils and the rock in my belly expands. *She's innocent*, I want to scream. *She's innocent.* But it's Baba or Nate, and my lips simply won't move.

Then I hear her voice again, urgent and loud. *Quickly, Little Flower, there is no time. I was not lying, my powers have dimmed, the future is no longer mine to see. But I can feel it. I can feel the changes happening in this universe. A dark presence is at work, twisting our minds, reshaping our destinies. I know you have come here to save your brother, Violet. But I think perhaps, you must save the boy in this world before you can save the boy who sleeps back home.*

I study her face, the parchment of her skin, her eyes, swollen and green, unable to blink or protect themselves from the impending heat and terror. *But how do I bring him home, Baba?* I ask her. *How do I bring him home and awaken him in our world?*

I await Baba's response, but I can't hear her any more. I just feel so helpless. I wish I was stronger, braver . . . better. I wish I could stop the horror before me. But I learnt a long time ago, wishes are futile in this universe.

Thorn pulls a lighter from his pocket.

I swear I can hear the scratch of that metal wheel grinding against the flint, smell the earthy scent of freshly extinguished matches. The tiny flame sticks to the lighter in spite of the wind. And it occurs to me how something so very small can become something terrifying and all-consuming in only a matter of seconds. As if proving me right, Thorn tips the lighter so that it touches the end of the cane. Within a heartbeat, he holds a blazing medieval-style torch.

The crowd gasps. A few Imps begin to cry.

'This ain't right,' somebody shouts. 'It ain't right.'

Thorn approaches the giant wood stack. Flames and menace light up his eyes. He passes the torch between his hands, quickly and precisely so that the fire leaves a single, orange streak. He grins. 'This is what happens to traitors, Baba.'

For a moment, I think I've started to scream. Then I realize it's Saskia, her voice fraught and high. 'No, no. Please, God, no.'

It seems so selfish in the circumstances, but I ask the question anyway, guilt pooling in my stomach. *How do I get home? There's no canon, no story to complete.*

Oh, my child. There is always a story. And in our world, you are the one true saviour. You must do what you've always done – save the Imps.

From what? I ask.

Thorn stands beside the mound, his head level with Baba's feet. He raises the torch high above his head, perhaps for drama, perhaps so the flames are in her line of sight.

I must break our connection now, she tells me. *Or you will feel what I will feel.*

But I can hardly make out her words. *No, Baba. I can't bear this.* Tears stream down my face and it feels like somebody's sitting on my chest.

She smiles. *Do not fear for me. The greatest story I know is not one of sacrifice, but one of rebirth. Remember that, my child.*

You will be reborn? I ask. But as the pain lifts entirely from my eyes, I know she can no longer hear me.

Everyone seems to hold their breath.

The only sound is the torch as it crackles and snaps like a pack of hungry dogs.

I wait for the flames to fall towards the wood.

But instead, Thorn turns to Nate and says, 'It has to be your word.'

Nate pushes his hand into his hair, lifting it from his sweat-drenched brow. And that's when I see it. A tiny mole just above the inside of his wrist. The same mark as the Gem President. A single word repeats over and over in my head: *Traitor*. My heart darkens with rage.

Nate pauses, his face caught between horror and acceptance. Then, his features seem to reconcile. 'Let them burn,' he says.

I'd expected a sudden movement, a vicious jab. But instead, Thorn touches the flame to the wood slowly,

97

almost lovingly.

Once the kindling grabs hold of the fire, there's no stopping it. A dreadful whooshing noise fills the air as the flames sweep around the stack, immediately transforming it into an ocean of reds and yellows. Lapping higher and higher.

And finally, Baba begins to scream.

A noise as thick and black as the smoke itself.

13

ALICE

I tear through Fanboy's final post, completely hooked. Baba takes the blame for Nate. She protects him. She dies for him. Thorn burns her at the stake. And Nate lets her burn. *He actually lets her burn.* The guilt he feels is overwhelming, but somehow he manages to twist it in his head. He thinks he's setting her free. Free from the prison of her body, old and disabled. Where have I heard that before? *We're setting him free.* The exact words Violet's parents used about Nate. Very strange.

I wipe my eyes with trembling fingers. Violet and Katie are there . . . right now . . . and Nate, he's there too . . . it's not his fault Fanboy is turning him into a massive dick. The three most important people in my life are in the most dangerous place I can imagine. And what with Thorn setting his mates on fire and Howard Stoneback plotting to destroy the Imps, the danger has just multiplied tenfold.

I try and control my breathing. Maybe I'm jumping the gun. Maybe this is as crazy as it sounds . . . I need to see the tattoo for myself to know that it's real.

The reporters are at the hospital already. They've obviously been banned from the building, so they hover at the main entrance like the vultures that they are. I walk past and they shout questions and snap away at my face.

I stare at the ground, but I don't shield my face with my hands celebrity-style. I've got a good profile . . . they can have that for free.

The receptionist recognizes me immediately. She's the one Violet always calls 'Crazy-mop-top-Millie'. I've no idea what her actual name is, but I don't think it's Millie somehow. Violet's got this lovely way of poking fun at people without being harsh. If I were to do that, it would come out bitchy.

'They're in the ICU,' Millie says. Her eyes bulge with sympathy. She looks like a bug in a wig.

'Thanks,' I reply.

'Do you want someone to go with you? It must be tough, you know . . .' she tails off.

I force a smile. 'I'm fine.'

Everyone stares at me as I make my way to the ICU, where Katie and Violet are. I'm used to people staring, like I said, but I will never get used to the whispers. I expect the usual. *Well, she clearly thinks she's God's gift; I bet she goes like a bunny; She obviously isn't a natural blonde.* And my all-time favourite: *Somebody really should tell her that the* Baywatch *auditions were last century.* But today, nobody whispers. They know who I am: the only member of the Comic-Con four who isn't in a coma.

I don't stay with the girls long, because that's not really why I'm here; not today. I take a deep breath as I enter Nate's ward.

I sit beside him for a few minutes, my heart beating in my mouth. If that tattoo is on his arm, then it means two things:

1. Nate is alive in the world of *The Gallows Dance*.
2. Fanboy is changing the world of *The Gallows Dance* with every post.

I take a deep breath and rotate Nate's arm so I can

100

see the underside of his wrist. There's a little black loop all right. Time seems to slow down as I grab my phone from my bag and do exactly what Violet must have done only yesterday, take a picture so I can enlarge it.

It's a rat eating its own tail. Ew!

This confirms *everything*.

The world around me blurs, my head begins to throb. I feel completely overwhelmed and consider just running out of the hospital there and then. Just heading home, downing a bottle of fizz and falling asleep in a sweet fug of nothingness. But I need to help my friends. I need to be strong. I take a few deep breaths and try to think clearly.

Nate is alive. OK. This is awesome.

Fanboy is cocking everything up. Anything but awesome.

I need to contact this Fanboy and convince him to stop posting. And I'm Alice Childs, author of *The Gallows Song*. That must mean something. And if it doesn't, if he won't stop, well, I'll hunt him down and grind his bloody keyboard to dust with my Jimmy Choos.

I go straight to the Fandalism site on my phone. The barbed wire motif suddenly seems all the more jagged, all the more dangerous. I scroll with urgent fingers. There isn't a contact page. I do a bit more snooping, but he isn't on social media or the internet more generally. The guy's a cyber ghost. How on earth did he get so popular?

This complicates things.

Deep breaths. New plan.

I need someone to help me. I'm hopeless with computers. Which sounds daft coming from a girl who spends most of her spare time glued to one. But that's different, that's writing. I know diddly about how to track down another user.

What I need is an IT nerd.

I open Facebook and follow a friends of friends trail until I find the perfect geek. A nerd who I really owe a drink, and who, historically, owes *me* a favour.

That night, I meet Danny in a gastro pub. Without his Gandalf costume, he looks younger, the slightness of his build more apparent. He sees me and smiles.

I slide into the seat opposite and lean over the table, offering him my cheek to kiss. I've spent way too long with editors and bookish people, because he clearly has no idea what to do, and a little awkwardly places his cheek against mine. He smells of paper and mint.

I grin at him. 'Thanks so much for meeting me.'

'No problem.' There's a slightly awkward pause. 'So how are Violet and Katie?' he asks.

'Still unconscious, but they're stable . . . whatever that means.'

'Good,' he says. 'The stable thing, not the coma thing.'

Another pause. I want to tell him how much it meant to me, him being there when I found my friends unconscious. He felt familiar, safe, an anchor when I felt I might just drift away. I can't find the right words, so I settle on, 'Thanks for helping at Comic-Con. Sorry Russell was a bit of a twat.'

He grins. 'A bit?'

'He got worse in the car, talked about movies the whole way to hospital. I swear he's on another planet.'

'Yeah, he did seem a bit me-centric,' Danny says, laughing. He has a lovely laugh, almost musical. Slowly, his face falls. 'I really am sorry about your friends. You must be beside yourself.'

I nod, tears immediately filling my eyes. I grab a menu and pretend to read it, desperate to change the subject. 'So . . . what you up to these days?' I ask.

He must realize I need the distraction, because he plays along without question. 'I'm working at a Tech firm down the road – they're going to fund my uni place, so long as I return there after graduating.'

'That's amazing.'

'Yeah.'

I look up from the menu. He's studying my face, looking confused. Eventually, he says, 'So you said in your message you needed my help again?'

'Yeah. Sorry, I know it's a big ask considering I haven't seen you in a year, except for yesterday, and you barely spoke to me at school.'

He frowns. '*You* didn't speak to *me* at school.'

'Did too. I asked to borrow your calculator. Three times.'

'I'm not sure that counts,' he says, smiling. 'It's OK. I think I would have freaked if you'd spoken to me back then – you were super scary at school.'

'I wasn't scary.'

'You wrote all that amazing fan fiction that everyone loved, and you were taller than everyone else in the year by the time you were twelve, and you were so pretty . . .' His eyes drop to his hands, which I notice are fiddling like crazy with a sachet of sugar.

'That doesn't make me scary,' I reply.

He grins. 'Maybe not to you. Vampires aren't afraid of vampires. Zombies aren't afraid of zombies.'

'So now I'm a zombie?'

'A metaphorical zombie, yes.'

I smile. 'You read my fanfic?'

'Course, I was super curious. A glimpse into the psyche of the elusive Alice Childs. It was really good, I was quite surprised.' He has this eager way of talking which totally makes up for any rudeness.

I burst out laughing. 'You were surprised?'

'Yeah, well, you look like –' he points the mangled sugar sachet at me – 'that.' He fidgets in his seat. 'Sorry, that was so not cool. I'm just really nervous.'

His honesty really appeals to me. I would never dream of admitting I was nervous – it's like admitting you're weak, and weak people lay themselves open to attack. But telling me this, Danny doesn't seem in the least bit weak. It's as though labelling the emotion takes away some of its power.

The waiter comes over, notepad and pen at the ready. My stomach rumbles, so I order a veggie burger with extra chips. Danny follows suit.

The waiter leaves and Danny raises an eyebrow. 'So, I'm assuming the help you want isn't exactly above board.'

'What makes you think that?'

'You wrote an international bestseller, which was very good by the way.'

'*Surprisingly* good,' I say.

A grin flashes across his face. 'Anyway, I'm guessing you can afford to pay a professional. But instead, you came to me, which means you want it off the books . . . excuse the pun.' He rips the sugar sachet by mistake, sending a shower of crystals across the table. 'Thank you for what you did for me, back in Year Eight, by the way.'

It catches me a little off guard. I didn't think we would actually *talk about it*. I assumed it would just be this unspoken debt he would silently pay off. I mean, he already chipped away at it at Comic-Con, for sure, but my spare-calculator-lending Comic-Con saviour is, on balance, probably still in *my* debt. He doesn't exactly look comfortable, brushing the sugar away and avoiding eye contact, but all the same, he's putting it out there, on the sugar-coated table.

'It was nothing,' I say.

'You really think that?' He looks up at me. He doesn't have a perfect cupid's bow, Nordic cheekbones, or a jawline from the Hemsworth gene pool, but his eyelashes are immense.

I shrug. 'OK, it was kind of cool.'

It *was* kind of cool. We were at Sara Cummings' birthday party back in Year Eight. Sara was one of the mean girls – she was beautiful, clever and made it perfectly clear she thought she was better than everyone else. I was friends with her for a few weeks, trying on the 'popular' girl thing for size, but she was *horrible*. Bullies who look like princesses are the worst kind, because nobody expects Lady Diana to gob in your drink. Plus, her parties sucked and she didn't like Harry Potter. I soon found my way back to Violet.

Anyway, God knows how Danny ended up invited to Sara's party – he must have been friends with one of the hot boys – but there he was all the same, sitting opposite me in a circle, playing spin the bottle. And when it was Sara's turn, it landed on Danny. She started to laugh and said, 'I'm not going into a cupboard with *him*.' And then she whispered, really loud so everyone would hear, 'He'll make it stink of jerk chicken.'

Danny's family are Jamaican, so this comment was bang out of order. 'She was an evil witch,' I say, suddenly guilty I'd willed Danny to remember this just so he'd feel compelled to help me out.

But Danny's eyes are alive and filled with joy. 'You took my hand and led me into the cupboard and shouted over your shoulder –' he does this high, girlie voice – '"There's only one jerk around here."'

I cover my face with my hands. 'Christ, Danny, I'm so sorry. I'd hoped you'd remember so you'd help me, but now you're saying it out loud—'

He cuts over me. 'Don't apologize. I was a king amongst the geeks for the rest of high school because of you.'

We stayed in that cupboard for the full seven minutes. We didn't kiss, we didn't even touch. We just stood there grinning unashamedly at each other, breathing really heavily and revelling in our victory over the horrid Sara Cummings.

I think maybe *this* is why I wanted Danny's help more than anyone else's. Not because he owes me, not because he helped me out at Comic-Con, but because he didn't try anything in that cupboard. Because he helped me remember I was so much more than a pretty girl at a party. And I realize how the scales are really looking . . . I owe Danny.

He places his hands on the table and leans towards me. A hint of peppermint moves through the air. 'You were awesome.' He has beautiful hands, his skin darkening at the knuckles and nail beds.

That familiar guilt squeezes my stomach again. 'I don't know, I didn't feel very awesome, I ditched Violet for that party just so I could hang with the mean girls.'

'But that's the thing, you could have been a mean girl, but you *chose* to hang with nerds.'

'Like when Harry was sorted,' I say, without thinking.

He scrunches up his face and does the best sorting hat impression – possibly the only sorting hat impression – I've ever seen. 'Not Slytherin, hey? Are you sure? You could be great, you know.'

Hold the phone. He speaks Harry Potter.

I burst out laughing and then mutter, 'But I am Slytherin, you know that, yeah?'

He drops his voice to a whisper. 'Your secret's safe with me.'

The food arrives. The chips taste amazing, and Danny obviously thinks the same, nodding his approval and shoving several into his mouth at once. He swallows. 'So what do you need my help with?'

'I need to find someone.'

'Wouldn't a map be more helpful?'

I waggle a chip at him. 'No, no. I need to find someone online. I need to know who they are and where they live.'

'Who they are may be tricky. You can be anyone online. Where they live should be easier.'

I grin, not caring that I've just taken a bite out of my burger. 'Well that's the most important thing. I need to be able to find them.'

'Just how illegal is this?'

'I want to talk to them, that's all,' I say.

His eyes widen. 'Who?'

'Some blogger called Fanboy, he's messing with my ratings, and more importantly my characters. He's writing a fan sequel to *The Gallows Song*.'

'You're not going to go all badass on him, are you?'

I wink, trying to close the conversation down the only way I know how: flirting. 'Now we both know my ass could never be bad, don't we?'

He looks a little uncomfortable, spends way too long dipping his chip in his ketchup. 'Sorry, Alice, I didn't mean it like that . . .' he tails off.

'Relax, I'm just messing.'

He clearly doesn't relax, not straight away at least. Now here's a slight problem: Danny is immune to my superpowers. And I'm not getting a gay vibe from him. I think, maybe, Danny is a gentleman. The kind of prince who would wipe away the dragon's blood before kissing the princess. I should have known this, based on the cupboard experience, yet still it comes as a surprise. Because Danny doesn't make me feel power-less, quite the opposite; he makes me feel like I can be a good person. Like I can put this Fanboy mess right.

'I can find Fanboy's IP address for you,' Danny says, finally. 'But why don't you fight fire with fire?'

'What do you mean?'

'Beat him at his own game. Start writing fanfic again.'

I almost choke on a chip. Why didn't I think of this before? If Fanboy can influence the world of *The Gallows Dance* through fanfic, then so can I.

Danny Bradshaw is a genius.

14
VIOLET

A riot breaks out around us – some Imps are trying to reach Baba and Saskia and Matthew, who are screaming on their pyres, but others are fighting back. I grab Katie's hand and together we scramble up the bank, away from the fighting. I don't know where we're going, only that we need to escape the smoke, the screams, the crack of moist wood.

Footsteps beat the ground behind us as we reach the top.

'Katie, stop,' I manage to say. 'We need to stay here. We need to help Nate – however much we want to run.'

We stumble to a halt as Thorn thunders up beside us, several Imps in tow. They surround Katie and me, yanking at our arms with gruff movements. Pain shoots into my shoulder, panic explodes in my chest.

Thorn looks at me and smiles. 'You must be Violet.'

I blink in astonishment. A thousand questions drown out the terror. How does he know my name? Does he remember me from last time I was here? Is he aware of the loop? Is he one of the Gems with enhanced memories?

He studies my face. 'Baba told me you were visiting.'

I try and make sense of his words. What has Baba told him? I'm scared of saying the wrong thing, so I offer a stilted nod.

He turns his attention to Katie. His features momentarily freeze up, and then his expression transforms into one of yearning and loss. He's remembering his murdered lover and his unborn child – Katie's potential resemblance to the latter brought him up short last time we were here too. It's impossible not to feel a stab of sympathy, even as his face re-hardens into something cruel and cold.

He spins to face me, any sign of his vulnerability gone. 'Tell me, Violet, why were you running? Only the guilty run.'

My heart beats wildly beneath my shirt, and he must be able to sense my anxiety, because he smiles like he's enjoying it.

'Scared people run too,' I reply, cursing my words for trembling so. 'And watching your hostess roast is beyond scary.'

'She said you were coming to save the Imps?' A thin note of danger taints his voice.

When I don't reply, he begins to laugh. The Imps join in, even Katie offers a nervous chuckle. But my face doesn't even crack a smile.

'Relax,' he says. 'You'd be dead by now if I truly suspected you. I took the opportunity to question Baba when she told me of your imminent arrival. She said you were harmless, that you weren't in on the betrayal. She said you were here to learn about the London Imp–Gem alliance. And at that point, I think she was beyond lying. Removing body parts has a way of cutting through the bullshit, wouldn't you say?'

I swallow, clearing my mouth of the rage, the distress, the terror, desperate to keep me and Katie off his kill list. 'She was telling the truth,' I say. 'There's so much we could learn from your alliance. It's the flagship of Imp–Gem treaties, after all.' Silently, I thank

Baba for telling him this. It gives us an excuse to be here, to spend time with Nate.

Thorn nods. 'Well, Ash and Willow can show you around when they return from the Pastures. You're welcome to look around, but you must stay out of my business.' He extends his hand towards me.

Every fibre of my being screams at me to stop, and yet I take that hand in my own. It sits in my palm like something hot and unsafe. His fingers curl around mine and almost crush them. I force my face to remain still; I won't give him the pleasure of seeing me wince.

'You will stay with me, obviously,' he says. I open my mouth to object, but he cuts across me. 'I won't take no for an answer.'

So I do the only the thing I can. Nod.

I hate this place.

ALICE

Danny lounges on my bedroom floor, his face reflecting the light from his laptop. He kicked off his trainers before he came up and his socks are mismatched and riddled with holes. He's scrolling through Fanboy's site with interest. 'The graphics are dope.'

I sigh. 'I know, right.'

'Nothing we can't handle. If you want, I can help you set up a new site, give it a new look?'

I flush with gratitude. 'Thank you.' I'm more than capable of setting up a site, but it's so nice having someone on my side.

'No problem.' He begins tapping away on his laptop. 'So, what do you want to call it?'

I shrug. 'Something classy. No puns allowed. It

needs to show that we're fighting back, the Fandom, I mean. We won't let Fanboy ruin our utopia. We're rising up, we're revolting.'

'Maybe leave out the revolting bit.'

I laugh, an idea forming. 'The Fandom Rising,' I say, loving the way it sounds when I say it out loud. 'The Fandom Rising, like we're a flock of birds taking off. It's perfect.'

Danny nods. 'Yep, that sounds great . . . and the graphic?'

'Birds, let's stick with the bird thing. It fits for lots of reasons. It's not just about the Fandom rising up, it's the freedom of the Imps, and it ties in with *The Gallows Song*, which was meant to be the final book, the swan-song if you like.'

'You want swans in the graphics?'

I shake my head, excitement zinging through my body. 'No, not swans, swallows. They've got an amazing silhouette, they'll look really striking.'

'Are you a secret birder or something?'

'Maybe.' I wiggle my eyebrows then laugh. 'Nah. Winter 2015, the swallow print was everywhere.'

Danny sits next to me on my bed. He pulls up some images of swallows on his screen and we spend a few minutes picking out our favourites. 'There's something I need to ask,' he says, turning to look me in the eye. 'Why the sudden interest in Fanboy? Violet and Katie are unconscious, and suddenly you want to track down a mysterious fanfic writer.'

What can I say? I want to tell him the truth. But he'll never believe me. God, this is how poor Violet must have felt when she was trying to tell me about *The Gallows Dance*. I open my mouth, ready to just tell him the whole mixed-up story, when I see those gorgeous dark eyes staring back at me. I stop. I don't want Danny to think I'm mad. I wave my hand in front of my face. 'He's messing with the Fandom, that's all. Violet would hate it, and so would Nate. I mean, he's actually making Nate bad, can you imagine that? Nate is the best person I know.' My voice snags on the lump in my throat.

'I remember Violet's little brother. He was a cool kid, really good with computers, better than me.'

I can't hold them back any more. The tears begin to fall down my face and I don't try to stop them or dab at them. I just let them fall. 'He's the best. They're turning off his life support in a few days.' I snort back a sob. 'He's going to die.' I bury my face in my hands and weep like a child.

Danny lays a hand on my back and I'm surprised by how light his touch is. 'Alice, that's just . . . well, it's just awful. I'm so sorry.'

I cry for a while, and Danny just leaves his hand on my back, not speaking, not moving. The warmth from his palm gives me comfort. Eventually, when I'm all cried out, I look up at him. He looks really beautiful, nothing like Willow, or any other Gem for that matter, but beautiful all the same. 'Everyone I love is unconscious in that bastard hospital, and I'm still here. How has that happened? How am I still awake?'

He breathes in long and slow. I'm expecting words of comfort, words which match the lightness of his touch. But I'm learning that Danny has this bluntness which he isn't afraid to wield, even in the presence of a weeping damsel. 'A better question would be – why is everyone you love unconscious?' He studies my face. 'What are you hiding, scary Alice?'

I choke back another sob. 'It's complicated. I'm not even sure I understand, but Fanboy has something to do with my friends being in comas, I know it sounds insane . . . I need to find him and make him stop.'

His brow creases beneath his mess of black curls. 'OK. Well, if that's the case, we better find out who he is.'

15

A L I C E

I leave Danny working and fetch some drinks. I'm just firing up the coffee machine when Mum glides in, dressed head-to-toe in lycra. She's either heading for a late-night workout or an eighties revival concert.

'Who's the boy you came in with?' she asks, grabbing a couple of mineral waters from the fridge.

'Just a friend.'

She raises a pencilled brow. 'He's not your usual type.'

'I don't have a type.'

She laughs. 'Yes you do. And they're normally at least three inches taller than you.'

'And that's worked out just swell, hasn't it?' I give her a cheesy thumbs up.

She sighs. 'Well, you're an adult now, Alice. I can't tell you what to do. Just make sure you use protection.'

'Jesus, Mum. The only protection we'll need is Norton spyware.'

She scowls, her foundation cracking between her eyes. 'Spy what?'

God, she pisses me off sometimes. Telling me who I can and can't fancy, sticking her nose into my sex life. I can feel the anger heating my cheeks. 'You know I'm not seeing anyone at the moment. Violet's probably getting more than I am, and she's in a coma.'

'Alice, what a terrible thing to say.'

The anger turns into embarrassment; it was a terrible thing to say, she's right. I slide a cup beneath the coffee machine and push the button, letting the gurgle of liquid drown out my shame.

'See you later,' she calls over her shoulder as she leaves the room.

The gurgling stops and I shuffle back to my room, slopping coffee on the cream carpet and not giving a crap. *Why does Mum turn me into this pathetic version of myself?*

I hand a coffee to Danny, who smiles gratefully at me. My Mum-induced downer begins to lift.

'Take a look,' he says, angling the laptop so I can see.

I sit beside him on my bed and look over my sparkling new site. He's already done an amazing job. 'Danny, you are quite simply the best.'

'It still needs some work. Why don't I finish it off while you do your creative thing?'

'What?'

'Fanfic. We can copy and paste it in when we're both done.'

'Great, thanks.' I pull out my laptop, which has actually gathered a little dust, and set myself up at my desk. I listen to Danny tapping away on his keyboard and I begin to relax.

OK. I need to undo the damage Fanboy has done.

But how?

The calmness I felt listening to Danny's rhythmic tapping has gone. My fingers begin to tremble as I think about the enormous responsibility of the situation. I could so easily screw this up. And it will be my friends who feel it. My mouth dries and my forehead pricks with sweat.

I need to stop thinking about the bigger picture. I need to focus on the screen before me . . . think like a

116

writer, not a saviour. Writing, I can do.

Deep breath.

OK. Let's stop Nate being such a tool.

Changing Nate back to a good guy can't be too sudden, that would be unbelievable and the readers won't buy in. I need to start by building empathy, all the best redemption stories do this. And what better way to build empathy than to help the reader understand *why* Nate turned traitor in the first place. Fanboy touched on this, but I can flesh it out, make it zing, because if anyone understands what it's like to not fit in, it's me. I focus on the words as they spill from my fingers on to the screen.

It's time to tell Nate's story.

NATE

Most people, most things, belong somewhere. Books on shelves, flowers in beds, laughter in children. We all need family, friends, groups of people who make us feel accepted and part of something bigger than ourselves.

Not me. I've never belonged anywhere, not really.

My name is Nate, and I'm an Imperfect. And may it be said quite rightly that my body, face and immune system are, indeed, imperfect. But my brain – my big, beautiful brain – is as perfect a specimen as you'll ever know. I've always been clever. Some say I'm a genius. But the problem remains that I'm an Imperfect. And in spite of the Imp–Gem alliance, the words Imp and genius remain paradoxical.

And this haunts me every day.

I'll start at the beginning. You see, I've never had a

family; I was orphaned when I was very young and was raised by the streets of London. It quickly became clear that I was brighter than the average Imp. This helped me make friends. After all, I could con bread from a starving man if I had to. But these so-called friends did not love me for who I was, they loved me for what I could provide. And that is not belonging. That is bribery.

I thought becoming a rebel would fill the hole. A ready-made family bound together by a united goal. I spent years imagining the day I would be old enough to join the cause. The comradery, the friendship. The belonging. But when that day finally came, the only rebel who truly accepted me, who wasn't threatened by my big, beautiful brain, was Thorn.

Thorn. The Gem.

And that got me thinking.

There are lots of Gems beyond the streets of London.

Maybe I could belong.

I sit back, feeling happy for the first time in ages. I'd forgotten how much I enjoy writing fanfic.

Danny watches me for a moment. 'Wow, you look completely zen.'

'Call me Gandhi.'

'Can I read it, Gandhi?'

I nod, eager to see what he thinks. He crouches beside me and falls silent, his eyes moving rhythmically from side to side. When he's finished, he grins his lovely grin. 'It's really good. You've totally got inside his head. But it reads like he's still going to the dark side – I thought you didn't want that.'

'Yes, but this is just step one in a bigger plan. You see, I need to help the Fandom understand why Nate went bad in the first place, you know, build empathy. Once they feel sorry for him, they'll not only invest in his redemption story, they'll positively beg for it.'

He smiles. 'You've got it sussed, Al. I'll finish the site tonight, send you your login details, then you can hit that publish button.'

He called me Al. Literally nobody has ever called me that. I kind of like it. 'Thanks so much, I really don't know how I can ever repay you.' I want to kiss his cheek, but something holds me back. I settle for squeezing his arm.

He blushes. 'Meh.'

True to his word, Danny sends me my login details later that night.

The site looks incredible. He's really talented. There's a cloud of swallows climbing upwards against a black background, the words *Fandom Rising* above them in gold. He's left a space for me to write something under the header. I bite my lip. I want to write something which Violet would like, something which makes her feel closer. I stare at the cloud of swallows and it suddenly seems so obvious. Her favourite song from when she was a kid was about swallows. I wonder if I had this at the back of my mind all along. Jane used to sing it to us at sleepovers after we'd overdosed on Haribo and Stephen King movies. It's one of those boring, folksy songs the Girl Guides probably still sing around a campfire. I quickly google some of the lyric fragments.

I find it with ease. My throat begins to ache again. It's prettier than I remember – no wonder Violet loved it.

I type out a verse:

Let me fix your broken wing,
A swallow should fly free, my love,
For you were born to dance and sing,
And you will soar with me, my love.

Then, I write my message to the fans:

You've all read Fandalism.

The tale of a lost Imp who turns traitor. The tale of
a utopia rotting from the inside.

Now it's time for Nate's story.

There. Let's see if I can't start a fanfic war. That will
help my ratings at the very least.

I copy and paste in my first chapter, check it over a
few times, then I hit publish.

I message Danny.

It's alive. It's alive. IT'S ALIVE!

Well done, Dr Frankenstein ☺

I tweet the link to my followers, with a message
saying *Anime Alice is back! Check out my new fanfic site,*
Fandom Rising.

Quickly, I update my other social media accounts,
and then, like a total Kardashian, sit back and watch
the views on the webpage. They tick upwards, but way
too slowly to be any use to Violet and Katie. I need
someone to help with promotion. There's only one
obvious candidate, though it pains me to say it: Russell
Jones. I drop him a quick message on Twitter, dangling
the carrot of that third book he kept blathering on
about.

Hey Russell, thanks so much for helping me today. It was so kind of you. Sorry I wasn't very chatty, I'm sure you understand. I would really appreciate some boosting, trying to get back in the fanfic saddle. It could provide some inspiration for that third book we were discussing

He replies a few minutes later, in spite of the late hour.

Sure thing, beautiful.

Slightly patronizing, but he does retweet my post.
It works. Within an hour or so, views are in the thousands.
Game on, Fanboy.

16

VIOLET

We sleep at Thorn's house. An old red-brick terrace with balconies which were once painted white and adorned with flowers. There's no torture chamber, no creepy stuffed animal heads. It's almost an anti-climax. Katie and I share a double bed which feels like a spring could burst free any moment, impaling our spines, but it's a huge improvement on the Imp-hut from my last visit. Still, knowing Thorn sleeps only metres away makes me crave that hay-dusted bench back at the Harper estate.

I console myself with a single thought: tomorrow I'll see Ash.

Katie turns down the paraffin lamp so I can just make out the edges of her face. She stares at me, blinking slowly. 'Well, today sucked.'

This almost makes me laugh, but the scent of roasting flesh still sticks to my hair, and I can't quite muster a smile. Instead, I drop my voice low. 'The room could be bugged.' I glance quickly at the walls, suddenly regretting how readily I flung my shirt off. The shabby furnishings, the lack of electricity, the general poverty combines to make you forget about the Gem technology which could be hidden anywhere.

'How could it happen?' Katie asks, her voice barely a whisper. 'How could he do that?'

'You mean Nate?' I say, afraid to use the word traitor,

especially now the bug idea has lodged in my head.

Katie nods.

'Someone must be writing that third book,' I say.

There's a long pause. So long, I wonder if Katie's fallen asleep. Finally, she whispers, 'Do you think it's Alice?'

'No. We doubted her last time we were here, and she proved us wrong, remember? There must be some crazy author back in our world who's turning Nate . . .' I tail off, glancing into the blackness with paranoid eyes.

Katie squeezes my hand under the covers. 'Let's hope Alice works out what's going on then. She must have at least figured out you're not mad, now we're back in comas again. Maybe she'll hunt down the crazy author and make them stop.'

I instinctively touch my split-heart necklace, running my finger along the jagged edge. 'We can but hope.'

ALICE

The first thing I do when I wake is check my views. Fandom Rising has really taken off. Russell has actually been pretty cool, helping publicize my links across all his social media channels. I can't work out if he wants to get inside my pants, or if he wants me to write the third book. Well, he should be so lucky, on both accounts.

Spurred on by my growing popularity, I decide to post again. *How else can I help Violet and Katie? What damage has Fanboy done to their universe, apart from dark-siding Nate?* Quickly, I scroll through the Fandalism site, frowning so hard I swear I'll need botox before I hit twenty. My gaze settles on her name. Baba. Of course. Didn't Violet say the old woman visited her in her dreams? The one person who can help her, who can tell her the future, has gone. My scowl morphs into the smuggest of grins, because my next post is going to be nothing short of genius. Not only can I tell Nate's story, I can give Violet another precog.

NATE

I stare into the embers of the bonfire, tears stinging my eyes. I didn't want Baba to die. She was always so good to me. I'd come to think of her as a surrogate grandma. But it was me or her. And I must confess, death terrifies me, and whilst I am lots of things, I am not ready to die.

The crowd scattered many, many hours ago, but guilt and grief have prevented me from leaving, and now I am the only one left here, shivering in the dark. I've curled into a ball on my side. Maybe, if I curl up tight enough, I can just disappear. All this will stop. The pain, the guilt, the betrayal.

Through the smoke, through my tears, I see a figure.

And as it moves towards me, an inexplicable calmness spreads through my body.

The silhouette must belong to a precog.

I begin to visualize an old lady with no lips and sealed-up eyelids. Maybe Baba's long-lost twin or something. But then I remember, I can write my new precog any way I please. There's no reason why replacement-Baba can't be a dude, hotter than the sun, with a six-pack to rival Dwayne Johnson's. Pimp my precog. I'm quite literally cackling at my screen as I begin to write. Violet is so going to thank me for this.

He is a man so beautiful he makes me forget the ugliness inside my soul. Tall, East Asian, with black hair and piercing brown eyes. The smoke folds around his broad shoulders in layers of grey.

'Hello, Nate,' he says. 'My name is Yan.'

'Hello, Yan,' I whisper back. I know I should run away, but I feel so calm, so peaceful. Surely this stunning man couldn't possibly hurt me.

'Why so sad?' he asks.

I pause. 'I . . . I did something terrible.'

'I know.'

I rub my eyes, blinded by the grey and my own tears. 'Who are you?'

Yan smiles. 'I've been sent by a friend.'

I want to sit up . . . I want to sit up and walk towards him, but my body won't move. 'Why?'

'To help,' he replies simply.

'To help destroy the Imps?'

He blinks. 'No. To help you remember.'

'Remember what?' I ask.

'To remember who you really are.'

I squeeze my eyes shut, trying to stop the stinging of the tears. And when I open them again, Yan has gone.

I close my laptop, still smiling to myself. Baba just got an upgrade.

You're welcome, Violet.

17

VIOLET

Thorn walks us to the church in the diluted, post-dawn sun. I'd forgotten how the stink of the city permeates every part of you, how the cold gets beneath your skin and makes your bones ache. And I'd forgotten the soul-sucking greyness of it all. What I wouldn't give for the red of a double-decker bus, the crisp multicoloured stripes of a shop's awning, the turquoise pop of a little girl's pinafore. Black and white movies are only cool when you're not stuck in one.

We approach the church, and Thorn presses his thumb against a pad mounted beside the wooden door. The pad emits a beep and the door springs open. We step inside. The scent of incense-infused stone fills me with terror and nostalgia all at once. I quickly take in my surroundings. Headquarters looks slicker, cast in the artificial blueish glow of overhead spotlights. The desks have been upgraded, laden with hi-tech computers and gadgets, and the chairs look padded and comfy. When Alice and I changed this place into the HQ of the Imp–Gem alliance, we didn't upgrade it like this.

My eyes instinctively search for the pew where I laid out Nate's waxy, still body. But the pew has gone. Something fat and ugly swells in my stomach, a noxious mix of anger and vengefulness. Somewhere in this universe is the man who shot my little brother . . .

Howard Stoneback. And if I ever meet him, I think I may kill him.

Thorn sits on a nearby chair and smiles at us. 'Ash and Willow should be back soon. Then they can show you around the city.' He busies himself with a nearby blueprint.

Katie and I stand side by side, fidgeting and awkward. Even though I'm dreading the moment Ash returns and realizes Baba, Saskia and Matthew are dead, I find myself wishing he would just hurry up. As if on cue, footsteps sound from outside the church. My skin bristles. Something about those footsteps is familiar, confident and yet gentle. The keypad beeps. I inhale a lungful of bittersweet church air and hold my breath . . . *Is it him?*

He walks through the door. His winter eyes – stark and glassy against the peach of his skin – cause my insides to knot.

'Ash,' I whisper, savouring the shape of his name in my mouth.

Nothing separates us except several metres of air. Until this moment, I'd never noticed how insubstantial air is. Basically, *nothing* stands between us. I want to run to him and wrap him in my arms, breathing in that heady scent of woodsmoke, soap and sweat. It's like something's reaching inside me, hauling me towards him. I have to resist it with every inch of my body.

His eyes fall on Thorn, who he acknowledges with a terse nod.

I wait for his gaze to move to mine, for that powerful click when you can almost hear two souls connecting. I stare at his pale, irregular face, just willing him to look at me. And suddenly, he does. It's the simplest thing, just the tiniest of eye movements, and yet everything feels different. I smile at him, I mean, really smile. I can't help it. Being held in his view and knowing that my face fills his mind is enough to make me forget, at least for a moment, the mess I'm in.

I anticipate his lazy smile leaning up one side of his face, that shiver down my spine. Is it just me, or is there a flicker of recognition in his eyes?

'That's *Ash*?' Katie whispers.

'Yep,' I reply.

'He's *improved*.'

I see what she means. Undeniably, his colours remain the same; if I squinted, blurring the edges of his face into an Impressionist painting, he'd be the boy I fell in love with. But *The Gallows Song* clearly suited him. He's gained a little weight, muscle bulk rather than flab, and he looks broader in the shoulders. The slight hollow-waif look has vanished from around his eyes. In spite of the heat gathering around my neck and thighs, I can't help feeling a little put out: he looks better without me.

'Hi,' he says.

At first, I half expect him to do a double take, his face transforming with joy as he realizes who I am. But of course, he hasn't a clue – and the glint of recognition in his eyes quickly fades. The boy who loved me, who offered to die in my place, doesn't even know me. It takes everything I have to keep on smiling.

'Hi,' I reply.

Thorn rises from his chair. 'Ash, this is Violet and Katie, Baba's friends. They want to know more about the London alliance.'

He shakes my hand, gently, steadily. His lips move slightly, a mere tremor, and his eyebrows pull together for the briefest of moments. It's one of those micro-expressions, revealing more about his feelings than a thousand words. He's completely floored. 'Sorry,' he mutters, controlling his features. 'You just . . . really remind me of someone.'

Does he remember me after all?

Thorn laughs. 'Yes, her likeness to Rose is rather striking, but Baba assured me it was no more than a coincidence.'

Katie grabs my arm. 'Who is *that*?'

Willow walks through the door. Even cast in the artificial glow of the church, he seems to radiate sunshine. I'd forgotten just how attractive he is. I get this strange squirmy feeling in my gut. Dammit. It's like he's got superpowers or something, and I remind myself what a coward he was, how he failed to say his lines when I stood waiting to be hanged.

Katie makes this strange sound, halfway between a swallow and a swear word. I've never seen her dumbstruck by a man before. I press my lips together in case I laugh.

Ash watches her, his smile finally edging up one side of his face. 'Yeah, he has this effect on people. It's really annoying.'

Willow walks towards us, and then stops mid-stride, mouth hanging open. He stares at me. The emotion must overwhelm him so that he forgets himself, and he begins striding towards me with purpose. Urgently, he cups my face in his hands, his eyes digesting my every line. 'You look just like her,' he whispers.

Ash gently pulls his hands away. 'There are similarities, I agree, but don't be weird about it, yeah? This is Violet.'

Willow's hands fall from my cheeks. There's a flicker of embarrassment, before he arranges his features into a perfect smile. 'Forgive me, Violet. You must think I'm mad.'

I shrug. 'It's cool.'

Ash turns to Thorn. 'So there was a mix-up with that meeting you wanted us to attend, turns out you got the wrong date.' He looks around. 'Where's Baba?'

My heart sinks. In a few seconds, that lovely half-smile will disappear entirely.

Thorn smirks. 'She . . . had to leave.'

'What do you mean?' Ash asks. 'We've only been gone a night, she never said anything about leaving.'

'Maybe she doesn't tell you everything,' Thorn replies.

Ash blinks, confused. 'When's she coming back?'

'She isn't,' Thorn replies, clearly enjoying the power.

Silence hangs in the air. I feel sick. Really sick. I consider just blurting it out, unable to watch Ash's confused expression, knowing what's about to come. But Thorn scares me. His size, his intensity. And I can't bring Nate home if I'm dead.

Willow steps forwards, suspicion darkening his copper eyes. 'What do you mean, she isn't coming back? Did you tell us the wrong date on purpose?'

'Oh Thorn, what did you do?' Ash asks, his voice rising with panic.

Thorn shrugs, and then says in an almost nonchalant tone, 'She betrayed us, so I killed her.'

Time seems to stop. Even the stone seems to hold its breath.

I expect Ash and Willow to explode, a flurry of movement and swear words. I brace myself for the outburst, but instead, Ash simply whispers one tiny, lost word: 'How?'

'Fire,' Thorn replies. 'Down by the river. It was quite the show.'

'You bastard,' Ash whispers. He takes off, sprinting from the church, Willow close behind.

Katie and I run after them, grateful to escape the sound of Thorn's laughter as it morphs into the shriek of gulls. We reach the site of the execution in mere minutes. The crowds and the flames have long gone, leaving an empty silt beach, so black, so scorched, it looks no more than a charcoal drawing. Three burnt stumps wilt where the posts once stood proud, and there's no sign of the victims – my friends. For a moment, I think maybe they escaped, then reality kicks in and I remember their remains – bones, tendons, teeth, the bits that don't burn – have probably fallen into the charred stack below. I shudder, bile rising in my throat.

Ash and Willow stand on the outcrop overlooking the scene, exactly where Katie and I stood yesterday. They don't speak, they don't even cry, they just stare. Without thinking, I begin moving towards Ash, my arms outstretched, wanting to comfort him, wanting to share his pain. He turns and for a second, I think it's really going to happen – he's going to wrap his arms around me. But a voice cuts through the quiet. 'Ash, Ash.'

A young woman with bronze skin and dark, flowing hair dashes from the city towards us. A panicked look grips her face, yet it's still obvious just how gorgeous she is. She has large oval eyes, heavily lashed and filled with kindness.

'Oh Ash,' she says. 'They told me what happened.' She reaches Ash and he looks at her the way he used to look at me. And even before he extends his arms and they embrace, I know that they're going to slot perfectly together. But it still breaks my heart when they do.

'Daisy,' he whispers into her hair.

I look at her. It's like someone gave me a magic wand and asked me to fix everything about myself I hated.

And, Cinderella-style, I twizzled that wand above my head, releasing a cascade of sparks. My legs lengthened, my eyelashes grew, my hair de-frizzed.

Only I didn't have a wand, I had a pen.

The jealousy which explodes through my veins surprises me. It's hard and angular, strong enough to temporarily drown out my sorrow for Baba's loss, strong enough to swallow up my anger towards Thorn. I wrote Ash a girlfriend, and I made her PERFECT. I made her a Gem, for God's sake. I would kick myself if my legs weren't too short to reach.

Katie studies my face, then whispers, 'Careful there, Othello.'

She's got a point, but I can't do anything to tame that green-eyed monster as I watch Ash sweep the hair from Daisy's face.

'It's my fault,' he says. 'I should have known Thorn was up to something when he asked us to go to the Pastures for the night.'

I force myself to look away, the jealousy threatening to consume me entirely.

That's when I see him: Nate. He sits on the very edge of the beach, almost hidden by some rocks. He stares at the sooty remains of the bonfire, his sandy hair stirring in the wind. His face is stained with tears. I can see where they've dried and new ones trickled, leaving streaks of salty residue. The jealousy, the anger, all just flakes away and I'm left only with a need to rush to him – to this strange, almost-Nate –and tell him everything's going to be OK. But he looks at me like I'm a stranger. To him, I *am* a stranger.

I suddenly feel very guilty for writing him such a sparse backstory. He had no family and lived as a street-Imp most of his life. The rebels took him in and became his family. But now, he looks like he needs a mum and dad more than anyone else in the world.

He wipes his face on the back of his shirtsleeve and stands to leave. The movement draws the attention of the others.

'That's right, run away,' Daisy shouts.

'What's Nate done?' Willow asks.

Daisy releases a sob. 'It's just too awful to say.'

Ash loops an arm around her graceful neck and pulls her head into his chest. They're so close they could almost be one person. 'Hush, it's OK,' he whispers into her hair.

Daisy stares at Nate, and even in the morning light, I see an uncharacteristic hardness in her dark eyes. 'Coward.' She spits the word like a snake spits venom.

My gut clenches. *Does she know that Nate's the traitor?*

Nate rushes past us, knocking my shoulder as he goes. I lay my hand on the spot where his body touched mine. I want to run after him, but I have no idea what to say or how to make it better.

Daisy watches him leave. 'He's been acting strangely the past few weeks, and now this.' She swings her arm, gesturing to the shadow of the bonfire below.

Ash rubs her back. 'Dee, it's Nate. *Nate.* He's one of the good guys.'

I don't know which upsets me more: hearing Ash use a cutesy nickname for her, or hearing Ash defend Nate. I must make a sort of whimpering noise, my body unable to contain all of the horrible feelings. Daisy looks directly at me. Has she noticed that I look like her short, pale, ugly sister? I want so badly to hate her, but it isn't her fault I made her everything I longed to be. It's nobody's fault but my own.

She catches my eye and smiles. It's a tired, broken smile – she's trying to be kind. 'You really have picked a terrible time to visit.'

'Understatement,' Katie replies.

A tiny laugh escapes Daisy's lips. 'I know you're staying with Thorn, but if you'd rather, you can stay with me and Ash. We've got room.'

'Thanks,' I manage to squeak.

She touches my upper arm, a gentle squeeze, and then does the same to Katie. It's a small and yet surprisingly intimate gesture, an attempt to reassure us, a genuine act of compassion when her heart must be breaking. 'Anyway, see you soon,' she says, before setting off back to the buildings.

I expect Ash to follow, but instead, he seems to study my face. I'd forgotten just how achingly pale his eyes are. I suddenly notice how cold it is; the tiny hairs on my neck begin to prickle.

'Who are you?' he asks. I can almost feel the warmth of his breath on my cheek.

I want to tell him I'm the time-travelling assassin. The girl he showed the Dupes to. The girl he offered to die for. But all I can do is stare back at him.

'Ash,' Daisy calls.

A smile ghosts across his face, a smile which I can't for the life of me read. And then he walks away.

'*Henpecked*,' Katie sings.

'She seems nice,' I say.

'She suspects Nate though,' Katie replies. 'We need to be careful.'

'Agreed.' Because despite what Nate did to Baba, despite the rat tattoo festering on his arm, he's still the only hope I have of saving my little brother back home.

'Who's that?' Katie asks, pointing to the river. Almost directly in front of us, halfway towards No-man's-land, bobs a rowing boat. I swear it wasn't there a moment ago. Even stranger, standing in the boat is a tall, black-haired man. He doesn't seem to move, as if he's somehow immune to the motion of the water. I can just make out his face. Defined, beautiful, East Asian. He's undoubtedly Gem, his features symmetrical, his suit tailored and expensive. He blinks at me, slowly, knowingly, perhaps.

'Where did he spring from?' Katie whispers. 'That is just creepy-weird.'

He begins to wave. No, not wave . . . beckon.

'Is he . . . ?' I ask, tailing off.

Katie nods. 'I think he wants us to follow him.'

If my heart wasn't beating so hard, I would laugh. 'What? Just wade into the Thames and climb aboard?'

A sudden noise draws our attention: the trill of bird-song and the swoosh of wings. We look up to see a flock of crescent-shaped swallows passing overhead. They move as one, heading over the city and into the distance.

And when we look back to the river, both the boat and the beckoning man have vanished.

18

VIOLET

I'm floating. Suspended in a pool the exact temperature as my body so I can't tell where my skin ends and the water begins. For a moment, I wonder if I am water, unable to hold any shape or form. *Am I dreaming?* My eyes are closed, and when I open them, the face which hovers above mine takes my breath away, reminding me that I am so much more than the water which surrounds me. It belongs to the beckoning man. I start to marvel at the fact his hair isn't falling forward, in spite of the fact he's suspended over me. Then I realize we're both standing upright and the world makes a little more sense. There is no pool. Just an endless stretch of black. I glance at my feet and see that there's no ground. And when I look up, he's smiling.

'Who are you?' I ask.

'Yan,' he replies, taking my hands in his.

'Yan,' I repeat softly. Then I say it again, a little stronger. 'Yan.'

'You need to trust me, Violet. Can you do that?'

'I . . . I don't even know you.'

He laughs. 'Not yet, but you will. I've been sent by a friend.'

'Baba?'

'Perhaps.'

As he looks around him, colours begin to appear,

swirling around each other like paint in water, shapes gradually taking form. We're standing in the orchard, in Baba's favourite spot. His presence only draws attention to her absence, making my chest sting with loss.

Tears spring to my eyes. 'Why did she save Nate?'

'The same reason you're trying to. Because of love.'

My emotions overwhelm me and I have to gasp for air. It hits my tongue – fresh, sweet and tart all at once. 'Can I bring him home?'

'I believe so.'

Warmth seems to run through my veins. *There's still hope.*

Yan smiles. 'The transfer process *should* work. Though they are very different boys right now: the boy asleep in the hospital bed and the boy who just betrayed Baba.'

'Is that what Baba meant when she said I had to save the Nate from this world?'

'I think so,' he replies.

I rub my eyes, hope quickly turning into frustration. 'Can you tell me how the story ends? So we can get home.'

He shakes his head. 'I can tell you no more than Baba.' He sees the disappointment on my face and rests a hand on my shoulder – calmness spreads through me, radiating from his fingers like warm nectar. 'I'm sorry, Violet. The future is so difficult to see at the moment, there are too many different outcomes battling for space, it is impossible for me to carve a clear path. I do have an important message for you though.'

'From Baba?'

He smiles, lowering his voice so I can barely hear it above the breeze. 'See the red-breast bird take flight. Count to three, move to the right.'

I let the words hang between us, hoping Yan will

elaborate, or at least explain further. But he just looks at me with his lovely brown eyes.

'What does it mean?' I eventually say.

'I don't know.' He looks upwards. A flock of birds pass overhead, swallows I think, and he whispers to them in a faraway voice, 'You must save the boy in this world before you can save the boy who sleeps back home.'

'That's what Baba said.'

He grips my arms with strong, precise fingers. 'Hurry, Little Flower. There isn't a second to lose.'

And suddenly, I'm standing on the shore looking out over the river. The dark of night surrounds me, but I can just make out Yan beneath the moon. He stands in a little boat, halfway towards to no-man's-land, and very slowly, he begins to beckon.

I wake with a start, the walls of Thorn's spare bedroom barely visible through the fuzz of sleep and a single, dying candle. Yan's words beat in my head, over and over. *Hurry, Little Flower, there isn't a second to lose.* I find Katie by touch and shake her awake.

'What . . . what? Violet?' she mumbles.

'Come on, sleepyhead. I've just had a visit from a brand-new, alarmingly sexy precog. It's that beckoning boat-dude. Long story short, we need to find Nate.' My eyes grow accustomed to the murk, and I can just make out that she's blinking.

'What, like, now?' she says. 'It's the middle of the night.'

I press my finger against my lips, aware that only a thin sheet of bricks separates us from Thorn. 'Exactly.'

'Wait . . . you've got a new precog?'

'Yep.'

'And he's . . . sexy?'

'I'll tell you more on the way.' I throw the covers off the bed, hoping the blast of cool air will help rouse us.

'On the way where?'

I'm already slipping my feet into my shoes. 'Keep up . . . to find Nate.'

'But he'll be asleep.' Even as she says this, she's busying herself with her shoes, as though already resigned to losing the argument.

'Will he? If Nate's the traitor, he must be communicating with the Gems somehow, and he couldn't risk using technology – Thorn will have all sorts of gadgets to detect that. So he's doing it the old-fashioned way.'

'Carrier pigeon?'

'No, you plonker.' I love that Katie can always make me laugh. 'Face to face.'

'But we don't know anything . . . like where or when.'

I'm pulling my shirt over my head, my voice catching in the folds of cloth. 'He said he saw Baba in No-man's-land. That's why he was Thorn's witness at the burnings – I heard some Imps talking about it earlier.'

Katie smiles, connecting the dots. 'You think it was the other way around? Baba saw Nate in No-man's-land?'

'It's worth a shot, and if they were going to meet, it would be under the cover of darkness.'

'This is a lot of *ifs* to be getting out of bed for.'

I head to the window, sliding it open as gently as I'm able. 'I think it's why Yan was in the river, beckoning to us. He was leading us to Nate.' I lean out into the night. The air feels fresh, even though it tastes of sewage and cold. 'The house is alarmed downstairs, windows and everything. There's only one way down.'

'You've got to be shitting me,' Katie mutters.

Climbing down that knackered drainpipe is almost as difficult as climbing up that bastard tree the first time I was here. It threatens to fall off the wall every time I put my weight on it, and I end up using the pits in the mortar to get my footing. It's only two storeys high, which goes some way to calming my nerves; falling would probably result in a few broken bones, and not immediate death, but I'm still ridiculously relieved when I reach the ground unscathed. I look up at Katie, who leans precariously from the window. She offers me a crooked smile, and I wonder if she's appreciating the fact that it could only be in this universe that a few broken bones seems like the better of two options.

Katie's about as athletic as me, and she seems to really struggle even getting out of the window. At one point she sends a shower of brick dust into my face, her footing giving way beneath her weight. She hangs for a second from her hands, and I position myself under her in case she falls, but somehow she manages to right herself.

She reaches the ground in one piece. 'OMG, we did it,' she whispers.

'Don't get too cocky, we've still got a long way to go.'

We softly pad through the streets. Thankfully, the clouds are fine, so we have some ambient light to help us navigate.

'How will we find him?' Katie whispers.

'He'll need a boat.'

She grins. 'And we know where they're docked, because we used them the first time we were here to escape across the river.'

As we head towards the river's edge, I tell her about the strange riddle Yan told me. She repeats the words a few times, frowning. 'I guess the red-breast bird refers to a robin,' she finally says.

'I guess,' I reply.

'Well, other than that flock of swallows, so far I've

only seen some evil-looking gulls and some scrawny pigeons.'

The water comes into view, a great trench of black, catching the stars on its surface and shaping them into something even more beautiful. Urgently, quietly, we wind our way towards the docking bays. Alleyways and arches all look kind of similar, especially at night, and I worry for a moment we'll get lost, but the landscape soon begins to change, the buildings seemingly appearing from nowhere as we reach the part of the city where the bombs didn't reach.

My heart begins to thump against my ribs, my legs begin to shake. What if this entire expedition is for nothing? What if Thorn discovers we're missing and we still don't find Nate? By the time we reach the stretch of bank where the boats are docked, I've convinced myself this was a waste of time and that Thorn will already have sent out an angry search mob. Tentatively, I peer over an outcrop of rock and spot a jagged line of tarpaulin covers – the rowing boats. There's no sign of Nate, and I'm flooded with exhaustion and disappointment. The scent of oilcloth and fish calms me for a moment; our campsite in France smelt just like this.

'We should go,' I whisper to Katie.

She takes my hand and squeezes. 'No pigging way, I got out of bed for this shit, we are going to sit this one out and see if Nate shows.'

We settle on our bellies hidden behind some shrubs – a mesh of branches segments the riverbank into a patchwork of greys and blacks. My heart rate slows and my breath settles, the earth reassuringly solid beneath my chest. We wait for what feels like an age. The night grows cold, and whilst I was grateful for the poor cloud coverage when we needed the light, I now curse it, the clear sky allowing the day's heat to escape into the cosmos. Katie and I still wear our summer clothes from Comic-Con. I can feel her shivering beside me.

'Maybe we've missed him,' Katie eventually says.

My heart sinks. 'Or maybe he just isn't coming. Never trust a sexy precog.'

Defeated, I'm beginning to lever myself upwards when I hear a voice in the distance, singing a familiar lilting tune. It belongs to a male and contains more sorrow than a single voice should ever hold. I squint into the night and see a figure – a patch of dark within the dark. He moves closer and I can just make out the words to his sad lament. My heart feels like it's about to burst, and not because of the anguish running through every line, but because I know that song. Mum used to sing it to me.

She used to sing it to Nate.

'Let me fix your broken wing,
A swallow should fly free, my love.'

He drops from the steep bank on to the beach. He must be dressed in black, because when he turns towards us, his face shines like a plate in the moonlight. It's definitely Nate. His tawny brown eyes glisten with tears. I suddenly feel a huge swell of pity for him. What if I'm right and a crazy author from our world made him betray the Imps and blame Baba, and now he has to bear the weight without ever knowing he's just a puppet. It's such a horrific thought that I almost can't bear it. I'm suddenly glad for the cold; the unforgiving pain in my body makes me feel closer to him.

Nate begins flipping the tarpaulin from a nearby rowing boat, still singing Mum's song.

'For you were born to dance and sing,
And you will soar with me, my love.'

Does he remember things from his other life? Is my little brother in there after all? Excitement chases away the cold in my bones. He crouches down, using his weight to pull, and begins edging the boat towards the river. It's tough going on his own, and the big sister in me wants to rush over and help him. I have to focus on tensing my muscles until the urge passes. He reaches the shore, and then does something really strange. Instead of pushing the boat into the water so that it bobs free, he pushes it only partway into the river. Then he climbs into it and pushes the oars into the mud of the shore, inching it slowly the rest of the way.

'Is he seriously worried about getting his trousers wet?' Katie hisses.

I shake my head, confused. We wait for him to finally float into the water. He pauses for a moment, probably catching his breath, then he begins to row. The rhythmic splosh of his oars gradually fades as he moves away from us.

Silently, we drop down on to the beach and set about uncovering another boat. There aren't any. The other tarps are covering stacks of wood and salvaged debris. This wasn't part of the plan.

'Now what?' Katie says.

I look at her and shrug. There's only one answer.

'No twunting way,' she says.

'Come on, we survived it once.'

'Barely,' she says. 'And if memory serves, you got heaved out by a hovercraft.'

'We're both strong swimmers, the night's still and the current's weak.'

We look at the river. It looks wider than it did a second ago . . . wider and choppier.

'We can drown in this world, can't we?' Katie asks.

'Only if we sink.' I begin pulling off my clothes.

Katie does the same, and we strip till we're down to our undies. We both put our shoes back on – they'll slow us down, but not as much as a piece of glass or a jagged rock. The last thing we need is an open wound in this water; it looks and smells like a sewer. We take small, shaky steps into the river. It's so cold it takes my breath away. Something slips past my ankles, a piece of polythene or something more disgusting like an eel or a water rat. I just want to turn around and run back to Thorn's house, but then I think of my brother, laced up with tubes, and some form of courage solidifies in my stomach. We *have* to do this.

We walk until we're waist deep. I'm shivering all over and can hardly breathe. My teeth chatter – I hadn't realized that actually happened.

'We need to start moving or we're going to freeze to death,' Katie manages to say, though her voice stop-starts.

'For Nate,' I say.

She nods. 'For Nate.'

We push into the water together.

Icicles drive into my naked skin. The pain makes me gasp and my mouth immediately fills with river. I splutter and swallow. It tastes so much worse than it smells. I manage to stop coughing and move my limbs even though every inch of me stings.

We make good headway, both naturally adopting breaststroke because it's easier to keep our heads out of the water. I've always enjoyed swimming; the rhythmic action becomes almost soothing, like being rocked. But I'm used to the swimming baths, where the water's near body temperature, smells of chlorine and isn't the colour of tar. Where the echo of children's laughter bounces off the tiled walls and the diving board twangs. Right now, all I can hear is my rasping breath, sucked immediately into the night sky. And yet there's something strangely beautiful about that sky. There's no light pollution, no clouds, and the stars burn vivid and true.

It isn't far, but swimming against the current, weak though it is, robs all the strength from my muscles. I can tell we're drifting downriver. I risk glancing back over my shoulder and I see that the beach where Nate hid his boat is nowhere to be seen. I'm about to tell Katie when something floats past. It's one in a list of many items, some of which have bumped up against me or wrapped themselves around my shins. Generally, I've tried to ignore them, averting my gaze and letting my brain infer that it's seaweed, plastic, debris or lumps of human waste. But this item really catches my eye. It's a human arm. Grey and mottled with some of the flesh gone; I can see each of the fingers, each of the nails. I inhale a mouthful of water. It stings my throat and goes up my nose, burning my sinuses and my eyes. I cough it up again.

'What was it?' Katie asks.

I somehow manage to swallow. 'Just a branch,' I lie.

I've never been more relieved than when my feet hit solid ground. It squelches beneath the soles of my shoes, and I let myself fall forward so that the water still supports me a little. My whole body shakes with cold and exhaustion.

'We've lost him,' I say, hopelessly looking up and down the shore.

'He's there,' Katie says, pointing upstream.

In the distance, I can just make out the lines of a tiny boat.

We stagger on to the shore. I suddenly remember we left our clothes on the other side of the river. Katie and I are both really pale and our skin seems to glow beneath the starlight, turning us into giant white targets. We're like half-drowned swans just waiting to be shot. Feeling very vulnerable, we crouch low and track the shore towards the boat.

No-man's-land looks nowhere near as menacing close up. The dark, twisting shapes are just bombed-out buildings and crumbling walls, same as the city we left behind. But there's no polythene, no rags, no lines of smoke or bursts of laughter this side of the river. It's still and silent and stinks of death. It feels like a window into the Imps' future somehow. An eerie snapshot of their non-existence. It's spooky as hell, but I can't deny, the silence makes it easy to find a boy lugging a boat on to the shore.

Once Nate's cleared the boat from the water, he sets off in the opposite direction from me and Katie. We creep after him, stopping only when a speck of light disrupts the black, a distant *thrum* filling my ears.

'What's that?' Katie asks, her whisper almost unintelligible.

I peer into the light. It's a tunnel of yellow, a cone, brighter at its point of origin. Behind it, I can just make out the glint of metal, the shape of something large and curved.

'A Gem helicopter,' I reply. I'm amazed my voice comes out at all. My breath seems to burn the lining of my mouth.

We crouch low and squat behind a block of concrete, shivering and pressed together for warmth. I've never been so cold. The water has mostly evaporated from my skin – which looks more like blue corrugated metal beneath the stars – but it hangs in my hair and to my underwear. I would give anything for a blanket right now.

The helicopter lands, the noise blasting my ears and temporarily distracting me from the pain. Katie and I wriggle forwards, trying to get a better view. Two men step from the chopper. The first man steps in front of the light; I can see his profile and his halo of blond curls. It's Howard Stoneback. The man who shot my little brother. My insides seem to open up, split in two by a giant crevice. My heart begins to race, my breath quickens, and I forget completely about the cold and the fatigue. My body fills with red-hot rage and I begin to violently shake. I want to kill him. I want to make him bleed the way he made my brother bleed. The fury surprises me, but this does nothing to dampen it.

Katie rests a hand on my shoulder. 'You OK?' she mouths.

I manage to nod and focus on my breathing. In, out. In, out.

The other man steps into the light. He has his back to me but he's a Gem without doubt: tall, broad shoulders, thick brown hair.

Katie and I shuffle a little closer so we can just pick out their voices over the gentle lap of the river, the ringing in my ears and the scratching of rats. The man with his back to us speaks first. Something about his voice is oddly familiar.

'It was quick thinking anyhow, Nate. Well done.'

Nate looks at his feet. 'I didn't think he'd . . . kill them. It was awful.'

The man with his back to us touches Nate on the arm, and in doing so, shifts his body so that I should be able to make out the three-quarter angle of his face. But the way the helicopter light falls, his features are just one large shadow. 'The Imps are savages. Surely you know that by now,' he says.

'You forget that Thorn's a Gem,' Nate says.

The faceless man adjusts his posture, and I can tell he's slightly annoyed at being challenged. 'Yes, but an Imp by heart. Just as you, it seems, are a Gem at your core.'

'I still didn't mean for her to die,' Nate says. 'Or

147

Saskia and Matthew. They didn't deserve that.'

The faceless man speaks softly. 'Of course you didn't. But now you must focus on the future, Nate. We've come so far. Just think, our actions will cement the fate of the Imps for ever.'

'I know,' Nate says.

At that moment, the faceless man moves and his features emerge from the shadows. Every one of my muscles freezes.

It's Willow.

19

VIOLET

I clamp a hand over my mouth, biting down on my knuckles with rage. That two-faced, wormy, weasel of a bastard. How could he work against the Imps, after pretending to be part of the alliance, after clutching Rose's body to his chest?

Willow speaks again. 'And one day, everyone will thank you for what we are about to do . . . even my son.'

I peer through the darkness, trying to stop my face from trembling so I can get a proper look. Although the resemblance to Willow is striking, this man is older, his skin stretched as though it's had the wrinkles smoothed away, and his eyes hold none of the warmth or kindness. Even though he's stepped from the shadow, the light doesn't reach his eyes, and I doubt it ever will.

'Who's that?' Katie mouths at me.

'Willow's dad,' I mouth back. 'Jeremy.'

'Dilf!'

We turn our attention back to Nate. He looks awkward, small.

'What news do you bring?' Howard asks.

'Two girls have arrived,' Nate says. 'Young women. Late teens, early twenties. They're both Imps, and they're kind of . . .' He pauses for a moment. ' . . . familiar.'

I gaze at Katie. A flicker of a smile crosses her face, making her freckles dance.

'Baba was expecting them,' Nate says. 'They're

researching the London alliance. They seem harmless enough.'

Jeremy Harper nods. 'Well, Oscar's been working night and day. Night and day. And soon, the solution to our little infestation problem will be ready.'

'Did you plant the canister?' Howard asks Nate.

'Yes,' Nate says. 'At Headquarters, they don't suspect a thing.'

My brain works slowly, numbed by cold and exhaustion. Canister? Does it contain a toxin of some kind?

Howard reaches out and pats Nate's back, as though he's a proud dad at a football match. I want to run up to Nate and shout: *He shot you. He killed you. Run away from him as fast as you can.* But I'm paralysed by fear and ice and rage.

The three figures move closer together for a moment and I can no longer hear what they say. They shake hands and Jeremy and Howard step back into the helicopter. Katie and I scrabble beneath a sheet of scrap metal as the helicopter takes off, just in case the lights find us, hunched and shining in the dark. The chug of the blades sounds deafening after straining in the silence for so long, and the ground around us illuminates so that I can see every speck of dirt. I fear that the light is so fierce it will somehow penetrate through our metal shield, revealing our semi-naked bodies. But it dims and the chop of the rotor falls into nothingness.

We lie completely still. I don't feel cold any more. I just feel really, really tired. Like my body is filled with weights and I'm sinking into the ground. The world closes in around me as I drift off to sleep.

'Violet?' Katie whispers. Her voice sounds far, far away. 'Violet? You need to wake up now.'

'I am awake,' I reply. Or maybe I just think the words. The line between reality and dreams becomes flimsy, permeable, like a piece of tracing paper.

'Violet,' she snaps, her voice suddenly loud and close in my ear.

I open my eyes with a start.

'Where were you just then?' she asks.

'I don't know, I . . . I just wanted to rest,' my voice sputters out.

She grunts. 'Great, hypothermia. Come on, we need to get back before we both pass out.'

I stumble into the river, barely aware of the silt beneath my shoes or the water lapping against my skin. I watch my arms extend before me. They could be someone else's arms. Two dead, corpse arms stuck to my body, moving of their own accord like they're possessed.

I think I'm kicking but I can no longer feel my legs . . . I can't feel anything.

I'm about half way to the shore now . . . the river is at its deepest . . . the expanse of water beneath me must feel so soft and still.

My eyes flicker shut, my corpse arms float at either side of me, my legs give up.

The comfort of dreams awaits me now. No more exhaustion, no more cold, no more fear . . . only the gentle push-pull of my breath as I slip into unconsciousness.

A L I C E

That evening, Fanboy posts again.

A tiny drone flew through the open bedroom window and hovered before Nate. He thought for a moment that it looked like a massive bug, and wished he could swat it with his shoe. But instead, he plucked it from the air, pressing a fingertip against its glossy side. The drone emitted a faint beep, as though acknowledging Nate's identity, and then unfolded in his palm to reveal a tightly rolled note.

Nate smiled. All this technology and it still boils down to note passing.

He read the words with nerves growing in his stomach.

Tomorrow night, 12 a.m. Bank Station.

Beneath the writing sat the tail-gobbling rat. Nate traced the shape of it with his finger.

His first Taleter meeting.

Howard smiled as the gadget in his hand lit up, confirming that somewhere in the stinking Imp city, the Imp-boy known as Nate had received his message successfully. Howard reclined in his oxblood chair, swilling back a glass of Scotch. Tomorrow he would finally reveal the last piece of his plan.

And then nobody could stop him.

He closed his eyes, tears of joy threatening to tumble down his cheeks. In just a few days he would achieve his one, true goal: the annihilation of every Imp on the planet.

Horror forms in the pit of my being. I can't swallow, I can't move. I can hardly breathe. The words begin to merge together on the screen so they look like a load of lines and dots. The annihilation of every Imp on the planet. In just a few days.

Violet. Katie. Nate.

Holy shit.

I slam my laptop shut, sweat and tears mingling on my face. *What the hell am I going to do?* I have to get Violet and Katie to that meeting so they know what they're up against. Could I write some more fanfic? *No.* There's no guarantee that would work.

I have to send Violet a message.

I pull on a pair of jeans, borrow Dad's argyle sweater and tuck my hair into one of Mum's berets. At a glance, I'll pass beneath the radar.

Just before I leave the house, Danny messages. His name lights up my phone and my chest in equal measure.

Al, I've found the IP address. I reckon
Fanboy's using a local internet café.
You fancy a stake-out tomorrow? x

Sure thing ☺ x

Bloody Fanboy, if I find him at that café I'll wring his scrawny neck.

I get to the hospital in record time. Crazy-mop-top-Millie doesn't wave at me like she normally does, which means I've foiled at least one person. I glance at my watch. If I've learnt one thing hanging out with Nate, it's when the meds trolley does its rounds. I pull my beret over my ears and head to the ICU, expecting the normal glances, but it seems my outfit has succeeded in making me invisible. I've got the same brain, the same personality, the same body. I'm still me. Funny how a few items of clothing can make such a difference.

I approach the ICU. There's the trolley . . . sitting, waiting, inviting me to knock it over. So I bide my time, ignore the palpitations in my chest, and watch as the nurse pops into the ward. Then, I storm down the corridor and shove into the trolley with all my might. There's a loud crash, followed by the pitter patter of pills scattering across the tiles. I duck inside the ICU and conceal myself behind the nearest partition curtain, too scared to even breathe.

The staff rush to the commotion, cursing their bad luck.

Quickly, I stride towards Violet's bay. Adam is fast asleep beside her bed. Bollocks. I really didn't think this through. But if trolley-gate didn't wake him, I doubt my next move will. I study his sleeping face, unable to stop the jealousy growing inside – my parents never slept beside me when I was unconscious. My mouth fixes in a thin, determined line. I realized a long time ago that my shit parents don't matter, my *friends* matter: Nate, Katie and, of course, Violet. I run my fingers through her thick, dark waves, releasing the scent of flowers.

When I was there last time, in the world of *The Gallows Dance*, I gave up everything to save her. Living as a Gem. Willow. And I'd do it again. In a heartbeat. I'd do anything for her.

Even if it means hurting her.

I pull a small kitchen knife from my handbag. The blade catches in the glow from the corridor, and for a second, it looks like an angry, sharpened tooth. My stomach hurts, my throat burns, and yet I have to do this. Because if rat tattoos and bullet wounds can cross between worlds, then so will this.

I kiss her on the forehead and carve the words 'BANK, MONDAY, 12 A.M.' into the fleshy part of her forearm. And then, just in case she doesn't work it out, I carve my initial.

20

VIOLET

I don't remember reaching the shore. I have a strange, broken image of two pale hands reaching towards me, their touch so hot it made my skin ache. Then there was the slap of wood against my stomach as I landed on something dry and hard. The distant swish of oars in water. The stars seemed to stretch further than the darkness which held them; the sky becoming nothing more than the spaces in between.

The next thing I'm aware of is this pain in my arm. Like a knife, stabbing into me again and again. I try to scream, but my mouth fills with river water, cold and bitter as it sprays on to my face. I try to move my arm, try to wrench it away from whatever it is which is making it hurt, but it's like my corpse limbs aren't connected to my body any more, and all I can do is lie there, limp and half dead, coughing and aching, my arm on fire. I suddenly wonder if Baba didn't die in the flames, if I'm somehow still feeling her pain. Then I must pass out.

When I wake, Ash leans over me so his face is all I can see. He rolls me on to my side, the riverbank slipping beneath my body, and thumps my back. Painful, deep wretches threaten to rip me in two. My arm feels like it's been dipped in magma, and I swear I can feel something warm flowing over my hand and seeping across my body.

'What the hell were you thinking?' he whispers to me.

I try to answer, but the slightest movement of my throat makes the coughing start again.

'We were following Nate,' Katie says, laying my clothes over me. My skin's so numb from the cold, I feel only a strange, dull pressure, as though the river anaesthetised me.

'Katie, don't,' I manage to say.

She laughs, a sad exhale, and begins pulling on her own clothes. 'I think we're a bit past that now, Vi. If it weren't for Ash, you'd be dead.' She turns to him. 'How did you find us?'

'Thorn planted a tracker in your clothes. Don't worry, I re-routed the signal so it reaches me first. As far as he knows, you're still in bed.'

'Why?' I manage to croak. 'Why are you helping us?'

'You kinda look like you need it.' He looks down at me and almost smiles. 'And Baba made me promise.'

I grab at my arm and groan; pain strikes beneath my muscles again.

'Christ, you're bleeding,' Ash says. 'You must have cut your arm pretty bad.' He presses his hand on to my arm and I feel myself push back slightly, grateful for the blunting of the pain.

'You can't go back to Thorn's like this,' he says. 'We need to get your arm fixed up, and he'll smell the river on you. Then you'll be answering his questions instead of mine.' He moves his head from view, and I see the stars again. I let my lids half close so that the clear boundary between light and dark disintegrates.

'Nate,' I whisper. 'We have to help Nate.'

Ash bites his lip for a moment. 'Come on, let's get you back to mine. You need a hot shower and some food.' He lifts me with such ease I feel like I'm flying,

156

and I let the gentle rocking of his step lull me into a trance.

The next thing I know, I'm lying on a sofa and he's tucking a heavy blanket around me.

'Who are you?' he whispers to himself, brushing my skin with his fingertips as he folds the fabric beneath my shoulders. 'Why do I feel like I know you?'

'Ash . . .' I begin, but talking still hurts, my tongue weighed down by exhaustion.

'It's OK,' he says. 'Just rest.'

My eyelids gratefully lower, and yet my lacerated brain can't stop thinking about Nate. *Who is Oscar, and what is the solution to the infestation problem? And what's in that canister Nate was talking about? What have you got yourself into, little brother?*

'Vi?' Katie says.

I open my eyes. Katie stands beside me, her hair dulled by the water and a towel thrown around her shoulders. She looks like a piece of marble. Pale and veiny and like she'd be cold to the touch. But I guess she still looks better than me. 'Vi, you massive waffle-crust, it was your idea to swim across that bloody river, and I ended up having to drag you the last half.'

'Thanks,' I manage to squeak.

'If Ash hadn't spotted us I think we would have drowned,' she says.

My eyes flick around the surroundings. I'd expected to be back at Ash's ma's house, which I visited last time, even though that would have made no sense – it's half a day's walk from the river. But this looks like part of a warehouse, the front converted into a sitting room. I notice the feminine touches – flowers in a teapot, sketches on the wall – and try to swallow down that unwelcome jealousy. He lives here with Daisy. Of course he does.

'Just stop making out you're Superman,' Katie says gently. 'You're clearly more Captain Underpants.'

'What are you on about?' Ash asks. He sits beside me on the sofa so that I can feel his back against my stomach. It feels like a hot-water bottle, and I have to resist the urge to curl around him. He pulls back the blanket and begins to clean my arm with a wipe which smells strongly of antiseptic. 'They're Gem wipes, they should stop it hurting so bad.' As he strokes my skin, the pain begins to fall away from me. I suddenly feel lighter, like maybe I can move again.

'So Nate's the traitor,' he says, almost to himself. 'I should have listened to Dee. He's been acting so differently these past few weeks.'

'Please don't tell anyone.' My voice sounds small, pleading.

'Why not?'

'Thorn will kill him.'

He exhales, his breath hitting my cheek, hot and quick. 'You're right. I've seen enough of my friends die at Thorn's hands.'

'Someone is making him bad, I just know it,' I say.

'Who?' he replies.

My eyes swivel to Katie, begging her for a clever response. The cold has slowed my brain and other than blurting out *an evil author from another dimension* I've got nothing.

Katie looks blank. There's a long pause.

Ash studies my features. 'You can tell me when you're ready.'

I stop myself breathing a huge sigh of relief.

I'm about to thank him for being so understanding, when he grips my arm. 'What on earth?' He's pulled the wipe away and is now blinking fast and hard. He continues to rub my wound, this time a little more vigorously. 'Katie, pass me another wipe.' He chucks the first one on the floor and begins wiping again. 'Violet, who did this to you?'

'I must have cut it on some glass or something,' I manage to say.

He fixes me with his bluer-than-blue eyes. 'I don't think so, somehow.'

He and Katie stare at me with such intensity, I start to feel a little on show. I see the shock in their faces before I hear their gasps. Immediately, I strain my head so I see what they've already seen.

Carved into my arm are letters. I blink rapidly, bringing them into focus, allowing my brain to catch up. It's writing: BANK, MONDAY, 12 A.M.

'What the hell?' Ash says. 'They're letters, aren't they? You need to tell me what's going on.'

'It's a message,' Katie finally says. 'From the other side.'

'Which *other side*?' Ash asks. 'You make it sound like you're angels or something.'

Katie looks at him. 'Angels would make a lot more sense.'

'What does it say?' he asks. He begins to spell it out, slowly. He's been learning to read.

'Please.' I cover the letters so he can't see. 'I promise I'll tell you, just not now. It's not the right time.'

He studies my face, and then says reluctantly, 'You need stitches. I'll go get the kit. I'll grab you some of Dee's clothes too.'

I watch him leave the room, and I swear the ache deepens just a little. I hate not telling him the truth, especially when he seems so close to remembering me. But I need to focus on Nate, I need to focus on getting us home.

And then another searing pain hits me. Deep in the

bone. And it appears before our eyes, a bright red line, opening across my skin as the blood springs up, at first in tiny scarlet balls, which quickly join together and tumble down my forearm.

'What the hell?' Katie whispers.

'Make it stop,' I scream. 'Make it stop.' I wriggle into an upright position and kick my legs so I'm pressed against the arm of the sofa, as though trying to get away from my own body. I stretch my arm out in front of me, as if I can distance myself somehow from the pain. Another line opens up so a small triangle is formed. And then another. It's an A.

'How is that happening?' I shout.

Katie throws her arms around my neck. 'It's OK, Vi, it's OK, remember, the tattoo, the bullet wound? It's coming from the other side, from *our* world.'

But I'm too busy screaming, too busy kicking myself away from the blood to process her words.

Katie grips my hand, the one belonging to my bloodied, letter-emblazoned arm. In one firm motion, she clamps a wipe over it, and I feel the numbing lotion work its magic, the pain leaking away from me. 'It's OK,' she says. And the way her voice sounds, sure and confident, makes me believe her. I stop writhing and nod. Slowly, she pulls back the wipe.

I study the marks like they don't belong to me, like they're written on a piece of paper.

'Who would do this?' she says. 'Who could possibly know that marks transfer between our bodies?'

I look at that A and I begin to smile. 'Alice. She's trying to tell us something – maybe she's found the third book. I think maybe she wants us to . . . go to the nearest bank, at midnight tomorrow?'

Katie laughs. 'No, you giant dildo, she means the tube station.'

21

A L I C E

I wake early, images of knives and blood flashing through my dreams. First thing I do is check behind the radiator. The knife is still there, wrapped in a pink silk scarf and shoved as far down as it would go. Eat your telltale heart out, Edgar Allan Poe. Soon as I'm dressed, I manage to retrieve it and zip it into a side compartment of my handbag. I know I could probably just wash it and pop it back it in the knife drawer, but I've watched too many crime dramas – there'll be some fancy way of identifying blades from their incisions. And I just want it out the house. Out of my life. I *had* to cut Violet, but it is not a moment I want reminding of every time I slice an apple.

I leave the house and walk down the backstreets where the bins get left. Several streets on, I find what I need. A bin which is already full, the lid pushed up and overflowing with rubbish. I glance around me – there's nobody to be seen, and I'm not particularly overlooked by windows. I work fast, unwrapping the knife and sliding it into one of the bags, careful not to slice the plastic. Then, avoiding the grime stuck to the rim of the bin, I shove the bag further down so it doesn't fall out.

Except for my lack of hand sanitizer, I already feel better. It's bin collection day tomorrow, and then the knife will be out of my life for good.

*

I wait for Danny outside the café. The traffic crawls past, windows wound down in the summer heat. The discordant sound of three different radio stations hits my ears. I feel unsettled, nervous. Last night I carved up my bestie's arm. I'm officially a psycho-bitch. A fist tightens around my heart. I catch sight of my reflection in the glass of a double-decker; I look like one of those celebs sneaking out of rehab with my dark glasses pulled down, wearing a cap and hoodie. I even left my favourite lipstick at home. Mum would flip if she saw me.

Danny approaches. I've never noticed what an easy walk he has, like his leg joints have been oiled. Just watching him makes that fist loosen a little.

He grins at me. 'Looking good, Agent Childs.'

'I'm trying to blend, but now I'm thinking I've achieved the exact opposite.'

'Maybe lose the cap,' he says helpfully.

I clutch at my head. 'But it pulls the whole look together.'

He begins to laugh.

'No, seriously,' I continue, spurred on by his generous smile, 'it's the focal point of the whole ensemble.'

'OK, OK, leave the cap. Maybe ditch the glasses. It's the double whammy that's making you look a bit . . .'

'. . . Britney circa 2007.'

He grins.

I pull the glasses from my face and he nods his approval. I follow him into the internet café. It's painted sage green and has rows of super-modern desks. I love that it still smells of coffee and biscuits, in spite of the rows of monitors. We choose a computer at the back of the room, in the corner, so we have a good view.

'Now what?' I whisper to Danny.

He shrugs. 'We wait and see if he posts. I can't track the exact computer, but when we know he's here, we can take a quick walk and check out all the screens. We'll soon find out who he is.'

I order us a couple of drinks and we settle into the wait. We flick through webpages, chatting about our favourite movies, books, things which piss us off. Normal stuff. People underestimate the importance of normal stuff. It's when we start moaning about parents that Danny tells me about his brother. 'My parents separated a few years after my brother died. Dad moved out; I think being together reminded him of what he'd lost, if that makes sense?'

'Your brother died?'

He nods, breaking eye contact. 'Yeah, I was only little, he was a few years older. I don't remember much about him to be honest.'

'What do you remember?'

'Daft things, things you can't see in a photograph. Like . . . he would have sold his soul for a Crunchie, and he always smelt of Christmas.' He presses his lips together. 'And if I was ever cold, he would always fetch me a blanket. That's how I picture him now, holding out a tartan throw with a smile on his face.'

'Danny, I'm so sorry, that's so sad.'

'Yeah. But I forget to miss him sometimes, is that weird?'

I touch his hand. 'No, I don't think that's weird at all.' There's a really long pause, which gets a little too long and I start to feel like I have to say something. 'Do you still see your dad?'

'Yeah, all the time. Dad's the best.'

'I wish my parents would separate,' I find myself saying.

He looks at me sideways. 'Are you even allowed to think that?'

'Better two happy homes than one miserable one.'

'Is it that bad?'

I sigh, not wanting to whinge about my life when Danny's just told me about his dead brother. 'I'll introduce you to my parents one day, then you'll see what I mean.'

My phone buzzes in my pocket. For a second, I think it may be Violet, but then I remember she's in a coma and my heart sinks. 'Sorry,' I mutter, checking the screen. It's a message from a number my phone doesn't recognize. I open it up and each word makes my heart beat a little faster.

Did you enjoy watching her bleed?

The world looks fuzzy, my palms bead with sweat. Someone knows. They must have seen me. But who? And how did they get my number? I blink the lines of my phone back into focus.

'Alice?' Danny's saying my name. 'Al? Are you OK?'

'Yeah,' I say, arranging my face into a smile. 'It's just . . . a fan.'

I can't tell him the truth. Normal girls don't get hate mail. Normal girls don't hack messages into their best friend's arm. Quickly, I shove my phone right to the bottom of my bag, beneath all my shit, wishing I could literally bury it. The image of the knife in the bin flashes into my mind.

'Are you sure?' he says, his brown eyes filled with worry. 'You've gone kind of pale.'

'Yeah, sure I'm sure.'

He opens his mouth, perhaps to challenge me, when my phone buzzes again. My heart flips. I desperately want to ignore it, but Danny is looking at my bag with interest. I try and act natural, pretending my face isn't sweating, and retrieve my phone.

I check the screen. Relief floods my body. It's just an alert telling me Fanboy's posted again.

Then I remember the significance.

Fanboy's posted again. He's here, in the café, right now.

'It's Fanboy, he's posted,' I tell Danny. I scan the people at the computers. It could be any of them. There's a middle-aged man in a cheap suit, a teenage girl with too many piercings, a group of young men who look like tourists. My money's on cheap suit. Never trust a man in a cheap suit.

Danny's already booted up his laptop, keeping it low and on his knee, presumably so Fanboy doesn't see. He taps on his keyboard a few times, his frown deepening. 'Nope, sorry, Childs. His IP address has moved.'

'Moved?'

'Yep. He's blogging from somewhere else.'

'Can you find him?'

He shakes his head. 'He's subnetting something rotten. It's like he doesn't want to be found this time. Dammit, this is going to take a bit of time.'

I think of Nate's life support about to be turned off, about Howard Stoneback plotting the death of every Imp, including my friends. 'I don't have time,' I whisper.

Danny looks at me, his dark eyes filled with concern. 'Alice, please, tell me what's going on.'

I want to tell him, I really do, but I can't bear to watch his face as he realizes what a fruit loop I am. I shake my head. He'll be angry, I reckon, or at least pissed off, but that's better than the alternative.

He sighs. He doesn't look anything other than worried about me. 'I'll find you that address, I promise.

Now go home, get some rest, maybe write some more.'

I smile at him, though it feels strained. 'Thanks, Danny.'

*

As soon as Danny's gone, I log on to Fandom Rising, trying to think of a way I can help Violet. My mind reels back to Danny and the loss of his brother. It sparks off an idea. Nate had such a lonely backstory in *The Gallows Song*. No wonder his loyalty to the Imps dwindled. But what if he once had a sister? Surely his redemption would be more believable if he had a long-lost Imp sister. I position my fingers over the keyboard and begin to smile. What if I take it one step further? What if Nate's long-lost sister looked a bit like Violet? Maybe when Nate meets Violet, he would want to help her.

I position my fingers above the keyboard and begin to type.

NATE

Forgive me. I lied when I told you I had no family. It's true, I was orphaned when I was little, that I was raised by the streets of London, but one family member survived.

My sister.

I don't remember much about her, as we were separated when I was only about five. I don't even remember her name, but this is what I remember:

She was several years older than me. She had pale skin, brown eyes, and wavy, dark hair which always felt soft to touch and smelt faintly of flowers. She would give me her extra blanket when it was cold, give me her last bit of bread when I was

166

hungry, and she would rock me to sleep whenever it thundered.

She made me feel like I belonged.

And sometimes I think that's worse. Love and loss. For my heart never truly hardened like it needed to. Like I wanted it to.

Because I still pray that someday she will find me.

I arrive home feeling tired and desperate for a shower. I love central London, but it always seems to leave an invisible coating of pollution and sweat on my skin. Violet called it her second-city skin, and I always knew exactly what she meant. I'm halfway up the stairs when I notice how quiet the house is. Just the tick of the hall clock and the soft hum of a car passing outside. Normally at this time in the evening I can hear Mum's favourite TV show, punctuated by Dad complaining about mindless tripe. I do a U-turn and check the fridge. Sure enough, Mum's left a note. She always leaves them stuck to the fridge, appropriate considering how chilly they are.

Gone to the spa for the night. Use my tab for takeaway. Mum.

The lack of kisses makes me feel like an abandoned toddler. My eyes begin to prick. Not just because of the note, but because I hate being on my own in the house. It's way too big for one person, and I've watched way too many slasher movies. It's always the lanky blonde who gets hacked up first. That hateful text has made me even twitchier. My stomach sinks. I would normally go to Violet's house, but I can't for obvious reasons. Jane and Adam would probably welcome me with open arms, but I'm the last person they need to see, completely awake and alert. Talk about salt in the wound. So instead, I do something I haven't done in a very long time. I get a pen out of my handbag – an eyeliner to be precise – and I draw three kisses at the bottom of the note.

Christ, I'm tragic.

I head upstairs for a shower, banning all thoughts of *Psycho* from my head. Maybe I'll ring Danny later, see how his IP hunt is going. I pause in front of my bedroom door. It's open. Strange, I'm sure I left it shut. Anxiety flutters in my stomach. *Don't be silly, Alice, Mum probably went in my room for some reason.* But Mum never goes in my room, not even to clean or gather up laundry, she pays someone else to do that, and it isn't the cleaner's day today. Breath is trapped in my lungs. My hearing sharpens: a car passes outside, my alarm clock ticks . . . something creaks. My heart stops. *Who's been in my room . . . are they still there?*

And I know I should turn around and run down the stairs. I've just received a threatening message off a random number, and now my bedroom door is mysteriously open. *For Christ's sake, Alice, you left your door open and forgot. Stop being so melodramatic.*

So with my heart hammering against my chest and my mouth dry with fear, I step into my room.

Always trust your gut, especially when you're the lanky blonde.

Scrawled across my dresser mirror in my favourite lipstick are the words:

I BET YOU BLEED TOO.

22
ALICE

Someone's been in my room, touched my stuff, written on my mirror. A boil pops in my stomach, releasing a load of poison into my system. I call out for my parents, then remember they're at the spa. I pull my phone from my pocket, shaking so badly I almost drop it. The realization hits me. I've got nobody to ring. Violet and Katie are in comas. I'm completely alone.

Except for Danny.

He answers the phone after one ring, almost as if he was ready and waiting. *'Agent Childs,'* he says.

I try to talk, but only a strange noise comes out.

'Alice?' he says. *'Al, what is it?'*

I manage to speak. 'Someone's been in my room and written a horrible message on my mirror.'

'What? Oh my God, are you serious?'

'Uh-huh.'

'Are they still there?' he asks.

This sentence immobilizes me. 'I don't think so.'

'Where are your parents?'

'They've gone away for the night.'

He pauses. *'Go wait at your neighbours and text me their house number. I'll be over straight away.'*

I wait for Danny at the bottom of my drive. I don't know my neighbours and I'm too shook up to make small talk. He pulls up about ten minutes later in a red Corsa. He rushes to me and places both arms around my neck. I lean into him, grateful for the warmth and the human touch. He doesn't say anything for what feels like an age, he just rubs my back until I can breathe steadily again.

Finally, he says, 'Do you want to stay at mine tonight? Mum's making her famous spicy chicken wings. She'd love to feed you and tell you embarrassing stories about me. They're her two favourite hobbies.'

I sniff. 'That would be good, thanks Danny.'

He pauses. 'Do you want to show me the message?'

'OK.'

We head back into the house. Danny goes first, even though it's my house.

We enter my room. The message is still there, blood-red on the glass.

He draws breath over his teeth. 'That is messed up. I think we should phone the police.'

'No,' I reply quickly.

He glances at me. 'Someone has broken into your home and threatened you. We should phone the police.'

What with everything that's going on, the message on Violet's arm, the last thing I need is police in my business. 'Please, Danny, I don't want the police involved.'

'Do you know who did this? Are you protecting them?'

'No, no, of course not, I just . . . don't want the police here.'

He exhales slowly through his nose. 'OK, scary Alice. But you need to tell me exactly what's going on.'

'I will,' I say, my eyes flicking back to the greasy red letters. 'But can we get out of here first?'

Danny's house isn't that far from Violet's, so I immediately feel safer. The house itself is small, clean and fragranced with delicious cooking smells. We kick off our shoes and his mum welcomes me into the kitchen. She has the same slight build as Danny, the same heavily lashed eyes set against the same dark skin. She smiles at me with her soft mouth, a smile which reminds me of Jane. She does exactly as Danny promised, piling chicken high on to my plate and launching into a series of embarrassing stories. My favourite one is about Danny painting a piece of sweetcorn with Tipp-ex so he could con an extra quid out of the tooth fairy. Mrs Bradshaw was so proud of his initiative, she left him a fiver.

It feels so natural, sitting here with Danny and his mum. I don't even resent their bond. For the first time ever, I actually pity my mum. We could have had this . . . if she'd only spent less time at her spin class.

By the time we've polished off dinner, the sky is growing dark. Mrs Bradshaw doesn't ask me or Danny where I want to sleep, she just tells Danny there's extra bedding in the cupboard and leaves us to it.

'Thanks for dinner,' I say to her as she leaves the room.

She smiles at me with her lovely soft mouth. 'Any time, sweetie.'

Danny makes up the couch and lets me have his bed.

I finish using the bathroom and find his bedroom. It's an ode to all things Fandom. I'm talking *Lord of the Rings* figurines, *Game of Thrones* posters, *Dr Who* memorabilia.

He pokes his head round the door. 'You got everything you need?'

'Yeah. Me and Frodo are just fine, thanks.' I pause.

'Will you sleep in with me?' I don't mean sex. It's the last thing on my mind, well, maybe not the last thing, but Danny's flushed cheeks make me clarify. 'Just for company, you know. I'm still a bit freaked out.'

'Sure. I'll sleep on the floor,' he says.

'Thanks.'

He reappears a few seconds later with the duvet from the couch. He wraps the covers around himself and sits cross-legged on the carpet. 'Sorry about Mum.'

'What? Your mum is lovely.'

'God, but those stories.'

'Seriously, when my mum saw you, she asked me what protection we were using.'

'Norton spyware?' he says.

I laugh. 'That's exactly what I said.'

He lies down. 'Al, don't forget, you said you'd tell me what's going on.'

'I will,' I mumble. 'I promise, when my head isn't so mashed.' I nestle into Danny's bed. It smells of him, and sleep closes around me quickly.

VIOLET

The next evening, we wait till the sky darkens and the house falls quiet, then shakily pull on Daisy's clothes. The tops have hoods, which will come in handy if we want to hide our faces, but most importantly, they aren't fitted with trackers.

I've clearly got better at climbing down the drainpipe; it's like my feet know how to find the holes in the wall, freeing up my brain to concentrate on my hands. By the time I reach the ground, I'm overflowing with adrenalin. My knuckles and shins have been scraped by the bricks and the river-tainted air is pricking at the inside of my nose. Katie jumps down a few moments later. We head down the street, striding as quickly as we dare, careful not to wake the Imps with the slap of our feet against the tarmac. But it's like every noise is magnified by the night – my heart thumping in the gaps between my breaths – and I remain convinced every window we pass will light up, followed by the cry, 'What are you doing out of bed?'

Katie grabs me by the hand and begins to pull me down a side street.

'This isn't the way to Bank,' I say.

'Yeah, I know. We can't very well rock up unannounced – we haven't a clue what we're getting ourselves into. We have to sneak along the tunnels, we're less likely to be spotted.'

I nod, impressed by her sudden metamorphosis into Nancy Drew. 'And you know the way through the tunnels how exactly?'

'When we moved from Liverpool, Mum made me learn the map, she was so paranoid about getting lost.' She taps the side of her head. 'It's all up here.'

'Maybe we'll find out what was in that canister Nate planted at HQ,' I say.

'Do you think it's a bomb?'

I nod, afraid to even whisper the word *yes*, afraid to admit what my brother has got himself into.

We walk until we approach a giant mouth, yawning across the street. It looks like there used to be a building over it, the shadow of foundations just visible in the dark, but any recognizable walls have long gone. A carefully constructed heap of rubble suggests the opening was cleared fairly recently, within the past few years at least. Steps lead down into the blackness, even darker than the sky above. It must be an old tube station.

'This must be what's left of Moorgate,' Katie says,

switching on a torch she pinched from Thorn's house. I'm not sure if it's super powerful or if my eyes have just grown unaccustomed to light, but it makes me wince all the same. The triangular beam reaches into the black mouth with precise yellow edges, illuminating the steps before us. We begin to climb down. The stairs seem to go on for ever, and the lower we go, the louder my heart beats, until I swear it matches my footsteps in volume. My breath quickens and I worry that between us, Katie and I will steal every lungful of air from the tunnel, until we're left mouthing helplessly, gaping like fish out of water.

The temperature drops and the air grows dank as we enter the cavern which used to be the station. I used to love the smell of the underground – oil and paper – it smelt of travel, of possibilities. But now it smells of rot and sewage and dead meat. Katie swings a torch around the walls. A couple of the mounds slumped against the wall move and we both gasp. They're Imps – sheltering, hiding, dying. It's best not to ask.

Katie leads me to the right platform, her hand slippery with anxiety sweat. I imagine I can feel the waft of air against my face as the ghost of a carriage moves towards us. But no trains have run down here for centuries, and I doubt the air has moved either. It sits, stagnant, like water in a blocked drain.

It's counterintuitive, crossing the line where the platform ends and the tracks begin. I've stood on platforms many times, my toes inches behind the yellow line, marvelling at Alice as she stands so confidently close to the edge, even in her killer heels. I never thought I'd purposefully be dropping on to the tracks. But I do it all the same, the concrete ledge crumbling as quickly as my nerve as I lower myself down.

We walk between the metal tracks, until the platform's behind us and a tight tunnel closes around us, reflecting the torch beam so it feels like we're walking in a bubble of light. And even though I know it's silly, I keep expecting a tube to come hurtling towards us.

We walk until my feet ache and my nose finally accepts the stink in the air. Eventually, Bank station sits before us – a giant chamber smelling of earth and burnt wax, and cast in an orange glow. We creep closer until I can see hundreds of tea lights lining the platform, the odd torch angled upwards and spotlighting the ceiling. It's strangely beautiful, and I suddenly feel like a small child approaching a Christmas window display in the depths of winter. Only the sound of distant voices, of Katie's breath increasing in speed, reminds me of the imminent danger.

Katie kills the torch and we crouch low, still concealed by the gloom of the tunnel. There's a rusted old carriage halfway along the platform, leaning slightly to one side and looking more like a sunken shipwreck. Dark shapes move inside, no more than shadows behind glass. Katie and I pull our hoods up and begin to sneak along the side of the train, tiny curls of ancient paint brushing our cheeks and catching on our clothes. The voices inside sound hushed, secret, like they know the walls have ears. My pulse drums in my ears and Daisy's jumper moistens from my sweat.

I suddenly wish Alice were here. I remember leaving her on the platform only days ago, having bitten her head off about the contract. I wish we hadn't parted on such bad terms. The thought of never returning home and never seeing her again fills me with dread and sorrow in equal measure. I push her from my mind. I need to focus on Nate right now.

Katie turns and looks at me. She tries to smile, even though it looks more like a grimace. *You got this*, she mouths. I nod and we continue to creep until we come to a crack in the metal shell.

We peer through, the tinny scent of rust filling our nostrils, forcing us to hold our breath. The light of several flashlights whizz by, causing shadows to dance and my eyes to water. Still, I can just make out a blur of cloaks and faces. There must be about thirty people crammed into the carriage, some sitting on seats, others milling around. Most of them are Gems, I can tell from their height and build.

'What is this?' Katie whispers. 'Some sort of secret Gem society?'

Oh Nate, what have you got yourself into?

Through the smeared window, I see a figure approach the carriage. My heart stops. Even though his face remains obscured by darkness, I know that it's Nate; I'd know that walk anywhere. The cloak drowns him, so that he looks like a kid playing dress-up for Halloween – so small in comparison to his Gem counterparts. He holds out his arm and a cloaked figure runs a scanner over his loop tattoo. The rat eating its tail . . . it must be some sort of identifier.

Nate makes his way to the back of the crowd, stooped and slow like he wishes he wasn't there. My chest hurts with yearning. Suddenly, the whispers fade and everyone turns to face the front of the carriage. A hooded figure takes centre stage. He stands tall and throws back his hood, revealing a mass of blond curls.

Howard Stoneback.

I bite down on my lip until I taste blood, a familiar rage throbbing in my gut.

The audience pull back their hoods one by one, revealing a sea of perfect Gem faces. Howard raises his voice, addressing the crowd in an infuriatingly sonorous voice. 'Welcome to the thirteenth meeting of the Taleters. A meaningful number for some. My uncle, President Stoneback, apologizes for his absence, but he felt it was too risky to attend. Still, the news of his escape is wonderful.'

Katie and I share a worried glance. The President has escaped from the prison Alice and I wrote him into. This is bad news. Clearly the government are keeping a lid on it, not wanting to panic the Imp masses.

'Who the hell are the Taleters?' Katie whispers.

As if to answer her question, Howard continues. 'We have been meeting ever since the Imp–Gem treaty was put in place, and we are mere days away from fulfilling our shared goal.' He raises his voice. 'We shall rid this planet of its Imp infestation problem. Permanently.' The next word which falls from Howard's mouth both shocks and incenses me. 'Nate.'

The Taleters turn and stare at my brother. I can barely keep myself from screaming at him: *Run away, Nate. Save yourself.* But I dig my fingers into my palms and order myself to remain quiet and still.

'Do the London alliance have any suspicions?' Howard asks.

Nate shakes his head. 'None. They're clueless, as ever.'

A light chuckle ripples through the crowd.

Howard pushes his hair from his eyes. 'Excellent. Same as the government, it seems. I will hand you over to Oscar, who will reassure those of you who expressed concerns to me. Sadly, he couldn't be here in person due to the approaching deadline, but we have a live call.' Howard retrieves what looks like a marble from inside his cloak and throws it into the air. It hovers before him and projects a beam of light upwards. We watch as a 3-D image begins to form just below the ceiling of the carriage.

Katie leans into me and whispers, 'This is our most desperate hour. Help me, Obi-Wan Kenobi.'

'Katie,' I hiss.

'Sorry,' she mutters. 'I'm just so creeped out right now.'

I find her hand and squeeze it. The image sharpens – it's a Gem, in his late twenties at a guess, but it's hard to know with Gems. He's stunning, butterscotch hair waving around his face, and these amazing grey eyes. He's in some sort of laboratory. The clean lines of the white surfaces, the blank stretches of wall and the carefully arranged equipment only serve to heighten the sense of something more organic, something grimy, lurking just out of shot. A sense of dread fills my chest, freezing up my lungs.

He begins to speak with his full, wolfish lips.

'Greetings, fellow Taleters. Apologies for my absence, but my work must take priority, I'm sure you understand. Some of you have worried about the impact of our weapon on your loved ones. I am no fool and I realize that some Gems have inadvertently married Imps, perhaps have Imp lovers, or half-blood children. So you can now rest easy knowing I have found a solution to this little problem. Our weapon can be used effectively against the Imp population, with your Imp loved ones now being protected. And Nate, this will be your reward for helping us. It will give you what you want most in the world. But enough talking, allow me to introduce Subject 21.'

He leans forward, giving a quick close-up of his beautiful lips, and then scoops the camera up. Slowly, he pans around the room. I was right, something organic was lurking out of shot. I see a line of beds, and lying in each bed is an Imp, strapped down and fed by tubes.

The camera moves to the nearest Imp. She has long,

mousy hair which spills across the pillow, allowing only glimpses of the crisp, white cotton below. She can't be much older than fifteen. She's crying, but she has something in her mouth so she can't scream. She wears a white robe which reminds me of NHS hospital gowns.

Oscar approaches her. *'So, a simple injection. I find intravenous is the quickest and most effective, though I am very close to achieving an oral solution.'* He leans over the girl and swiftly sticks a needle into her neck. Her body arches and begins to convulse. Oscar turns to the camera. *'This is the worst bit. So far, I have about a seventy per cent success rate, but I'm hoping this will reach about ninety. The unsuccessful die. But the successful benefit from all DNA reconfigurations internally. Improved immunity, slower aging, increased muscle density and synapse speed. The external must be left to surgery and growth hormones, obviously, but that can be sorted at a later date. I'm aware, though, that some of you are less concerned with the general use of this serum, and more concerned with the specifics. And the answer is yes. Any Imps retrofitted into Gems will survive the Imp-targeting viral attack.'*

I turn to Katie, my eyes wide, my throat tangled with panic. *An Imp-targeting virus?* I mouth.

She shakes her head, horrified, like she can't quite believe it.

The girl continues to convulse behind Oscar, but he doesn't even look, like she's nothing to him. Then, just like that, she stops. The machine continues to beep. The girl opens her eyes and Oscar strokes her hair. *'It's OK, little one, don't be afraid. You made it. You're a Gem.'*

An Imp-targeting virus.

That's what is in the canister Nate planted.

'That's it,' I whisper to Katie. 'That's the ending. Baba said I had to save the Imps again; I have to stop that canister from exploding, then we can go home.'

Katie's about to reply when a series of footsteps strike terror into us both. They're coming from outside the carriage. We pull our eyes away from the crack and begin slinking along the side of the train, unable to blink or breathe from panic. We reach the end of the carriage, only metres from the mouth of the tunnel. The safety of darkness beckons. Katie makes a break for it. I follow, but my feet catch in the metal tracks. I stumble. Pain envelops my ankle and I release a strangled cry. And suddenly, strong hands are pulling me back, gruff voices shouting in my ear: 'Come here, spy.'

Katie turns. Even in the murk of the tunnel, I can see her mouth's open, like she's about to scream.

Go, I mouth. *Get help.*

She darts into the darkness, as I'm hauled back into the light.

23

VIOLET

The Taleters shove me into the carriage. The smell of the Gems – money and privilege, after-shave and port – makes my stomach cramp. Howard approaches, his twisted leer stuck to his face. 'And you are?'

I begin to see double. I open my mouth but no noise emerges, so I settle on blinking, hard.

'Nate, do you know this Imp?'

Nate walks towards me, dumbfounded. 'She's one of the visitors I told you about back in No-man's-land.'

'Pull back your hood, girl,' Howard says in a stony voice.

I obey, my hands trembling and the fabric of the hood sticking to my forehead. I really didn't think this through. Any of the Gems here could have enhanced memories and remember me from when I pretended to be Rose, and here I am, hood pulled back, face revealed, standing in the lion's den.

As if to prove my point, a voice rings out. *'Wait.'*

My head swivels, trying to find the owner of the voice.

'I recognize this Imp,' he says. *'The President will want to meet her . . . very much.'*

The voice is coming from above. It's Oscar, the light-projected scientist. He must have an enhanced memory. Shit. My eyes immediately scan the carriage for exits.

Howard tilts his face towards Oscar. 'What do you mean? How do you know this girl?'

Jeremy Harper steps forward. 'Who cares. She's clearly an alliance spy. She looks like she's about to soil herself. We should just kill her.'

'No,' Nate shrieks. 'There's some mistake.'

Everyone looks at him.

'I know this Imp,' he says. 'I mean . . . I really know her. I'm just not sure how.'

Nate knows me? But he didn't recognize me at Baba's execution. What's changed?

I hear the trill of birdsong and the swish of wings echoing through the station. I look through the mottled glass of the carriage expecting to see a flock of birds, but only my own terrified reflection stares back at me.

'*She's the insert,*' Oscar says. '*The Imp who took Rose's place during one of the loops. We should take her to the President, he'll know what to do.*'

But Howard laughs. 'My uncle would want her dead. Like all the other vermin.'

'*No,*' says Oscar. '*She may be more use to us alive.*'

Howard raises his voice, flecks of spittle flying from his lips. 'I am in charge in my uncle's absence.'

Nate looks at me, his face filled with panic. 'An insert? A loop? What are they on about?'

Suddenly, my jaw can move, and I whisper the words which have been building inside me ever since I arrived in this dump. 'I'm your sister, Nate.'

The sounds of Oscar and Howard arguing, the hum of disapproving Gems, drowns out Nate's words, but I can just about read his lips. 'My sister?'

'Nate, look at me.' I hold his face, forcing him to stare into my eyes. And then I begin to sing, quietly so only he can hear.

'*Let me fix your broken wing,*

A swallow should fly free, my love.'

'That song,' he says, his eyes filling with tears. 'How could you possibly know it?'

I don't reply, I just keep singing, every word burning my throat.

'For you were born to dance and sing,
And you will soar with me, my love.'

'Nobody knows that song except me,' Nate whispers. 'I hear it in my dreams.'

'Our mother used to sing it to us.'

An expression of such intensity grips his features, only bliss or the crushing pain of loss could cause it.

Just then, Oscar raises his voice, making the metal shell of the carriage reverberate. *'You will regret this, Howard. This Imp is important beyond your understanding. She isn't from our world —'*

'Stop questioning me,' Howard roars. 'You and your bloody loops. Funny how only a few of you remember this loop, but the rest of us can't.'

A murmur of agreement rises from the crowd. I hadn't realized there would be resentment between those who could remember the loop and those who couldn't. And right now, it's going to get me killed.

Howard swipes at the projecting marble still hovering before him, and the link to Oscar vanishes.

'That is enough,' Howard yells, white froth gathering in the corners of his mouth. 'The Imp dies.' He strides towards me and grabs my arm, dragging me from the carriage on to the platform.

'No,' I say. 'Please, Oscar's right.'

Howard responds by yanking my hair and shoving me further across the platform. 'All these bloody secrets,' he throws over his shoulder, as though Oscar can still hear him. 'Whispering with my uncle when you think I can't hear, you think I don't know? Well, maybe this will teach you to tell me what the hell is going on.'

My head feels like it's going to rip clean away from my neck. I try to scream but find my lungs are empty and tight.

'Wait, Howard. Please.' Nate hangs on to Howard's cloak, clawing his way towards me. The look on his face makes me want to cry. It's sheer terror.

The rest of the Taleters follow, pulling Nate back. Howard throws me into the wall of the platform. A tile snaps beneath my weight, pain shoots up my spine and I begin to feel light-headed and sick. Candlelight swirls around the tunnel; shadows and smoke twist around each other. Howard approaches, his blond curls so aglow he looks like a deranged angel. He leans in and I feel his breath against my ear. It smells of decay. 'Shame we can't hang you the old-fashioned way. I really miss watching the Imps dance. A bullet will have to do instead.' He turns back to the crowd. 'Bring me Nate.'

The crowd ushers Nate forwards so that he stands less than a metre away. He's so close I could reach out and touch him if my arms weren't pinned. I long to touch him. A reassuring squeeze of his shoulder. Tears stream down his face, and he's shaking his head like he can't quite believe what's about to happen.

Howard looks at him. 'You two seemed very cosy just now. What were you talking about?'

'N-nothing,' Nate stammers. 'I recognize her, that's all. Please . . . don't hurt her.'

'Are you a true Taleter, Nate?' Howard asks, his face relaxing into a dangerous smile. 'Do you want that serum so you can become a Gem?'

'Yes,' Nate answers without missing a beat.

Howard pulls a pistol from inside his cloak and

shoves it into Nate's hands. 'Then prove it. Put a bullet in the bitch's skull.'

Nate points the gun at me. Silence falls. His face contorts with grief.

'Do it!' Howard roars.

'I can't.' Nate's voice sounds small, but as he looks at Howard, strength gathers in his eyes. 'I *won't*.' The blast of gunshot rips through me. I brace myself for the pain, the mess, the loss of consciousness. But the bullet was never meant for me.

Howard drops to the floor, blood pooling from his stomach.

Before I can think or move, I hear Nate's voice. 'RUN!'

We drop down behind the carriage on to the lines. That's when the gunfire really starts. Exploding into the platform behind me, showering my face with shards of ancient paving. The ground around me erupts and the metal rails resound with terrifying pinging. Nate grabs my hand and we begin to tear down the tunnel into the black.

I look behind. Gems chase us, their cloaks fanning behind them, their faces battle-ready and thirsty for revenge. *They'll catch us, surely – they're Gems.* Up ahead, in the gloom, are several dots of light. Torches? Headlamps? It must be too soon for Katie to have summoned help. Regardless, I sprint towards those dots of light, knowing that they can't be any worse than what chases us.

The dots grow stronger, brighter. It's Willow, Ash and Daisy, clutching torches and running towards us. They pass us without as much as a glance, pulling weapons from their belts and coats. They're far outnumbered by the Taleters, but they have the element of surprise, and once they start firing, the Taleters retreat back to the station.

Our three saviours loop back towards us.

'Hurry,' Ash shouts. I can't remember a time I've been so pleased to see him. I throw my arms around his neck and squeeze with all my might, breathing in his safe and wonderful scent.

He drags me towards some motorbikes, ditched on their sides, engines still turning and stinking of diesel. Something about the lack of technology makes me feel secure, like a little piece of home is staring back at me.

'Hang on a second,' Willow says, pointing at Nate. 'Why are we saving him?'

Beneath the dust and muck, Nate's face drains of all colour.

I step in between them. 'He just shot Howard Stoneback. *Howard Stoneback.*'

Willow stares at me for a second. And then gestures for Nate to sit behind him. They zip away from us, Daisy close behind. Ash hoists the remaining bike upright, and I climb on behind him. He revs the engine and we squeal after the others. The headlights show every bump and crack in the walls, every decomposing rat corpse strewn between the rusting lines. But I'm so shielded by shock, so disconnected from reality, I'm oddly grateful to the choking dust and the ear-splitting roar of the engines, captured and magnified by the brick walls.

I hold on to Ash as fiercely as I can, unashamedly thankful for the excuse to lean into him. I savour the warmth of his back against my stomach, the hardness of his shoulder blades against my chest. The bike rumbles through the tunnel. The vibrations pass through my thighs and into my gut, masking the bubbling of residual adrenalin and the growing excitement that I'm clinging on to Ash.

We head back the way we came, but whereas the others follow the route for Moorgate, Ash takes another turn. I'm not sure where he's taking me, but I feel completely safe, and it barely occurs to me that this is a strange thing for him to do. *Of course we need some alone time. I nearly died.*

We draw to a halt. He cuts the engine and our strange, tubular world is plunged into eerie silence; I hear only the sound of our breath and the distant scratch of vermin. He leaves the headlamp on and grains of dirt swirl around us, catching in the light like flecks of gold. This tunnel has probably remained undisturbed for centuries; it feels like we're the only people in the world right now, and from the way Ash is breathing – deep yet unsure – I think he feels the same.

'The Gems won't follow us,' he finally says. 'We're well into Imp territory. We'll be safe here for a moment.'

We both dismount. But Ash doesn't look at me like I expect, rather he begins to brush the mud from the headlamp, his face tipped from view.

'Why did we stop?' I ask.

This forces him to turn. He's been crying. The tears have left clean tracks through the muck on his face, and his eyelashes are stuck together.

Instinctively, I reach out a hand and touch his cheek. 'What's the matter?'

'Violet, what were you thinking? You were nearly killed.'

'I'm sorry,' I blurt out. 'I'm so sorry. But I've found something out, something terrible.'

'I know, Katie told us. Fortunately for you, we were on our way anyway. My reading isn't great, but once I told Daisy what I'd seen on your arm, it didn't take much to figure out where you were . . . Who are you?'

'You really don't remember me?' I ask.

He stares at me. 'I think maybe I do.'

Something builds inside me, something strong and warm, threatening to spill out of me. I lean forwards and kiss him on the lips.

He pulls away like my mouth delivered an electric charge.

'Violet,' he whispers.

'I'm sorry,' I garble. 'I know you love Daisy, I know you do.'

'I do love her.'

The jealousy explodes inside me. I feel so petty – I've just uncovered a secret plot to exterminate the Imps, and all I can think about is Ash. But I'm starting to understand that jealousy sits on the surface like a blood blister, toxic and black, unable to heal. It isn't a single, clean slice to the flesh, not like the other dark emotions. It can't bleed out, it can't be wiped up or stitched back together. It festers and it broods and there's nothing you can do about it.

He takes my hands in his and smiles his lopsided smile. 'I do love her. But not like you think.'

'What . . . what do you mean?'

'There are many different types of love. I don't love Dee the way you think I love Dee.'

I shake my head, frustrated. 'What?'

'We're a symbol of hope, a union of an Imp and Gem. Willow introduced us, hoping we would fall for each other. But I just didn't feel it, you know. Dee's beautiful and kind, and she really cares about me, but something just isn't right.'

'But . . . you live together.'

'It's entirely for show; she's more like a sister to me. We've got separate rooms.'

I don't know what's going on in my body right now. It's like all the bitterness in my veins is being drained away, that blood blister receding so that I'm left with only skin. Skin which feels surprisingly warm, skin which longs to be touched. 'And what does Dee think about this?'

'She hopes that my feelings for her will eventually develop.'

'Are you just saying this? Seriously, Ash? Are you just saying what you think I want to hear?'

A hurt expression darkens the pale of his eyes. 'Of course not.'

But I can't bring myself to believe him, not yet, not when my heart hangs so delicately in the balance, and my instinct remains to protect myself. 'Well, maybe you will, grow to love her, I mean. She seems lovely, and she clearly wants you. It's almost your responsibility after all, providing a symbol for Imp–Gem unity.'

He stops me by placing a hand against my cheek. It's warm and soft and I can't help but push my face into it. I swear I would recognise the press of his skin even after a lifetime apart. 'Why do I feel so drawn to you?' he says.

I open my mouth to respond, but no words appear.

'Do you feel it too?' he asks.

'Yes.'

His mouth smiles, even though his eyes look sorrowful, desperate almost. 'I never believed in "the one", not until now. It's like I was numb, dead, until you turned up . . . and now everything makes sense.' He laughs a sad laugh. 'Everything and nothing.'

Tears spring to my eyes. 'Ash, I can't stay here . . . we can never be together.' Because one way or another, I'm leaving this place, be it by transdimensional tunnelling or by body bag. It breaks my heart to say it, but Ash and I will never have a happy ending. 'I don't belong here,' I whisper.

'Then neither do I.' And suddenly, he's kissing me.

It's a desperate kiss, filled with heat and love, sending waves of pleasure through me. I pull him close to me, and within seconds, I'm pulling off his shirt, my movements frantic. My hands move across his chest, tracing the abundance of freckles which cluster on his shoulders, and he kisses me again as his hands move beneath my top, gently feeling their way across my flesh.

I've imagined my first time over and over. It tends to involve clean sheets, soft lighting, the hot thrum of alcohol in my veins, and the gentle lull of music to hide my gasps. Not once did I imagine getting naked between the disused tracks of London's Underground, the hard floor scratching at my butt, and the noises falling from my mouth echoed back at me from the brick walls. Not once did I imagine my breasts, thighs, stomach . . . *everything* . . . exposed to the cold, stagnant air, illuminated by the glare of a motorcycle headlamp.

But since the day I met him, it always involved Ash. Even when I couldn't remember him properly, when he was just a shadow, a fleeting scent in my unconscious, it involved Ash. So in spite of everything – the dirt, the cold, the stark light – my first time is everything I'd hoped, because it's with him.

24
ALICE

I wake to the buzz of my phone. I blink, the artificial light stinging my eyes. It's super late, and I can hear Danny's soft breaths. I worry it will be another threatening message and my muscles tighten. But when I look, it's another post from Fanboy.

The meeting at the tube station.

I read it slowly, my trembling hands causing the words to blur on my screen.

Fanboy carefully documents the Taleters' plan to destroy the Imps. An Imp-targeting virus. Planted in canisters around the country, ready to detonate in mere days. They've developed a serum that can turn Imps into Gems, but that's only for a few favourites. For the rest . . . tears swell in my eyes as I whisper their names at my phone. *Violet. Katie. Nate.* They're going to die horrible deaths if I don't do something.

As I blink my vision clear, I notice a message from Russell. He must have sent it an hour or so ago.

> Hey, I love your new fanfic about
> Nate. Do you fancy meeting up to
> chat about publicity? I think we
> could be good for each other x

The last sentence jars a little. It sounds more like a come-on than an invitation to talk publicity. But maybe this is the best thing I can do. While Danny works on the IP address, I can work on winning the fanfic war, spreading Fandom Rising to as big an audience as possible.

I turn off my phone, glancing at Danny, sound asleep on the bedroom floor.

Guilt squirms in my stomach.

VIOLET

I wake beside Ash. It's pitch black here in the tunnel, but I can tell from the steady rise and fall of his chest that he's still asleep. We found an old blanket tucked in the storage box in the motorcycle seat, and this, combined with our clothes, is piled on top of us to keep out the cold. The warmth from his naked skin calms me like nothing else, and the darkness seems to accentuate his body heat. I imagine I can see us, two bodies forming a unitary glowing shape on the tunnel floor.

I reach for our torch and flick it on, positioning it so it points towards the ceiling. The beam reflects down on us, casting us in a strange, rippled light. I carefully check the battered old watch on Ash's wrist; 6 a.m. And for only a second, just because my legs are wound around his, I let myself believe that everything will be OK. I just need to find that canister and stop it from releasing the virus. I don't know which wakes Ash, the light or my movement, but he wakes all the same. He opens his eyes and smiles. He looks all sleepy and cute, his hair a ruffled mess, his face marked with a blanket crease. He's about to say something when we hear a gasp.

I sit up, without thinking, and the blanket flops away from me, revealing my bare chest. I gather it up as quickly as I can, my eyes focusing on the figure in the dark. I can just pick out Daisy's features, the look of horror and betrayal on her perfect face. I guess the others told her we got left behind, and she came looking. Maybe I knew she would. Maybe I wanted her to find us like this.

With a flash of guilt, I remember discovering Alice with Willow, the hurt and betrayal which ripped through me.

Ash props himself on his elbows and rubs his eyes. He sees her and the look on his face breaks my heart. It's one of shock and pain and fear.

She turns and runs back down the tunnel.

I pause, expecting a heartfelt 'Dee' to echo after her, resonating between her footsteps and sobs.

But it never comes.

Driven by guilt and shame, I hear my own voice call out, 'DAISY!' I stand, clutching the blanket to my chest, accidentally lifting it from Ash, so only his strewn-open jacket hides his modesty.

'DAISY,' I shout again.

She doesn't stop. I listen as her footsteps fade. I begin pulling my clothes on, desperate to chase after her, but Ash lays a gentle hand on my ankle.

'Let her go,' he says.

'But—' I begin.

He cuts over me. 'She needed to find out. I just wish I'd told her first. Please don't feel bad, it's my fault, not yours.'

I freeze, my right foot poised in the air, ready to pull on my boot, and I'm suddenly aware of my nakedness. 'What do you mean?'

He smiles. And then he says four words. Words I spoke to him a lifetime ago. Words whispered across the bow of a rowing boat. I still don't think he remembers exactly, but they must have lodged somewhere in his brain, because he says them back to me as his own. 'It's always been you.'

ALICE

In the morning, Danny drives me home and helps me clear the lipstick from my mirror. We use some water and a Mr Muscle window spray Mum has stuffed at the back of the cleaning cupboard.

I've been mulling over that message from Russell all morning, and I finally come to a decision. I'll help my friends, even if it means spending an evening with the delight that is Russell Jones. Danny heads to the bathroom and I whip out my phone, quickly tapping out a message.

Great, I'm free tonight.

Danny returns just as the phone rings. It's Russell. I hadn't expected him to call. I mean, who even does that these days? Caught off guard, I answer.

'Hi,' I say.

'Hey, beautiful. Just thought I'd see what you fancied doing tonight.'

'Dunno.' I glance at Danny, who studies me with curiosity.

'OK, well, I know a lovely little place in Hammersmith. I'll get my driver to pick you up. Message me your address.'

'Will do.'

'He'll pick you up about seven. Is that OK?'

'Yeah. Great, thanks.'

'Wear something lovely,' he says.

'I will.' I hang up pretty quick, worried that I'll back out if Russell keeps talking.

'Who was that?' Danny asks, picking up the red-stained cloth.

'Russell Jones,' I reply, trying to sound casual.

'*The* Russell Jones? The twat from Comic-Con?'

'Yeah, we're just organizing a meeting to discuss publicity stuff.'

Danny's face falls a little. 'Like, a date?'

'God no, nothing like that. I just need him to help me publicize Fandom Rising.'

'Makes sense, I guess.' He plonks the cloth on my dresser. 'So, are you going to his apartment or something?'

'He's staying in a hotel actually,' I reply, bristling slightly.

'OK. Well, I'll head off now and try and track down the IP address. Enjoy publicity and stuff.' He walks towards the door without making eye contact.

'Suit yourself,' I say, folding my arms like I'm a stroppy kid.

He closes the door, louder than is necessary.

I lie on my bed feeling like shit. I've pissed off Danny. The only person who can help me find Fanboy. Worst thing is, I don't even want to see Russell. A year ago, I would have been totally hyped if he'd asked me out, but now, a stern nipple waxing would be preferable. In fact, that isn't the worst thing. I take that back. Worst thing is, Danny was a complete knob right now.

The door reopens. It's Danny, looking very sheepish. 'I'm sorry, that was stupid of me. I think . . . I think maybe I felt a bit . . . jealous. But that's just ridiculous, you don't belong to me or owe me anything.' He meets my gaze and manages a shy smile. 'I just wanted to tell you that it's great you're meeting Russell tonight. And, you know, make sure you wear your cap. It will pull your whole outfit together.'

'Thanks, Danny.'

'Are you OK in the house on your own now?'

'Yeah, Mum and Dad are due back any second.'

He nods. 'OK, see you soon.'

He closes the door.

OK. It's official. I'm totally into Danny.

Even though I can't see those red letters any more, it's like they're still glaring at me from the glass. I move to Mum and Dad's room and shove a chair under the door handle. I only go in in my parents' room to raid Mum's perfume collection or borrow (steal) her expensive moisturizer; I never go in and just sit. It's beautifully decorated, a sea of duck-egg blue, but it lacks the personal touches of most rooms. There are no photos on the walls, no everyday clutter on the surfaces. It could be a showroom.

I settle on to their bed with my laptop, my eyes flicking to the door every other second. They should be home soon, then I'll feel less jumpy. I try and focus on the task at hand: another post for Fandom Rising. I rub my temples, the responsibility pressing in on my skull. *Think like a writer, Alice.*

OK. I've built empathy for Nate, showed why he went to the dark side. I've planted seeds for his redemption. Now it's time for a Snape-inspired U-turn.

NATE

I dream of my sister. Even though I know she must be an adult now, in my dream she is still a child. She's handing me her blanket and stroking my hair and telling me everything will be OK. Then, something changes in her face. Her eyes grow red, her nose begins to stream, her lovely, peachy skin begins to mottle with the beginnings of a rash.

'What's the matter?' I ask her.

But all she can do is cough.

I hear another voice. 'It's the virus, Nate.' Yan appears before me. He hands my sister a tissue and touches her lightly on the head. She coughs into the handkerchief and pulls it away to reveal a patch of blood.

Tears begin to fall down my face. 'I'm sorry,' I tell her. 'I'm so sorry.'

Yan holds my face in his elegant hands. 'It isn't too late. You can stop this.'

I wake as my sister begins to spasm, yellow froth spewing from her rosebud lips.

I'm sweating and screaming, trying to rid myself of the image.

I can't let this happen, I can't. Not to my sister, not to anyone.

So I'll retrieve that hateful canister and I'll smuggle it back to my lab.

I will find an antidote.

It finally makes sense: I wasn't born to belong with my people, I was born to save them.

I check over it a few times, then hit the update button.

The doorbell rings. I freeze. Mum and Dad wouldn't ring their own bell, and I'm not expecting anyone. I consider just hiding in my parents' room, door wedged shut. But maybe that would be worse, making people think there's nobody at home. I'll answer the door, phone behind my back, ready to dial 999. And if there's nobody there, I'll head straight over to Danny's house. *For God's sake, Alice, it's probably just the postman.*

I head downstairs, ignoring the nerves which flutter in my chest.

When I open the door, two police officers are waiting. A tall lady with light brown skin and pretty eyes, and a shorter man with red hair. They smile in stereo. Two police officers standing on your doorstep would freak you out even if you hadn't just knifed your bestie's arm and received threatening messages about it. In light of my current situation, I'm just about shitting my Victoria's Secrets. Maybe the stalker has told the police it was me who sliced Violet.

At least they're not going to murder me . . . I slip my phone back into my pocket – no need for 999 now – and make sure my mask is firmly fixed to my face.

'Alice Childs?' the lady says.

I nod, trying not to look in the least bit suspicious, guilty or anything other than completely calm.

'I'm Sergeant Singh,' the lady says, before gesturing to the male officer, 'and this is Constable Turner. We just wanted to ask you a few questions about your friend, Violet Miller.'

They both flash their ID, still smiling their reassuring smiles.

'Oh . . . OK.' I fish around for more non-suspicious, guilt-free words. 'Do you want to come in?'

'Thanks,' Turner says.

I lead them into the kitchen.

'Nice house,' Singh says. 'Do you live here with your parents?'

'Yeah,' I say. 'They'll be back any second.' I don't know why I said that, like I need a chaperone or something.

'Well, it's you we wanted to speak to,' Singh says.

I smile. 'Yeah, sorry, you said.' More sensible words please, Alice. 'Do you want a cup of tea?'

Singh nods. 'That would be lovely, thanks. We both take it with milk and one sugar.'

I begin filling the kettle. The officers sit at the kitchen table. I play a little game in my head, pretending they're just really convincing cosplayers. All I need to do is role play the shit out if this, and they'll leave me be.

Turner flips open his notebook. 'We just wanted to ask you about the assault against Miss Miller the other night.'

Do I act dumb? No, that would definitely be suspicious. I'm her best friend, I would know. I turn to get the cups from the cupboard, pleased for an excuse to hide my face. 'Yeah, terrible thing, her mum told me what happened.' *Too far, Alice, don't mention anyone else.*

Singh nods. 'So you haven't seen Violet since the assault?'

'No,' I say. Which is true.

'Do you know what happened?' she asks.

The kettle begins to hum. They're testing me, seeing if I slip up and know more than I should. I keep it vague. 'Yeah. Some whacko cut up her arm.'

They leave a long pause, probably hoping I'll fill it. But I busy myself with putting teabags in cups.

'Do you know anyone who would want to hurt Violet?' Singh eventually asks.

I begin to pour the water. 'No, everybody loves Violet. It was probably some sick fan.'

'A fan?' she says, her voice piquing with interest. 'What makes you say that?'

'You know, who else could it be?' I grab the milk, aware they can see every guilty line creased into my forehead beneath the glare of the fridge light. I slam the fridge door shut, quick as I can.

'Bank, Monday, 12 a.m. A,' she says. 'Mean anything?'

I turn to face her. 'No. Should it?' This is a risk. What if they've read Fandalism? And what if they've seen Fandom Rising and they already know that I'm in some weird fanfic war and therefore it must mean something to me. But that doesn't mean I cut Violet's arm, it just means I'm lying now. But why would I lie? All of these thoughts rush through my head even though my face stays completely still . . . I hope.

Singh shakes her head. 'No, it's just a strange thing to write. We thought it might mean something to you, what with you being her best friend.'

I shake my head, relief flooding my system. 'Nope, I've got nothing, sorry.' I bin the teabags and begin to pour milk into the cups, impressed by how steady my hand is.

'Did Violet ever work at a bank?' Turner asks. 'Or any other connection to banks we're missing?'

I pop the tea in front of them with the sugar. 'No, I mean, she used a bank I guess, but she never worked at one.'

Singh nods thoughtfully. 'OK. Thanks, Alice.' She stirs some sugar into her tea and sips it tentatively, like she knows it's going to scald.

'Well, I hope you catch them,' I say. 'Poor Violet, she's going to wake up with some butt-ugly scars now.'

'She certainly will – the cuts were deep and angry,' Singh says, studying my face.

I begin to make myself a drink, just so I can turn away again. The guilt is crippling my insides and I'm not sure how much longer I'll be able to keep my mask fixed.

Turner pipes up. 'And where were you Sunday night?'

Oh shit. The alibi. I forgot about the alibi.

'I was with Danny. Danny Bradshaw,' I say without thinking. Probably because he's the only person I've spent any time with recently who isn't in a coma. Still, it's stupid. They're bound to check with him, and I'm not sure how far his loyalty will stretch. Even if he covers for me, I don't know how believable he'll be. That boy is built from honesty.

They take Danny's details from me and finish their tea.

I watch them leave, my throat knotted with panic, then I ring Danny.

'Hey,' I say.

He doesn't reply.

'Danny? Are you there?'

'Yeah, I'm here.'

'What's up? You sound . . . different.'

There's a long pause. I can hear him breathing so I know he's there. Eventually he says, *'I read your post about Nate's sister.'*

Shit. Of course he did. He knows that I blatantly used his brother's death as fanfic fodder. Why did I not think this through? I open my mouth to reply, but I can't think of anything to say which doesn't sound pathetic.

'I don't expect everything I tell you to end up on the internet,' he says.

'I know. I'm so sorry, it was stupid . . . your story really got to me and I . . . I wasn't thinking.'

Another pause. Long enough for me to think he's about to hang up. Then he says, *'Well, I guess I should be flattered I provided you with inspiration.'*

'You're my official muse. But seriously, I promise I

won't pull a stunt like that again.' Now it's my turn to pause. 'Danny, the police were just here.'

'*About the mirror?*'

'No . . . somebody cut Violet's arm while she was unconscious.'

'*They did* what? *What kind of a sicko would do that?*' The disgust in his voice makes the guilt almost unbearable.

'Danny, they think it was me.'

'*That's ridiculous, why on earth would you do that? She's your best friend.*'

'Thing is, I needed an alibi . . .'

'*And you gave my name.*'

'Yeah.'

Shit, shit, shit. I hate talking on the phone. All these pauses are doing my nut right now.

'*When did it happen?*' he finally asks.

'Sunday night.'

He sounds practical, in control. '*OK. We went for a walk that night, you were bummed over your friends being in comas. We chatted it through and stayed out late. Nobody else saw us.*'

I want to cry. But instead I just whisper, 'Thanks.'

25

VIOLET

When Ash and I enter the church, all eyes are on us. I feel my cheeks swell with embarrassment. Katie rushes to me. 'What the hell were you thinking, you tit-turnip, worrying me like that?' She pulls me to her in an aggressive hug. 'We stick together, you and me.' Her gaze flicks between me and Ash, and her face bursts into a massive cheesy grin.

Ash squeezes my hand and darts off to talk to Willow. I can tell even from here that Willow's pissed at him, folding his arms and answering with pinched head-nods.

Katie leans into me. 'Sooooo, Violet the Virgin. Have fun getting down in the underground, did we?'

'Oh Katie, it was awful. Daisy found us, she was so upset.'

Katie chews her lip. 'Hmm, yes, I imagine that would dampen the mood.'

'Have you seen her this morning?' I ask.

'Not since yesterday.'

I drop my head into my hands. It feels strangely heavy. 'I feel just horrible.'

'Let's face it, Vi, nobody could compete with a good old time-loop romance. Girl meets boy. Girl hangs. Boy has memory wiped. Girl returns to boy. Boy is mysteriously drawn to girl. Girl humps boy. It's a classic. Poor cow didn't stand a chance.' She starts to laugh, it fills the church like a wind chime, and I find I'm laughing too.

But Katie's laughter comes to an abrupt stop. 'Jesus, Vi. You did use . . . you know?'

'Protection?' I ask. 'Yes, course we did.'

'Phew. I mean, imagine waking up in our universe, pregnant with Ash's baby. That would be all sorts of wrong.'

I don't know whether to laugh or cry.

I head to Nate's house. Ash handed me a crumpled note with a map sketched on it. The map's pretty clear and I reach Nate's house in about five minutes. Nate moved near to the HQ as soon as he introduced himself to Thorn and was recruited as part of the alliance. He lives in a modest bedsit, part of one of the buildings which hasn't fallen down on that street. I'm surprised he hasn't got somewhere a little nicer, a little more like Ash or Thorn's place. I don't think I wrote his accommodation into *The Gallows Song*. I wish I had now; I would have written him somewhere way nicer than this.

The door inches open from the pressure of my knock. I call out softly. When I get no reply, I slip inside. He sits at a desk in the corner of the room. There isn't much furniture, but the desk still seems too big and cumbersome for the room, like Gandalf moved his stuff into Bag End. Nate huddles over a very modern-looking computer. An incubator, half filled with soil, sits on the ground by his feet.

'What are you doing?' I ask.

He doesn't startle, nor does he look up from what he's doing. 'Welcome to my humble lab; it isn't much, is it?' 3D images hover before his eyes, and he inflates and contracts them with nimble fingers. A helix spins at the side of the image, modifying slightly with every one of his movements. 'I'm working on a new strain of crops which would need less light and water. We could grow them in the disused buildings, then make use of the land we've got. It would make the Imps more self-sufficient . . . and less hungry.'

'That's amazing,' I say.

He nods, accepting the compliment without thought.

'Why were you helping the Imps if you wanted to betray them?'

He removes the helix with an angry flick of his hand. The other images fade before my eyes.

'I honestly don't know.' He swings in his chair to look at me. 'It wasn't just maintaining my cover or anything. I really wanted to sort this out and help with the food shortage in the cities. It's not like I woke up one morning and thought, *I know, I'll betray my people.*'

He stands from his desk and looks at me. But his defiant expression is completely undone by the tears in his eyes. 'It happened gradually,' he says. 'The feeling of isolation, of being different, just seemed to grow inside me.' He looks at his feet. 'Sorry, you don't need to know—'

'It's OK,' I say, cutting through his apology. 'Go on.'

He sighs. 'I knew I'd only fit in if I became a Gem. And they offered me a solution, in exchange for my services. Of course, the need to help the Imps didn't just die inside me. I just carry two conflicting goals at once. It kind of sucks.'

He pulls open the door and begins to march down the street.

'Where are we going?' I ask, hurrying after him.

'I think better when I move.'

I struggle to keep up. 'Thanks for saving me back at the station.'

'Shooting Howard, you mean? I did it without thinking to be honest. I probably just signed my own death warrant – no side will want me now.'

'That's not true. Willow and Ash know you saved me, and they'll keep everything from Thorn. I know they will.'

'Do they know I killed Baba?' A strangled look of grief and guilt hangs on his face. And it's just not fair he should carry this burden. I wasn't going to tell him, but now, striding down this knackered old street, I know that I will.

'There are forces at work here beyond your control, Nate. Someone is inside your head, and they're making you do things.'

'A telepath, you mean? Someone like Baba?'

'Something like that. It's impossible to explain. But you are stronger than they are. I know you are, because I know you. You must fight back. Bloody balls of steel.'

He looks confused. 'Balls of steel?' he whispers.

I nod, a laugh catching in my throat. 'Yes. That's right. Balls of steel.'

'I've heard that somewhere before.'

'That's right,' I say. 'Balls of steel. Like Katniss. Like Tris.'

'I have no idea what you're taking about right now, you know that, yeah?'

I laugh. 'Yeah.'

He stops walking and looks at me. And then, totally unexpectedly, says, 'Are you really my sister?'

I nod. 'Yeah. Baba reached out to me in my dreams. She told me about you, about how you needed my help. You're the real reason I came here.'

He turns away without replying, and we continue to walk until we approach a break in the buildings. An expanse of rubble stretches before us, penned in by a low, uneven wall. I can tell it used to be a building, a large one. Nate climbs on to a higher part of the wall and reaches down to pull me up. I scrabble up the stone until I'm stood beside him.

'Come on,' he says. 'The view gets loads better, I promise.'

I follow him as we walk across the top of the wall, picking our way across the lumps and dips, the stone releasing particles beneath our feet. Finally, we reach a spot several metres above the ground. The sudden fear of falling causes my head to swim, and I find my hands reaching for Nate's arm. To steady myself, to steady him.

'Look,' Nate says, gesturing below.

I look down. The rubble forms the shape of a giant cross.

'It must have been a church,' I reply. 'A cathedral judging by the size of it.' I notice the outline of a broken circle right in the centre. It used to be St Paul's. I stare into the sky where the dome used to hang, and I suddenly feel very, very hopeless. If St Paul's couldn't survive the Gems, how the hell can we?

'We used to have hope,' Nate says. 'God, Buddha, Allah, Krishna . . . all different names for the same thing – hope. What have we got now?'

I take his hand in mine. 'We've got each other.'

'Not for long. Without that serum, we'll both die tomorrow.'

'Can't we just fetch the canister and disable it?'

He shakes his head. 'There's loads of them all over the country, all designed to go off at exactly the same time. I only know where the London one is.'

We sit on the wall and gaze across the scrappy rooftops of Imp London, the ruins of St Paul's at our feet. A cloud of birds passes overhead, the throng of crescent silhouettes dark against the clouds. 'Swallows,' Nate whispers. And as he watches them, a smile creeps across his face. 'I've just had an idea,' he says, clutching my hand.

'What?'

'We don't need a serum, we need an antidote. Then we can save all the Imps. I can retrieve the canister and get a sample of the virus. If I can get it back to my lab, I may be able to figure it out.'

'Isn't that dangerous?'

'Yes, but we're going to die anyway,' he laughs manically.

'Do you think you can do it today?' I ask, because as soon as that antidote is made, the story will end and we can go home. Then Nate will wake up before his life support is switched off.

Nate nods. 'For sure.' His tawny eyes are alive with life and for the first time since arriving in this world, I truly see him: the boy from my childhood.

My little brother.

ALICE

I remember Russell's stupid comment about wearing something lovely. It makes me want to pull on my jeans and my sloppy Hogwarts sweater. But I need to help my friends. So I choose my outfit carefully; only twenty per cent of sweet talking is done with the mouth, after all. Normally I would choose red, but it's the last colour I want to wear after the mirror message. So instead, I pick out a sky-blue dress.

All the time, I'm thinking about that horrible text and the writing on my mirror. Strange how both things happened just after I posted on Fandom Rising. I get this horrible squirmy feeling in my gut, like I've eaten a bad piece of sushi. *What if it's Fanboy? What if he's taking the fanfic war way too seriously?* I tell myself I'm being silly. *But who else could it be?* Well, I've just posted another story. Let's see if anything happens.

I told Russell I'd make my own way to the restaurant. Something about handing out my address made me feel nervous. And having myself delivered to him like some sort of present just didn't sit right. Also, I want to call by Danny's house on the way. It's only a bit of a detour and I want to tell him I'm glad he was jealous. You see, I'm starting to rethink that done-with-men thing, now that I know there are men like Danny in the world.

Danny's mum opens the door. Her face lights up when she sees me. 'Alice, you look beautiful. Are you and Danny off on a date?'

I shake my head, a little awkwardly. 'Uh, no. I just wanted to talk to him quickly if that's OK?'

'Yeah, course it is. He's just popped to the shops to grab some milk, but he'll only be a few minutes. Come on in.'

She gestures for me to sit on the sofa.

'Cuppa?' she asks.

I nod. 'That would be lovely, thanks.'

'We'll have to wait for the milk, but I'll boil the kettle,' she says as she disappears into the kitchen.

I'm left on my own in the sitting room. Just me and a load of family photos. I stand from the sofa and move to the mantelpiece. There's one of Danny when he was a baby. Christ, he was cute. Danny when he lost his first tooth (not just a piece of painted sweetcorn). A photo of him with his brother, dressed in matching outfits. A photo of Danny holding the science prize at school, looking ganglier than I remember. And a recent photo of Danny and his mum hugging, taken at a restaurant by the looks of it. I can't help but imagine a photo of me and Danny, holding hands, maybe going to a convention or something. What is wrong with me?

I move across to the sideboard to check out more of the Danny snaps, when I notice his rucksack slung on the floor. A piece of paper sticks out from it. I can just make out a face . . . Violet's face. My head begins to buzz with nerves. I slide the rest of the paper out. It's another photo, but not of cute babies or science prizes. It's a photo of me, Katie and Violet, cut from our last school yearbook.

At least, I'm guessing it's me.

My face has been scratched clean away.

A flash of horror, my legs almost giving way as if the bones have been removed.

Could Danny be sending me the threats? Surely not. All the way over here I'd convinced myself it was Fanboy.

A sinking feeling fills my chest.

Could Danny be Fanboy?

Has he been playing me the whole time?

I hurtle out of his house still clutching the photo. *I'm such a fucking idiot. Have I seriously just fallen for my stalker?* Tears are gathering in my eyes and it feels like my legs are about to give way. I round on to the street and run straight into him.

The milk goes flying, the bottle splits and white globs spray all over the pavement.

'Bollocks,' he says.

He sees the photo in my hand before I can hide it. 'Alice . . .'

'Was it you?' I say, my voice shaking.

His brown eyes widen, his palms stretch towards me. 'No, of course not.'

'Then why have you got this photo?'

He gently prises it from my fingers. 'I found it, stuffed through the letterbox when I left your house this morning. I didn't want to scare you, but I didn't want to leave you, so I hung around for a while, made sure no one was watching the house. I was going to tell you, to try and convince you to ring the police, but I thought I'd wait till after your date with Russell.'

'Why?'

'I dunno, I thought you deserved a night off.'

Can someone really be that good? I shake my head at him slowly, my breathing beginning to slow. 'So . . .'

'So . . . you need to tell me what's going on. The fanfic, the stalker, the police. Everything.'

We sit on the wall outside his house, watching the kids in the playground across the street. He's right, I need to tell him what's going on. But first, I need to apologize face-to-face for using his tragedy on Fandom Rising. 'Look, I'm so sorry about that post. I didn't even think about how it would affect you at the time. It was stupid and dumb, I'm really sorry.'

He nods. 'Thanks. I know you've got a lot going on right now, but I wanted you to know it wasn't cool.'

'Agreed.'

'OK. Don't think you can dodge the obvious.'

I keep my gaze fixed on the kids in the playground. Maybe if I don't see his reaction to what I'm about to say, it will be easier. I take a deep breath. 'This is going to sound crazy. I didn't believe it myself. But last year, when Violet, Katie, Nate and I were in comas, we were transported into *The Gallows Dance*.'

I wait for him to laugh, and when he doesn't, I risk glancing at him. He just blinks a few times like he's trying to make sense of it. 'Transported where?' he finally says.

'Into *The Gallows Dance*. Into an alternate universe where *The Gallows Dance* is real.'

'OK,' he says. His voice is a mix of confusion and disbelief.

'Violet, Katie and I woke up, but Nate got stuck there.' There's a long pause. 'He got shot when he was over there. Anyway, Violet and Katie are trying to get him back, but the problem is, Fanboy is ballsing everything up. He's writing Nate bad and making it really dangerous for them, releasing a virus which will kill them all. That's why I wanted to track Fanboy down and why I went with your idea to start Fandom Rising, to try and help Violet and Katie. Does that make sense?'

He has this startled rabbit look. He shakes his head slowly.

I look back to the playground. I wish I was six again, on the swings with Violet and Nate. 'That's why I need to find Fanboy, to stop him messing with their universe and to give them a fighting chance. I think it's Fanboy who's stalking me. It's just a sick ratings game to him – he has no idea what he's doing.'

There's a really long pause. His lovely face is creased with concern and disbelief. He runs his fingers anxiously through his dark curls.

'Danny?' I finally say. 'You think I'm mad, don't you?'

He bites his lip, the skin around his teeth whitening from the pressure. He's looking at me differently. Suspiciously. 'Alice, did you assault Violet?'

'What?'

'I need to know, did you assault Violet at the hospital?'

I can feel the panic starting to take hold of my lungs. I want to tell him. But I hear myself saying, 'No, of course I didn't. She's my best friend and she's unconscious. I mean, what kind of sick bastard does that?'

He looks relieved for a moment, but his face tightens again. 'The same sick bastard who leaves messages on your mirror and defaces your yearbook photo.'

I swallow down the guilt. 'Yeah,' I say. 'That would make sense.'

'You need to tell the police about the stalker, Alice. You need to tell them about Fanboy. He's dangerous.'

My phone buzzes.

Beautiful, where are you? x

'Shit,' I mumble, scrambling down from the wall. 'I need to go. I'll tell the police, I promise, just in my own time, yeah?'

'Are you seriously still meeting Russell, after everything that's happened?'

'I've got to,' I reply.

He doesn't look very convinced.

26
ALICE

I meet Russell at a bar called the *Willow Tree*. Jesus, he really is nothing without his screen persona. He sits at a round table in the centre of the room. He looks seriously hot, his white T-shirt pulled taut across his pecs, and I hate myself for noticing how ripped his arms look. He sees me and stands.

He kisses me on the cheek, his aftershave burning the inside of my nostrils. His hands slide around my waist and I have to stop myself from smacking them away. I haven't been pawed by a guy in ages.

I sit opposite him and smile my best smile. 'The Willow Tree, huh?'

'Yeah,' he says, pushing his hair from his eyes. 'I thought you'd like it.'

'I love it.' I'm still smiling my best smile.

'How are your friends?' he asks.

I shrug, ordering my eyes to stay dry. 'They're still in comas, but they're stable. I'm sure they'll be fine.'

'It's weird though, another earth tremor at Comic-Con, your friends going into comas again. You should write about it on that fanfic site of yours, now that would really notch up the views.'

I stare at him in disbelief. How did I ever fancy this guy? 'Erm, yeah, I guess,' I manage to say.

A waitress approaches us. She looks at Russell and a grin spreads across her face. 'Mr Jones, it's so lovely to see you again. What can I get you tonight?'

He orders me a cocktail I've never heard of. I prickle at the fact he didn't ask me what I wanted. The waitress beams at me like I'm the luckiest woman alive, having Russell decide what I'm drinking, then she leaves.

'Thanks for helping out with Fandom Rising,' I say.

He frowns. 'With what?'

'Fandom Rising,' I repeat. 'My fanfic site.'

'Oh yeah, sure. That's what friends are for.' He clearly hasn't read any of my posts. I didn't really expect him to, but it still stings a little. 'So where are you at with book number three?' he asks.

Christ, he doesn't hang around.

'I'm thinking about it,' I say, wanting to keep him on side. 'Fandom Rising is really helping me get creative again. It's actually honing some ideas, that's why it's so great you're on board with it.'

He smiles at me. This is going really well; if he thinks my fanfic will help him land another movie role, he'll publicize it no end. Fanboy doesn't stand a chance.

Russell slides a tanned and perfect hand across the table and rests it on top of mine. 'So tell me more about this fanfic site, Alice. What are you planning to write next?'

'Well—' I'm interrupted by my phone buzzing on the table. It's face down, so I think maybe it's a message from my stalker. Panic grips my insides. I wish that bloody cocktail would arrive so I could take the edge off.

'Sorry,' I mumble to Russell. 'I better check it isn't Timothy.'

Russell chuckles. 'Never stand between a girl and her editor.'

Quickly, I check my phone.

But it isn't the stalker. It's Danny. And the message

sends my heart spiralling out of control. No amount of
alcohol could take the edge off this.

Russell is Fanboy! Get out of there!

VIOLET

Ash and Katie are just laying out dinner when we arrive
back at Headquarters. The spread is small when
compared to the body of the church – just a single pot
of casserole and a loaf of bread – but the scent is huge,
barely held by the stone walls. My mouth instantly fills
with saliva. I haven't eaten all day.

I quickly count four places, so I'm guessing Willow
and Daisy aren't joining us. I can't help feeling a huge
sense of relief that I won't have to face Daisy. The guilt
has been nibbling away at my insides. I know she and
Ash weren't in a relationship when I slept with him, but
still, it was a bit of a sly move. And it does remind me of
finding Alice in bed with Willow. How hurt I was,
knowing she could betray me like that. And it makes me
realize not just how Daisy might be feeling right now,
but why Alice may have done what she did in the first
place. Because she really did love Willow. Just like I
love Ash.

Katie and Ash look up, and when they see me, their
faces light up. Nate by my side, Katie and Ash smiling at
me, food on the table . . . for a wonderful, fleeting
second, everything feels good.

Ash jogs towards me and takes my hands in his. He
leads me towards the table, as though there's only us in
the church, and Nate and Katie don't exist. 'I thought
you'd be hungry,' he says.

I reach the table, and Katie whispers in my ear,

'What with all the humping.'

I can't help but laugh.

'I made bread,' Katie says, pointing at a misshapen loaf on the table. 'From scratch.' She has a dusting of flour across her nose, which makes her look hilarious and adorable all at once.

'She's a natural,' Ash says.

Katie laughs. 'I just imagined the dough was Thorn's face and twatted the hell out of it.'

Ash pulls out my chair for me and winks. I feel my cheeks flush, and I can't help watch as he pulls off his jacket and his holster, resting them on the back of his chair.

'We can eat later,' I tell him. 'First, we need to find the canister.'

'Canister?' Ash says.

'I buried it beneath the church,' Nate says, grabbing my hand and leading me towards a wooden door. 'It's going to release the Imp-targeting virus tomorrow. I'm going to see if I can make an antidote.'

Katie must drop a fork; the sound of metal hitting china resonates around the church like an alarm bell.

Nate leads me through the door and down a stone corridor angled downwards. It's the same corridor from *The Gallows Dance* film, the corridor which led to Baba's cell. My heart still burns when I think of her, how I failed to help her as she's helped me so many times. The air thins in my lungs and cools against my face. If we can get that canister, if we can find an antidote, we'll be going home. I imagine my parents' joyous faces when Nate and I both wake up. I can almost feel the warmth of their arms folding around me. I swallow down the lump in my throat and order myself to focus – there are still a lot of ifs.

We enter a stone cavern, similar to the one Ash and

I were held prisoner in last time we were here. Nate lights a torch and the flames illuminate the walls, dappled with moss and pitted with time. He seems to count the bricks and then slips his fingers into a gap in the mortar.

'It's in here,' he whispers, easing out a stone.

We both peer inside the black hole.

The canister has gone.

The stone chamber seems to shrink, walls and panic closing around me until even my skin feels too tight. If we can't make an antidote, then we can't save the Imps . . . We can never go home. And it isn't just about going home. I can't bear the thought of all the Imps dying a horrible death. Of *Ash* dying a horrible death.

Of genocide.

But when Nate turns to me, his eyes hold a spark of excitement. 'There's still hope,' he says. 'If I can't make an antidote, I'll stop the launch.' He begins to jog upwards towards the main body of the church, and I follow, my head reeling.

'You can do that?'

'I know where the launch site is. We should hang fire till tomorrow morning though – word is, the President himself is coordinating the launch, so if we wait till then, we can cut off the head of the snake.'

Tomorrow is Nate's birthday. Which means one thing – his life support will be shut off and I'll lose him for ever.

Should we really cut it that fine? But Nate's right, killing President Stoneback is the only way of guaranteeing another virus won't be made. It's the only way of truly saving the Imps.

So, feeling completely torn, riddled with anxiety and fear, I whisper my response: 'OK.'

We burst into the main body of the church, Ash

and Katie waiting for us with hopeful looks on their faces.

'Change of plan.' I'm about to continue, when the sound of distant shouting cuts me off. We spin to the source of the noise. It's coming from outside, behind the great, wooden doors. The shouting grows louder. It's Daisy. Another voice joins her, deep and gruff, clearly angry. Thorn.

My skin hardens with fear, every hair on my neck raised.

The door opens and Daisy runs to Ash. Her face is soaked in tears. 'I'm so sorry,' she gasps, falling on to him as though she's trying to shield him. 'I was so upset about you and Violet . . . I didn't know what I was saying. I must have let slip that Nate betrayed us . . .' She looks behind us, eyes settling on Nate. 'I'm so sorry,' she says again.

Thorn raises a dark green box in front of him.

'The canister,' Nate whispers. 'But how did you . . . ?'

Thorn smiles. 'Looking for this?'

A L I C E

My face must fall. *Russell Jones is Fanboy.* My heart begins to pound.

'Are you OK?' Russell asks.

I force myself to smile. 'Yeah, yeah. It's just . . . my mum. Sorry, I better ring her back. She's freaking out about something.'

Russell rolls his eyes. 'Bloody mothers.'

I head to the toilet and ring Danny, my fingers trembling so badly I almost can't hold my phone to my ear.

His voice sounds urgent. '*Al, thank God. Are you still with Russell?*'

'Yeah. Well, I'm in the ladies.' I glance around the tiled room. I'm in luck, there's nobody else here. 'What do you mean, Russell is Fanboy?

'OK, so I was Twitter stalking him, not being jealous at all. I saw him tagged in a photo snapped by a fan. He was at the internet café the other day.'

'What?' My tongue turns into cardboard. I put the phone on speaker so I can scroll through my apps and still talk to Danny. I locate the photo quickly. It's several days old now. Russell's wearing sunglasses, but it's undeniably him. He's bent over a computer, surrounded by modern desks and sage-green walls. Danny's right; it's the same café he traced the IP address to.

'It can't be a coincidence,' Danny says. *'He wants publicity, he's helping promote your site – the fanfic war between Fanboy and Anime Alice is just a publicity stunt.'*

My heart rate soars and I can feel my dress sticking to my skin with sweat. 'Jesus, Danny. Do you think Russell broke into my house and wrote that message on my mirror?'

There's a pause. *'I don't know. Maybe. It doesn't make much sense though, why would he want to freak you out? That might make you stop posting on Fandom Rising, and that would be no good for him.'*

He's probably right, but I can't think straight. 'But what if he is? Maybe he hoped I'd tell the press and that would boost publicity even more. What if Russell's the stalker and he's poisoning my cocktail right now? I mean, that would be some pretty good publicity right there.'

'Ok, you've got a point. Which bar are you at?'

'The Willow Tree.'

Danny scoffs. *'Wow, he really is a dick. Look, stay put, I'll come get you.'*

'No, that will take too long.' I scan the room. Why didn't I leave the cocktail bar instead of coming to the bathroom? Now I can't leave without Russell seeing. And I can't face him right now. I'm a gibbering wreck. My eyes settle on the window. It's cranked open slightly. 'It's OK,' I say. 'I've found my escape route.'

By the time I get home, there's ten missed calls from Russell. He's probably never had a girl bail on him before. The thought makes me smile, but only briefly. I've just lost my best means of publicizing Fandom Rising, and Nate's life support is turned off tomorrow. A tight ball of grief forms in my stomach.

My only hope is stopping Russell. Stopping him from posting on Fandalism so that the virus isn't released, killing my friends. Even if he is my stalker, I need to speak to him and beg. I'll offer him a trade – I'll write the third book so long as he stops posting.

Mum shouts up the stairs. 'Alice, a parcel just arrived for you.'

I grab my phone and head down the stairs. It's nine at night. Who leaves post this late? The package sits on the kitchen table, a brown paper envelope. I turn it in my hands. There's no stamp, no return address. Just my name. I assumed it was from my publishers, but this must have been hand-delivered. My legs begin to tremble.

'Mum,' I ask in a small voice.

'Yeah.'

'Who dropped this off?'

'Dunno. It was left on the doorstep. I hope you haven't started mail ordering make-up again, you remember it was knock-off last time and gave you spots.'

'It was one spot,' I mumble.

She rolls her eyes like she's the teenager before leaving the room.

I'm left alone holding the package, thinking it could explode any moment. But still, I don't put it down. I'm that clueless girl in the movies, the one that makes everyone shout, *Don't do it, don't do it, step away from the envelope.* But I have to know what's inside. My hands are shaking and my heart is banging. Somehow, I manage to tear the paper open. I hold my breath. It doesn't explode. *Quit now while you're ahead*, I'm screaming at the stupid bimbo with the envelope. But instead, she peers inside.

It isn't a bomb. It looks more like the top of a pen or something.

I tip the contents of the envelope on to the table, too afraid to touch it.

It's the knife I cut Violet with.

My very own telltale heart.

Russell must have watched me put it in the bin.

Vomit rises up my throat. I'm about to chuck the knife back in the envelope before Mum reappears, when my phone rings.

It's Russell.

Probably not the best time to speak, because I'm sure only bats and dogs will hear me, but I need to know. So I answer the call and try not to puke into the speaker.

'*Alice, beautiful,*' he says. '*What happened? Are you OK?*'

I look at the bloodied knife on my kitchen table. 'Why were you at an internet café the other day?'

'*What? What does it matter?*'

'I need to know. Just tell me.'

He laughs, taken aback, the first time I've ever heard him anything other than smooth. '*OK, OK, if it matters that much. I was just looking at my emails, looking at naked people on the internet, you know. Why do you care?*'

'So you're not Fanboy?'

'*Fanboy, as in your rival fanfic writer?*'

'That's the one.'

'*Is that why you did a runner?*' He lets out a sigh. '*Thank God for that, I thought maybe I became less charming or something.*'

'Russell, I'm serious, why were you at that café?'

'*I was waiting for someone.*'

'Who?'

'*Alice, you're behaving kind of strangely.*'

Russell's either lying about not being Fanboy, or he knows who Fanboy is. I'm about to press him further when 'call waiting' beeps in my ear. It's Danny. 'Hang on,' I say. 'I've got another call.'

Russell starts to speak, but I cut him off.

'Danny? Danny, what is it?'

'*I tracked down the new IP address. I had a look on Google Maps and it's most likely a block of flats. Didn't you tell me Russell's staying in a hotel?*'

'Yeah.'

'*In that case, I don't think he's Fanboy.*'

27
ALICE

Danny pulls up outside my house. I offered to collect him, but he was having none of it. He's so gallant, definitely the kind of prince that wipes the blood from his face before kissing the princess.

I smell Mum's Chanel as she creeps up behind me. 'Good for you,' she says. 'Don't fall for a boy just because he drives a Porsche.'

'You did,' Dad shouts from the sitting room.

'And look how that turned out,' she mutters, just loud enough for me to hear.

Dad marches into the hall, newspaper hanging from his right hand. 'Is it the computer nerd again?' He stands beside us and glares out of the window. 'I hope he's got airbags in that tin can of his.'

We watch as Danny undoes his seat belt. He's not going to message, he's going to come to the door.

Pants. Suddenly, his gallantry seems less appealing.

'His name's Danny,' I reply, tight-lipped. 'And I'm sure he's got airbags, he's very responsible.' I pull my shoes on, fast as I can, desperate to avoid that awkward parents-meet-boy moment at the threshold.

'Well, Porsche or not,' Mum says, 'he's lasted longer than most of your boyfriends. This is what? Your second date?' She chuckles at her own joke and peers out the window. 'He's kind of cute.'

'See you later then.' I dash out the door.

I jump into the passenger seat, tingling with excitement. It's like my body is filled with electricity. I'm not sure if it's because I'm sitting beside Danny, I'm about to meet Fanboy, or because my mum and dad are watching me drive away in the anti-Porsche. I think it's all three.

'You ready?' Danny asks, pulling a scrap of paper from his pocket.

I take it from him. It's an address – Fanboy's address. The excitement turns into nerves. 'Ready as I'll ever be.'

He jabs the postcode into an old sat nav. 'So what's your plan?' he asks.

'I don't really have one. I guess I'll meet them and just ask if we can work together, or maybe if they'll tone down some of the stuff they're writing.'

'What if he's dangerous?'

The car splutters into life. I think of my parents, still watching from the hall window, and smile. 'Yeah, I'm not going to lie, that's a major worry, but it's a risk I've got to take. Nate's life support is switched off tomorrow and I'm running out of time.'

The car bunny hops for a few metres, before accepting its fate and settling into a dull trundle. Funny to think that only a few days ago, Danny was just some bloke I used to vaguely know, and now I can tell you exactly how many times he's touched me, how he smells, how many curls he has escaping on to his forehead.

'So you're not going to mention the fact your friends are in comas?' he asks.

I stare out of the window, hoping the question will disappear. But it doesn't. I let it hang there for a few more seconds. 'Nope. It's too bonkers,' I finally say.

'I like bonkers.' He offers me a shy smile. I think he noticed the crack in my voice.

We drive in silence. When I've been driven by boys before, they've always tried to impress me, revving the engine and accelerating from junctions like twats. One guy actually tried to woo me with a series of doughnuts in Tesco car park. I think he expected a blowjob, not a pint of vomit on his lap. But Danny drives like a dad. I love it. The evening sun catches his profile, lighting up his stubble and eyelashes. I inhale deeply. The scent of paper, mint and diesel make me feel safe, and I allow myself to run through the various scenarios when I reach Fanboy.

They all end with a door slammed in my face, or worse.

But I have to at least try and convince him to stop writing his blog, so my friends stand a chance.

Even the smell of Danny and his car can't stop me bricking it.

Danny must notice, because he says, 'Are you OK?'

'I'm fine,' I answer on autopilot.

He keeps staring at the road ahead, but answers simply, 'No you're not.'

This makes me smile. It's like he doesn't even notice the Gucci or the fact I exfoliate. I'm still smiling when the sat nav tells us we've arrived. Danny pulls up in front of a block of flats. I say block of flats – it's a load of converted warehouses, and they're stunning. Fanboy either lives with his parents, or he's old and minted.

I turn to Danny. 'The thing is, somebody left a knife in an envelope at my door.'

His mouth drops open. 'What? Are you OK? Did you ring the police?'

I shake my head.

'This has gone on too long, we need to ring the police. Now.'

I stare at my hands. Some lies are good. Some lies are bad. But Danny should know the truth, regardless.

'I'm the sicko.'

'Pardon?'

'The sicko who hurt Violet. It was me.'

Danny seems to flatten himself against the car door, like he's trying to merge into it or he's planning his escape. 'What? You cut Violet's arm? Why?'

'Because I needed to get her a message. I needed to let her know when the Taleter meeting was so she could learn about the virus.'

'You mean . . . the stuff on Fandalism?'

I nod.

'Alice. They're fanfic sites. They're not real. You assaulted your comatose friend.'

'I know, I know. But it *is* real, Danny. The earth tremors, the medically unexplained comas. They've happened twice now at Comic-Con, you don't think that's more than spooky?'

There's a long pause. 'OK. You've got a point. But cutting Violet's arm?'

Tears spring to my eyes. 'Please don't think badly of me. I couldn't bear it if you did. Everyone thinks I'm this stupid vain cow, but not you. Even my parents don't like me that much.' I sound pathetic, perhaps even a little manipulative, but I mean it. Every word. And I couldn't stop crying if I tried, the way Danny's looking at me right now.

But his expression relaxes, his dark eyes soften. 'It's OK, it's OK. It just goes to show how much strain you're under right now. I don't think badly of you, but I do think you need help.'

I swallow. 'I'll get help, I promise. When this is over and my friends have woken up, I'll get help. But right now, I need you.'

I don't think I've ever said these words before. Not even to Violet. I need you. I'm the neediest person I

227

know, yet I've learnt never to ask for help. Never to show weakness. I watch his face, anticipating the rejection.

'I'm here, aren't I?' he says.

I walk up the path with Danny. My legs shake with every step and I find myself noticing all sorts of random things. The path is cracked, the grass has been recently mowed, the street lamp is flickering overhead, the air smells like it might rain soon.

'How will we know which flat belongs to Fanboy?' Danny asks.

I shrug. 'We start by knocking on doors, asking questions, and seeing if someone acts suspicious.'

'And if that doesn't work?'

'We cry.'

My brain turns the thought-volume back up on my internal radio and my head floods with questions. What does Fanboy look like? How old is he? Will he know who I am? Is he actually a she? And what am I actually going to say to this genderless, ageless, faceless person who could be a psycho-stalker? *Please stop writing your fanfic, it's messing with the alternative universe where my unconscious friends currently reside.* Deep breath. At least this plan doesn't involve maiming my bestie, and at least Danny's here.

We arrive at the double doors which lead into the foyer. I try the handle, and unsurprisingly, it's locked. I run my finger up the bronze mounted grid of flat numbers.

I can barely look. Any of these names could belong to him.

A name jumps out at me.

'Jesus,' I whisper.

That's who Russell was waiting for at the café.

Timothy O'Hara.

My bastard editor.

'Alice?' Danny says. He sounds a million miles away. 'Alice, what is it?'

I watch my finger quavering over the bell, unable to press it. 'That arsehole,' I whisper. 'He's Fanboy. Timothy is Fanboy.'

'Who's Timothy?' Danny asks.

'My bloody editor, that's who.'

I watch my finger push against the buzzer, which releases a long, flat drone. I press for a long time, letting the anger pass through me into the metal. No reply. I pull my phone from my pocket and try ringing him. No reply. This pattern repeats a few times. Drone. No reply. Ring. No reply. Eventually Danny covers the buzzer with his hand.

'I don't think he's in.'

'Well, he'll have to come home eventually.'

'I've got some crisps in the car, we could have another stake-out,' he suggests helpfully.

I nod, and then try the buzzer one more time, just for good luck.

At least I know it isn't Timothy who's been sending me those God-awful things. He may be writing a fanfic blog, but he's not psycho-stalker material. So who could it be?

'Don't worry,' Danny says, as we walk back to his Corsa. 'If he doesn't show, I'll drive you to his office first thing tomorrow.'

'Haven't you got work?'

'I'll pull a sickie. I've never done that before, it'll be fun.'

'God, I'm such a bad influence,' I say.

He shakes his head. 'No you're not. Now get some sleep, you look exhausted. I'll keep watch.'

As I drift into sleep, I hatch a plan. I'll make a deal

with Timothy. The same one I was going to make with Russell. I'll agree to write the third book so long as he stops writing his bloody blog. Then maybe my friends stand a chance of coming home before Nate's life support is turned off.

The sound of my phone ringing wakes me. For a second, I forget where I am. I blink a few times. I'm outside Timothy's flat, sat in Danny's car . . . and my life is falling apart at the seams.

I pull the phone from my bag, the stark, electronic glare stinging my eyes. Could it be my stalker again? Surely they wouldn't ring. Still, it's a relief when I see that it's Jane, Violet's mum. But the relief is short-lived. Jane only has my number for when she can't get in touch with Violet, and as Violet's in a coma and it's late, I'm guessing something's very wrong.

I answer with a trembling voice, 'Mrs Miller?'

Jane's voice sounds like she's speaking through a radio, all hisses and gasps, like she's just been sick. *'Oh, Alice, Alice . . . I just don't know how to tell you this, sweetheart.'* She pauses to grab a breath and my entire body seems to go numb. But my brain feels like it's burning, catching fire, throwing out all these endless, terrible scenarios.

'Please, just tell me,' I manage to croak.

Danny is looking at me, his dark eyes large with concern.

Jane seems to gulp for air. *'I'm so sorry, Alice. I'm just so sorry. I have the most dreadful news.'*

VIOLET

Thorn passes the canister to an Imp behind him.

'Thorn, please,' Nate says. 'That canister—'

'I don't want to hear it,' he shouts. The pistol in his hand gleams in the evening sun as he gestures us outside with it. The church door clicks shut, sealing us outside. I remember too late Ash's holster, slung across the back of his chair.

Thorn points at Nate, his arm shaking, his beautiful face scrunched with rage. 'It was you all along. You were the one who spoke to Howard Stoneback.'

'Yes,' Nate says, his voice hollow.

I step towards Thorn, the glint of his weapon catching in my peripheral vision and sending my stomach into spasm. 'How did you know about the canister?' I ask.

He bats me out of the way. 'Let's just say a little bird told me.' He aims his gun at Nate's head. There is less than a metre of air between my brother and a bullet. The world seems to slow around me. Every pore, every hair on Nate's face comes into sharp focus. I swear I can see his pupils dilate with terror.

'You let me burn three of my most trusted Rebels!' Thorn shouts.

'Oh, come on,' Ash says. 'You were looking for an excuse.'

I clutch at my face in desperation. 'Please. Nate's helping us now. If you shoot him . . .' I want to tell him about the President, about the virus, about Nate taking us to the launch site, but the fury in Thorn's lavender eyes tells me this is futile. He wants blood.

Well, if he wants blood, he can have mine.

I step between the gun and Nate. I stand as tall as I'm able, puff out my chest, trying to make myself bigger than the target behind me.

Thorn seems to lengthen his arm, the space between me and that bullet decreasing even further. 'I only want the boy,' he says. He swings the gun away and fires a warning shot into a nearby alley. The blast disturbs a group of pigeons. The birds scatter into the air, the beat of their feathers barely audible above the drumming in my ears. And that's when I spot her, a slightly smaller bird, labouring under her own weight, struggling to rise from the ground. The feathers on her breast glisten with a wealth of tiny rubies. Thorn's bullet nicked her wing.

That rhyme Yan told me, the message from Baba. *This* is the red-breasted bird.

See the red-breast bird take flight. Count to three and move to the right.

I catch Katie's eye. At first, she frowns, like she's making the exact same connection as me. I think she may even mouth, *The robin.*

One . . .

Thorn looks at me, his eyes narrowed. 'Move.'

But I can't move, I can't. If I move, then Thorn will shoot Nate.

Ash and Katie say my name. Followed by another bark from Thorn, 'Out of the way, girl.'

I continue to shelter Nate with my body, shaking my head like a woman possessed.

Two . . .

I feel Nate pulling on my shoulders, trying to shift me, trying to save me. But I won't move or be moved – it's like my feet are nailed to the ground. I clench my fists, tighten my knees and I stand completely still.

'MOVE,' Thorn shouts.

Three . . .

If we were in a film, everything would slow down right about now. The second between Thorn shouting and Thorn pulling the trigger would stretch into minutes. I would see Katie's expression slip between one of determination and one of acceptance. I would see her lunging towards me at half speed. And for the last time, I would take in every flour-dusted freckle on her face, the smile lines still fresh from our time back in the church, and every strand of her hair, swirling around her shoulders as she slowly tumbled towards me.

But we aren't in a film. And that second is over in the thump of a heart.

Katie falls against me, a dead weight, causing my arms to unfold on their own accord, catching her and stopping her from smacking to the floor. Not that she would have felt it. Because she's already dead, she died in that quick, relentless second. My legs give way and I sink to the ground, cradling her in my arms. Her pea-green eyes stare into space, and the bullet wound in the back of her head, the missing piece of skull, lets more blood escape on to my lap than I ever imagined a single body could hold.

'Oh God,' Thorn whispers. 'What have I done?'

A L I C E

'What is it?' I ask. My breath labours, unable to keep up with my body's sudden need for air. Jane is weeping, she sounds like she may be gagging. *Oh God, please don't let it be Violet.* 'Please, Jane, just tell me,' I beg.

'It's Katie,' she manages to say. *'Katie's dead.'*

My entire body trembles, my insides scream. Katie can't be dead, she just can't be. All that life, all that warmth, surely it can't just . . . stop. I place my head between my knees, afraid my brain is about to shake itself to pieces. I can't breathe, my lungs are hungry, burning, but my throat has closed. She can't be dead. She can't be. I begin to gasp, cry, and my stomach begins to heave. I'm about to vomit. I *want* to vomit. Maybe then I can get rid of this awful panicky feeling like nothing will ever be OK again.

Danny leans on to my back, hugging me into his body. His arms seem to go on for ever and I feel completely held. 'Just breathe,' he whispers into my hair. 'Breathe, Al, breathe.' I manage to snatch a fleeting breath, then another, then another, until I get into some sort of jerky rhythm and my lungs stop hurting quite so much.

'Can you drive me?' I manage to gasp.

'Anything you need.'

Jane meets us in the foyer. She clutches me to her jumper and strokes my hair. 'Oh, Alice, sweetheart, I'm so so sorry.'

'What happened?' I ask.

Her words come out strangled. 'They don't know, some sort of brain haemorrhage.'

'Where is she?'

'She's still in the ICU.'

'Can I see her?'

She studies me with red, puffy eyes. 'Her parents said that was fine, but do you think that's a good idea?'

'I need to see her . . . to . . . to . . .' The panic is growing inside me again and I'm struggling to breathe.

Danny steps in. 'To believe it's real?'

I nod. And just before I tread the familiar path to the ICU, I can't help asking Jane, 'Are you still . . . you know . . . tomorrow?' I'm talking about the plan to switch off Nate's respirator, but can't bring myself to say the words.

Jane holds my gaze, her face twitching with guilt. 'Yes,' she whispers. 'Noon tomorrow.'

28

VIOLET

I look at Thorn, and see my own shock, my own devastation reflected back at me in his face. This wasn't supposed to happen. Katie wasn't supposed to die. Somebody begins to scream, somebody begins to weep, somebody begins to shake my body over and over. I spin my head, confused, before realizing it's me. I'm screaming and weeping and shaking. But my skin has thickened and I can't feel the elements on my face or the convulsions pushing through me. I don't own the screams bouncing back at me from the paving slabs. It's like I no longer exist in this world.

The only thing that reaches me in my cocoon of shock is the monotonous drone of the flatline, echoing in some faraway land.

Thorn's gun clatters on to the pavement beside me. Ash must have been holding me, because I notice when he moves to retrieve it.

I hear Thorn's words as though they're moving through something heavy and cold, a sheet of snow perhaps. No, not snow. Ice. 'Ruth, my sweet Ruth,' he murmurs. 'What have I done?'

I want to grab that gun off Ash. I want to grab that hateful gun and shoot Thorn in his hateful face. But it's like I'm trapped beneath that slab of ice, held tight in the freezing waters. Numb and statue-like, just watching the ghostly figures as they move above me.

Ash replies. 'Her name isn't Ruth. It's Katie.' The heat of his breath against my ear makes me notice a warmth gathering across my back, a reassuring pressure and the continuous thrum of two hearts. Ash and Nate are leaning into me, their arms wrapping around my sides and on to Katie, encasing us in something safe and protective. My skin thins and I begin to feel again, the drone fades in my ears, and I'm aware that I'm still sobbing, still shaking, tears and snot dripping from my chin.

My fingers hover over her face, and I wonder if they're too afraid to touch her, afraid she may shatter from the softest of impacts. But suddenly, they move on their own accord, sweeping her hair from her face and gently pushing her lids closed. She doesn't shatter. She doesn't do anything.

Why did Katie move? Why did she sacrifice herself? Was the message meant for her all along? I want answers, desperately want to understand, but my brain simply won't work.

'I will help you bury her,' Thorn says. 'And then I will accept my sentence.'

And because I don't care what happens to Thorn now, because I don't care about anything except the fact Katie is dead, I find myself just replying with a simple, 'OK.'

We bury Katie in the graveyard. A small patch of grass behind the church, overgrown and neglected. The repetitive chug of shovels against earth, the pain in my back and the sweat running down my face, are strangely soothing. With every shovel full of soil, I glance at the church and make a plea or a pact of some description: *Please let me wake up and Katie still be alive. If she's in a coma, I will come back for her, I promise. Please take me instead of her. Please.*

The church doesn't reply. *God* doesn't reply. We lower her into the ground; she lies in the trench like a broken doll. I reach down, crossing her arms over her chest and arranging thistles around her head so she looks like a sleeping queen from a fairy tale. Then, gently, I release a handful of dirt over her body. A few specks of soil land on her cheeks, adding to her freckles. I expect her to open her eyes, to tell me I'm a cunkwumble and laugh her lovely laugh.

But she doesn't.

I head into the church alone, leaving the others to finish the job. I wish I could stay and give Katie the beautiful ceremony she deserves, but it feels like my body is about to fold in on itself and just stop. I sit in the church at a random desk, and just stare at the stone walls.

I barely notice Daisy appearing before me. She kneels on the ground and looks into my face with her perfect, chestnut eyes. 'I am so sorry, Violet.'

I think I nod.

'Look after Ash,' she says.

And then I guess I must apologize, because she laughs a sad little laugh, tells me it's OK, and walks out of the church.

ALICE

Katie's parents lean over her body, so still they could be made from stone. Her mum sees me and begins to cry. It kills me how much like Katie she looks, same red hair, same green eyes. She pulls me into an awkward hug, her face knocking against mine. 'Thanks so much for coming, love. It would mean so much to our little girl.' Her voice collapses and she falls back on to her daughter.

'Of course,' I manage to say.

All of the tubes and drips have been removed so that Katie looks like she's asleep. But her chest isn't rising, her eyelashes aren't flickering. Her dainty, freckled face looks slack. But it's her hands which really get me. Katie's hands are never still, they're always drumming, tapping on invisible cello strings only she can hear. I can't help myself. I reach out and take a hand in my own.

'Oh sweet Jesus,' I whisper. How can someone so warm feel so cold?

Did I kill her? Did something I wrote result in her death?

My knees buckle at this thought, and Danny seems to appear from nowhere, placing an arm around my waist and holding me upright.

'I've got you,' he says, pulling my head on to his shoulder.

'Katie today, Nate tomorrow,' I whisper into his neck. 'Everyone I love is dying.'

Danny helps me up the path and unlocks my front door. It's still really early, and nobody's up, so he calls up to my parents.

'Mr and Mrs Childs. It's Danny, I've got Alice with me . . . something terrible has happened.'

My parents stumble downstairs, blurred with sleep.

I fall on to my mum, weeping.

She holds me close and stokes my hair. 'Alice, whatever's happened?'

I can't answer.

'It's Katie,' Danny says. 'She died last night.'

Mum tightens her grip on me. Then Dad joins in. They're both squeezing me so tight I can barely breathe. 'Oh Alice, I'm so sorry,' Mum whispers.

Dad is crying too, I can hear it in his voice. 'Her poor parents.'

I lie on the sofa with my head on Mum's lap like I'm three and Dad fetches us all a cup of tea. Nobody drinks it. Danny sits beside me and Mum, and I think he's stroking my hair too. Nobody speaks, there's no sound except for me, weeping and weeping until, eventually, I can't cry any more and the sun has lit up the sky.

The clock strikes seven. Katie died last night. Nate dies today. The grief gathers into a hard, little stone in my chest. I need to find Timothy, and I need to make him stop. I need to make him pay. I look at Danny. He has bags under his eyes, which turn his skin a bluish-purple colour, and his hair looks even messier than usual. 'We need to go,' I tell him.

Mum looks a little alarmed. 'Surely you should stay at home today. You've had such a shock.'

But I'm already beginning to stand, my legs weak and my body sore, that little stone knocking against my ribs. 'I need to find Timothy. I need to go to his office.'

Danny nods. 'I'll drive.'

'No,' I reply. 'It's too central, it'll be easier to take the tube.'

I hadn't realized Dad was standing in the doorway, mug of cold tea still clasped in his hands. 'Alice, we can take you to the hospital if you feel you need to do something. But visiting your editor, catching the tube . . . your mum's right, you're in shock.'

'I'm fine,' I say, walking towards the door, grabbing my handbag en route. 'I just need to find Timothy.' Obviously, I'm not fine, one of my best friends died yesterday. And she died doing the exact thing I should have been doing . . . helping Violet, saving Nate. But that stone clanking in my chest reminds me that I need to stay strong. I won't lose anyone else because of that bloody man.

'Well, we'll come too,' Mum says, dashing after me.

Dad follows, and it hits me that they're actually going to leave the house without styling their hair and brushing their teeth.

This makes me smile, but I still shake my head. 'It's OK. Danny will come.'

And I realize he's already beside me.

Timothy's secretary scowls when she sees me. The bitch never liked me. She never likes anyone.

'Alice,' she says. 'Timothy isn't expecting you today.'

'I know. But I need to see him, it's urgent.'

She looks at her computer screen, and then back at me, and then back at her screen. 'Have you heard from him this week?' she finally says.

'Not since Comic-Con.'

'I was so sorry to hear about your friends, Alice. I heard it on the news.' There's no feeling in her words – the sentiment is empty. It's the verbal equivalent of a 'thoughts and prayers' post online.

I ignore her. How do I tell her one of them died? How do I say it without dropping my little stone and allowing the grief to take control. 'Can I see Timothy?' I ask, simply.

'He hasn't been into the office. He emailed to say he was taking a week off to manage a personal crisis.'

Anger flares inside me. *Personal crisis.* He's holed up in his flat destroying Violet and Nate's chances of coming home. I take a deep breath and try to stop my voice from quaking. 'Have you been able to ring him?'

She shakes her head. 'I tried a couple of times, but he hasn't picked up. I'll ring him now, leave a message saying you're looking for him.'

'Thanks,' I mutter. I run out of the office, Danny close behind.

'Now what?' he asks.

'We go back to his flat and kick the bloody door in.'

By the time we've made it across London, it's well past 10 a.m. Panic is building inside me and I feel ready to blow. And this is *so* not the time for my crazy stalker to text me, so when my phone buzzes and I see the same unknown number, I'm unable to stop myself screaming, 'Not now, you nasty, stalking arse!'

'Jesus, Alice. It's not your stalker again?'

I nod. 'I can't cope with this right now.'

Very gently, Danny takes the phone from my fingers. He opens the message and I watch his expression darken. 'You better read it.'

They're my Fandom. Back off, bitch.
Yours, The Fanboy.

Fanboy *is* the stalker. Timothy is Fanboy. 'Holy shit,' I say, fury coursing through my veins. 'It was *Timothy*. He wrote on my mirror and sent me that knife. That sick bastard.' He must have read about the wound on Violet's arm in the papers and decided to spook me. But why? Was he really that pissed I refused to write the third book? And how did he know it was me who cut Violet's arm?

Danny lays a hand on my phone, as though he can protect me from the message on the screen. 'I'm ringing the police.'

But I'm out the car in a flash, running towards Timothy's building, my heels clacking against the concrete. I try the buzzer again. Nothing. I take my phone out of my pocket and try ringing him again. No reply.

'Al, we need to ring the police,' Danny says, catching me up.

I'm all out of ideas when a man with a briefcase pushes through the door, probably leaving to go to

241

work. Instinct, politeness, God knows what it is, but he holds the door for us. And as easy as that, we're in the building.

I take the stairs two at a time. We reach Timothy's flat and I ring the bell. It trills out in the stairwell. No reply. 'Timothy,' I call out. 'Timothy, it's Alice. I need to talk to you. It's really important.' I try to cap the anger in my voice. He's much more likely to answer the door if he doesn't think he's going to get an ear bashing.

But he doesn't appear, in spite of my logic.

I open his letter box and peer through it. This weird smell hits me. It briefly reminds me of the Imp city, a smell of decaying flesh and shit. My stomach clenches.

'Timothy,' I call through the letter box. I look at Danny. 'Seriously, get a whiff of that.'

'I can smell it from here,' he says. 'Smells like something died in there.' He rattles the door handle.

One good thing about being a writer – I know people. Timothy keeps a spare just where I would expect him to, tucked on the top of the light outside his door. Not as obvious as a doormat or a pot, but easily accessible. I stick it into the keyhole with unnecessary force, and one key-turn later, we're stepping into the hall.

29
VIOLET

The next day, Nate takes me, Ash and Willow to the launch site. The drive through the city passes in a flash, and I realize I've just been staring at my hands the whole time. Just staring at the soil which still lingers beneath my fingernails and in the grooves of my skin. Katie died yesterday. And today is Nate's birthday. His life support will be turned off. I notice a large tear splodge on to my hand, magnifying the soil from Katie's grave.

The Humvee pulls to a halt.

'We're here,' Nate says.

We're back at the Coliseum. The tall, circular walls fill me with dread. I imagine I can still hear the echoes of the crowds, baying for Imp blood. We step from the Humvee and the familiar scent of pollen sends my heart rate rocketing. I hold my breath as we push through the wooden side door, trying to force the image of the gallows from my mind. *They won't be there*, I tell myself. *Alice and I wrote them out.*

I stumble forwards, taking it all in: the circular stone wall, rows upon rows of raked seating, the smooth stretch of tarmac beneath my feet. My head hurts and I can hear my own pulse. It looks so different from the first time we crossed over. Empty and still, not a Gem in sight. Despite the brilliant circle of sky suspended above, I notice how cool the air feels against my skin –

it's like I'm standing in a bowl of shadows.

I'm about to turn to Nate when something catches my eye – a tall, jagged shape at the front of the Coliseum. The gallows. Just the sight of those wooden posts, those dangling ropes, and my body disappears, swallowed up by a layer of sweat. 'What on earth?' I whisper to myself. I approach the wooden stage, feeling strangely drawn to it. I can almost see the ghost of Rose – of *me* – standing on a trapdoor. My hands automatically clasp my throat. And as I get nearer, I can see that something's not quite right. The wood looks too clean – sanded down and slicked with varnish. I haul myself on to the stage with trembling arms.

'Violet? Are you OK?' Ash asks.

But I barely hear him. I kneel against the planks and run my fingers over the square outlines of the trapdoors. My nails bump up against globules of dried varnish, shining like amber beads between the gaps. The trapdoors are fake, no more than grooves, carved part-way into the wood and incapable of opening. I immediately look to the place where the hangman should stand, and I realize there's no lever.

'It's a replica,' Ash tells me. He gestures to the wall behind me. 'Look.'

I turn to see a giant bronze plaque. Thirty, forty columns of numbers and names rise up against the metallic glow, giving it the appearance of a cityscape at dawn.

'What are they?' I ask.

I trace a number with my finger.

Nate jumps on to the stage beside me. 'They're Imp numbers, followed by their name. It's a memorial for all the Imps that hanged here.'

I skim the nooks and ridges with my fingers, moving along the stage to the end of the list. 'So many Imps.'

My voice catches. 'Enough to fill a city.' I kneel so I can see the very last number; my face reflects back at me from behind the digits 753811. The last Imp to be hanged in this spot. I read her name aloud. 'Rose.'

Willow takes a sharp intake of breath.

I'm about to apologize when I hear a voice, smooth and calm, travelling from beneath the stage: 'The government built you a memorial, and the Taleters used it to conceal their laboratory. Typical.' Yan steps from behind the stage and leans against the structure like he's part of the wood.

'Who's this?' Ash says.

'It's OK, he's on our side,' I say, dismounting the stage and moving towards Yan. 'He's a precog, like Baba.'

Yan looks at Nate and nods. 'Nate.'

Nate smiles back.

'You two know each other?' I ask, confused.

Nate smiles. 'Yes.'

Yan doesn't acknowledge the others, but looks only at me, a frown gathering on his brow. 'Violet, what's wrong?' He brushes his fingers against my face. 'Oh Violet, I am so sorry.' Tears spring into his eyes as he realizes what happened to Katie. 'The rhyme . . . I didn't know . . .' he tails off.

'Did Baba plan it?' I ask, my voice cracking. 'Was Katie supposed to die?'

Yan shakes his head, a tiny tremor. 'Maybe.' He pauses. 'I can help?' It's a question rather than a statement. He's offering to calm me. But I want to carry the loss; it will keep me focused. We stop the bastard President and we save the Imps, we save my little brother both here and back home. It's the reason we came here, and it's the only thing that will make her death matter.

Yan nods like he understands. 'Come then.' He

opens a real trapdoor, hidden from view, at the side of the replica gallows.

'We must be careful,' Ash whispers. 'The President has a heart as black as they come. He'll kill us in a moment.'

I remember Stoneback's twisted grin. 'I know,' I say.

Yan leads us down some stairs. I hold Ash's hand, and I can't tell if the sweat comes from my skin or his. Probably both. We turn down a corridor. I anticipate the damp, earthy scent of stone, but the smell is cleaner, more medicinal, and I wonder if I'm getting crossover from my real-world body again.

We approach a door, the texture of wood barely visible in the gloom.

'The lab's in there,' Nate says under his breath.

Ash and Willow pull their guns from their belts. Yan follows suit. I begin to wish I was armed too, even though I'd probably shoot my own foot, I'd at least feel safer . . . stronger. Only a plank of wood separates us from President Stoneback. My legs begin to tremble.

Ash kicks the door and it flies open. 'Stop what you're doing!' he bellows. We enter a windowless room. Stark light hits my eyes and the scent of antiseptic fills my nostrils. I blink the dark splotches from my vision, my blood thrumming in my ears.

And there he is.

President Stoneback.

His head is bent low; his fingers tap wildly against a screen and his hair falls across his face in waves — it's grown since I last saw him.

'Very slowly, step away from the computer, Stoneback,' Ash says.

The man lifts his head, a wry smile stuck to his face.

A gasp catches in my throat. It isn't the President. It's the man from the light projection back at the tube station. The man who recognized me from the loop. Oscar.

He smiles at us with his full, greedy mouth. 'You're too late.'

'What do you mean we're too late?' Ash asks.

'Where's the President?' Terror forces my voice to spike as I realize the hateful snake of a man must be lurking somewhere nearby.

Oscar looks at me. 'Ah, Violet. The wanderer has returned. How's your friend? Alice, was it?'

The sound of her name on his lips sends a wave of nausea through me. I stride up to him, completely forgetting my lack of weapon. 'How do you know Alice?'

'I met her when she was here last time, though only briefly. I doubt she remembers me. I could tell she was an Imp straight away. Her thirst for perfection fascinated me. She gave me the idea for the serum.'

Ash puts an arm around my waste. 'Ignore him, Violet, we need to focus on stopping the virus.'

'As I said, you're too late,' Oscar says. 'It's launching in a few minutes. And nobody except me can reverse it, only I know the code.' He glances at the gun in Willow's hand. 'Go on, shoot, then you'll never know how to stop it, will you?' His long fingers reach under the desk and push something, just before Yan barrels into his shoulder and sends him reeling to the floor.

'He's pressed a panic button,' Yan mutters to himself. Then, louder, he says, 'Hold him down.'

Ash sits on Oscar's legs and Willow pins down his arms.

Oscar laughs at Yan. 'Of course, the replacement for the old woman. Baba. And what's *your* name, telepath?'

'It's Yan, if you must know,' Yan snaps, kneeling

beside him. 'Are you going to give me the deactivation code, or will I have to force it from you?'

'I'll never tell you, Little Swallow Bird,' Oscar spits. 'And I've strengthened my consciousness against people like you, so you'll never find out.'

'Good,' Yan says, laying his hands on Oscar's temples. 'I love a challenge.'

Oscar's features screw into a tight ball as Yan starts to attack his mind.

Little swallow bird? I turn over the words in my mind. Something about it doesn't sit right in my stomach.

Yan's engrossed in the task at hand – but this feels important. I watch as Oscar's left hand begins to twitch.

'Yan,' I say, softly, trying not to break his focus. 'Why did he call you "little swallow bird"?'

Without moving, Yan manages to hiss, 'It's my name. Yan means Little Swallow Bird in Chinese.' He applies more force to Oscar's face.

Little bird. Something clicks into place: Thorn's words. *Let's just say a little bird told me.* Rage rushes through me. 'Why did you tell Thorn about the canister?'

He doesn't look up. 'I needed you here, Violet. You and Nate. I needed you here in this lab, right now. It's the only way to save the Imps, and it's the only way to send you home. It will all make sense soon enough, I promise.'

I'm about to argue, about to press him further, when someone says my name. A sharp whisper in my ear even though nobody stands nearby. *Violet.*

I spin in a circle. There it is again. *Violet.*

'What is it?' Nate asks me.

'Yan, is that you?' I say.

But he's too busy with Oscar to reply. And it isn't his voice. It isn't even *one* voice — it sounds like several voices, talking in unison.

248

Nate takes me by the arms. 'What is it, Violet, what do you hear?'

'I can hear someone whispering my name.' I start to panic. Is it from the other side, from our world? I hear it again. *Violet.* But it doesn't sound familiar, it definitely isn't Mum or Dad, maybe it's the hospital staff. *Violet, come quickly.* The voice is moving away from me. *Violet, you must hurry.* It sounds like it's coming through the wall. I look in that direction. There's a door. And coming from behind the door is a faint, bluish glow.

'In there,' I say.

Violet, Violet, this way.

I move towards the voice, anxiety and dread causing my stomach to cramp.

Quickly, Violet, there's no time to lose.

'Is it coming from in there?' Nate asks, gesturing to the bluish light.

I nod, and without further thought, push open the door.

Behind it is one of the most disturbing sights I've ever seen: a vast room, carved from the stone like a crypt. And lined in neat rows, forming an endless grid, are Dupe tubes.

They stretch away from me, each filled with a body, floating in thick, transparent liquid. Some with limbs missing, some with patches of skin gone. Some, just children. Vomit fills my mouth as I notice much smaller tubes, some containing babies which have been transferred from one sack to another, never to open their eyes or their ears, stuck in a world of darkness.

The room hums with electricity, and the scent of medicine and blood is overwhelming.

'Oh my God,' I whisper. 'What is this?'

But I know the answer even as Nate replies. 'It's a Dupe storage warehouse,' he whispers, as though talking may disturb them. 'I had no idea it was here.'

'Why store Dupes *here*?' I ask.

'An endless supply of subjects to experiment on. I doubt their Gem owners know.'

'They were calling to me, Nate. The dupes were calling to me just now. They're . . . aware.' Tears slip from my eyes as I gaze from one tube to another. The people inside aren't vegetables; they're conscious.

Nate lays a hand on my shoulder. 'Maybe they've formed some sort of hive mind – then only a few would need to be telepathic to be able to reach out to you.'

'But why did they want me to find them?' I ask. I stop dead in front of one of the tubes. A cry escapes from my lips.

'What is it?' Nate asks.

But I find myself replying not to Nate, but to the naked body floating in the tube before me: 'You sneaky bastard.'

A L I C E

Timothy's flat doesn't look how I'd expected. Unopened mail forms a little pile on the mat, and the door to the living room is half open, revealing stacks of empty pizza boxes and unwashed plates. God, and that smell.

'Timothy,' I call out.

Danny looks up from his phone. 'He only posted about ten minutes ago, Alice. It's his final post too, the finale. He's definitely alive.'

I pick my way down the hall, stepping over a discarded jumper and a cup of what looks like cold tea. The milk's congealed on the surface. God knows how long it's been there.

'Timothy? It's Alice, are you OK?' Maybe blogging has been too much for him. Maybe the finale pushed him over the edge. Maybe he hit the 'publish' button, downed a bottle of vodka then passed out. I half expect to find him lying on the sofa with a needle hanging out of his arm.

Danny picks up the cup of cold tea so it doesn't get knocked. 'Shit, I'm definitely ringing 999.' He looks around for a surface to put the cup on, gives up, and places it back on the floor.

'To say what?' I reply. '"My friend's editor's flat smells of dead cat, so we broke in."'

'He's threatened you,' Danny says, his voice low. 'He broke into your house.'

I reach the living-room door and pause, bracing myself for the sight of my unconscious editor. 'Timothy?' I call out again. But where my voice had once been strong and challenging, it comes out wavering and scared. Danny must hear this, because he takes my hand in his.

We squeak the door fully open and step inside. It looks like a group of students had a party in one of their parents' house. The antique coffee table is littered with cups and plates and screwed-up balls of paper. There's a heap of clothes in the corner, and the telly has been left on silent. He must have been here fairly recently.

'Something isn't right,' I say to Danny, finally voicing that niggling fear. 'Timothy is not a slob, and that smell is not old pizza and cold tea.'

I pull my phone out of my pocket and call Timothy's number. The sound of an iPhone ringtone fills the hall.

Danny's hand tightens around my own. 'It's coming from the hall cupboard,' he whispers.

Still holding hands, we shuffle towards the cupboard door. The ringtone chirps out, completely at odds with the growing sense of dread and the stench of decay. It's beginning to feel like we're starring in our very own horror film. I half expect some blood-crazed clown to burst out of the closet, brandishing a dagger and a fist full of balloons. But grief and lack of sleep form a kind of protective barrier for me, and somehow it feels more like a dream than a movie.

We stand side by side, facing the cupboard door. The ringtone stops and the flat falls into silence. All I can hear is my own breath, my blood pulsing in my ears.

'You sure you want to do this?' Danny whispers.

The sound of his voice makes me start, but I manage a numb nod of the head.

I watch Danny open the cupboard door, and it's as if it's happening in slow motion, because I already know what's in there. *Who's* in there.

The door swings open, releasing the full stench of rotting flesh into the air.

His throat is cut open and yellow around the edges, and judging from the state of him, Timothy's been dead for quite some time. I scream. And then Danny's pulling me into him, slamming the cupboard door closed with his foot. A strange buzzing noise starts in my ears and I suddenly feel very far away, a cloud of shock cushioning me from the horror. I realize I'm still holding my phone in my hands. I begin to fumble with the keypad, frantically tapping out 999. I haven't even hit the call button when a nasal voice cuts through the buzz.

'I wouldn't do that, if I were you,' it says.

I turn to see a man. Tall, beautiful and strangely ghostly. His skin looks stretched, like he's had too much surgery. He leans against the door frame, and behind him, I see a small study. On the desk is a computer, the glow of the screen lighting up a chair.

His long, elegant fingers are wrapped around a gun, which he points first at Danny, and then me.

'Alice,' he says. 'It's about time we met.'

30
VIOLET

'Is that . . . ?' Nate begins.

'President Stoneback,' I finish for him.

'I don't understand,' Nate says. 'Why would a President keep his duplicate here – he must know they experiment on them.'

I circle the tube. 'It isn't the President's duplicate. It's the President. He's in a coma,' I garble. 'He's in a coma and he needed somewhere to hide his body so nobody would find it. Where better to hide an unconscious body than amongst a load of other unconscious bodies.'

'Why's he in a coma?' Nate asks.

I spin to face him. How can I explain? How can I tell him that the President is in *our* world? That he's crossed over just like I did, and left an unconscious body behind, just like me. I just shake my head and peer through the murky container. There's a tiny loop on the inside of the President's arm. 'Look,' I say, pointing for Nate's benefit. 'It's the real President, not a dupe.'

A flash of realization hits me, followed by a surge of adrenalin and a sudden clarity of thought. I look into his perfect face and I say, 'So *you're* the crazy author.'

ALICE

The beautiful, stretched man walks backwards to the

computer, always facing us, never lowering his weapon. I recognize him, but I can't quite remember where from.

Danny squeezes my hand. 'Do you know him?' he hisses.

I nod. 'I think I do.'

The man smiles. His teeth are so perfect they look fake. 'Come now, Alice. I'll be super offended if you don't remember me. Although last time you saw me I was on a screen at the Gallows Dance.'

I gasp. 'President Stoneback?'

He laughs. 'I'm afraid so, my dear.'

Danny shakes his head. 'President Stoneback from *The Gallows Dance*? You mean the actor? Alice, what's going on?'

Stoneback glares at Danny. 'He's an annoyance. Can I shoot him, Alice?'

'No,' I scream. I try and shove Danny behind me, but he resists with ease. We end up kind of grappling, trying to shield each other from harm.

'How sweet,' Stoneback says, covering the ground between us in two easy strides. 'A lovers' tiff.' He brings the butt of his pistol down on Danny's head so quickly, I barely have time to scream.

'Danny? Danny?' I kneel beside him, checking his pulse. It's there, but weak. I can see the red of his blood sticking his curls together and trickling down his forehead. I smudge it away with my thumb.

I look up at Stoneback, forgetting the gun in his hand. 'You leave him alone, you nasty shit.' I go for him, claws out, screaming. But the President is strong and fast, instantly showing me up as the Imp that I am. Within seconds, he has my arm wrenched painfully behind my back.

'So you're Fanboy?' I say.

He laughs. 'You are a beautiful ape, Alice, but you are an ape all the same. Did you really think your silly editor would destroy the Imps?'

'He wanted to put the diss back into dystopia,' I reply.

The President whispers into my ear. It sends a chill down my spine. 'The Fandom is a delicate beast, Violet. It wants conflict, but it also wants hope. I was able to get inside Timothy's head for a little while, but just like Sally King, he began to resist.'

'You mean Timothy *was* Fanboy?'

'Timothy started the Fandalism site under my influence, and it all seemed to go well. At first I thought the fanfic would pave the way for a third book. I got him to bribe that silly fansite, Daily Dystopia, to see if I couldn't persuade you and Violet to write something truly awful for the Imps. But after a while, Timothy began to rebel – he knew the Fandom would not respond well to full-on Imp genocide. It was only when I got here I realized I didn't need the third book. Fanfic was enough.'

'So why come over now?' I ask. 'Why not the first time round?'

'If you remember, we were stuck in a loop first time around – technology was limited by time. You build a machine as quickly as you can, only for it to disintegrate and reset as nothing. But you and Violet broke the loop, and suddenly we could progress. We could not only bring you to into our world, we could also cross into yours.'

'So you came over when, exactly?'

'You really are the lowest form of *Homo sapiens*, aren't you, Imp?' He laughs. 'I came over when the tunnel opened, when Violet and Katie crossed over.'

'At Comic-Con?'

'Yes, at Comic-Con, and what better place to arrive – the best cosplay ever. I'm even in a couple of – what are they called? – selfies. For such a bunch of ugly monkeys, you like looking at yourselves, don't you?'

My brain really is struggling to take this all in. 'But Violet said Baba visited her in a dream. I thought Baba wanted them to cross over.'

'She did. Oh, it has a wonderful circularity to it, wouldn't you say?'

'What has?' I say, frustration rising in my voice.

'The first time you crossed into our world, I brought you, and Baba piggybacked Violet in as well. She stole my idea of using you to write the sequel, but made sure you returned pro-Imp. Hats off to the precog, she had me fooled. Well, this time, I used her tunnel. She opened the tunnel to bring Violet and Katie across, and I linked in with my own technology, slipping into your universe undetected.'

'But Baba would know you were going to do that, surely?' I say.

'Her precognitive abilities faded, Alice. Old age, perhaps a little help from Timothy, who knows. Her precognitions of Fanboy were hazy at best. By the time she'd figured it out, it was too late. I was over here. And suddenly, I could influence my world via the Fandom in a way I'd only dreamed of before. The first thing I did after killing your silly editor was kill Baba . . . with my keyboard, no less. Such power, Alice. You have such power and you have no idea; to create worlds and people, to manipulate them like puppets.'

Tears well in my eyes. 'Nate is not a puppet, Willow is not a puppet, Violet –' I'm shouting now – 'IS NOT A PUPPET!'

The next thing he says breaks my heart.

'Well, puppets or not, they did exactly as I hoped –

they entered a world where I can wipe them out with the push of a button. All I had to do was get Timothy to start writing Nate bad, and plant a few thoughts in Violet's parents' minds about switching off his life support. You say you're not puppets, yet you were as easy to manipulate as pawns. I thought you'd cross over too, but no matter, I can just kill you now instead. Stop you writing another sequel and ruining everything with your bloody peace and love.'

'But they could still stop the virus, or get hold of the serum – survive as Gems,' I say.

'Ah yes, the serum. Oscar had that wonderful idea when he met you, in the loop you infiltrated. So thank you. The power to turn Imps into Gems. It's a hoax, you do realize that? The serum doesn't work. But we had to offer some sort of protection to the few, shall we say special, Imps. After all, no Gem would agree to wipe out *all* the Imps, not when there are so many Imps posing as Gems, so many Gem children with dirty, half-Imp blood. And by the time they realize the serum's a dud, it will be too late. The virus will be out there. It's time for a deep cleanse, Alice.'

Tears stream down my face. The last hope, that my friends could somehow survive by taking the serum, is shattered. I wriggle, trying to free myself from the President's grasp. A wave of pain shoots up my arm.

He must see my tears because he laughs. 'Oh yes, good old ape emotions. I sent you those threats hoping to throw you off balance, trying to stop your clever little Fandom Rising stint.'

He marches me to the computer, and I have no choice but to obey.

'Before I kill you, Alice, I want you to see how they will die.' He forces me to look at the screen, at his latest post on Fandalism, his fingers curling painfully into my

258

chin. Above the text sits a new graphic. A picture of a swallow, limp and dead, wrapped in Fanboy's signature barbed wire.

It's a symbol, a message.

Fandom Rising has failed.

Fanboy has won.

Nate stood beside Oscar.

'Are you ready, Nate?' Oscar asked.

'Let's do it,' Nate replied.

Oscar pushed the button. Nothing happened. But Nate heard him whisper the words: 'It is done.'

Nate imagined the viral canisters detonating all over the country. He imagined the viral particles spreading into the air and hanging like a mist, just waiting to be inhaled by unsuspecting Imps and Gems. And then, he imagined it being passed between the Imps like the deadliest of influenzas.

He ignored the burning guilt in his stomach and lifted the bottle of serum to his lips. It tasted sweet and bland and nothing like he expected. 'This is sugar water,' he said, fear catching in his throat.

Oscar nodded. 'My apologies, Nate. It's nothing personal, you understand.'

'But Howard said—'

'Howard has a message for you: once a rat, always a rat.'

'Is he talking about me, or him?' Nate said, sinking to his knees, overcome with grief, anger and guilt. He had helped destroy his people. The Imps. And now he would die too.

Nate looked at Oscar, tears blurring his vision. 'Just kill me now. Please, I beg you.'

Oscar smiled – a perfect smile, in a perfect face, on a perfect body, filled with a perfect immune system that would protect him from an imperfect fate – and he said, 'Now where would the fun be in that?'

The blog finishes.

Fanboy has destroyed the Imps.

'Violet,' I whisper. 'Nate. I'm so sorry.'

The President pushes me to my knees and presses the muzzle of the gun into my temple. My first instinct is to sob, to beg, and for a second, I think I may wet myself. But I look at Danny lying on the floor, his eyes beginning to open, and I feel something strengthening inside me. I will not give the President the satisfaction of seeing me afraid. I hold Stoneback's gaze with my own, and I force my lips to smile. Then I say, in a light voice, 'You know, that last paragraph was really over-written.'

VIOLET

'What do we do?' Nate says.

I remember the bullet wound on Nate's sleeping body, the flatline when Katie died, the writing Alice carved on to my forearm. If we kill him in this universe, he will die in ours. I can kill the President and I can stop him writing all his poison. Then we can stop the virus launch. I can save all of the Imps, I can save Ash, and I can go home with Nate.

'Violet?' Nate says.

I smile. 'We kill him.' I pick up a nearby fire extinguisher and smash it into the tube again and again. I pour every ounce of rage, of injustice, of desperation from my body into that metal battering ram, stopping only when the glass begins to splinter. The liquid drains away and the tube lifts, allowing the President to flop out. We catch him as best we can and lie him on the floor; the liquid streams from his skin and forms a puddle around him.

'We just kill him?' Nate says. 'In cold blood?'

I can't tell him about the crazy author, he would never understand. But that's OK, the President has numerous other crimes to focus on. 'He's trying to wipe out the Imps, Nate. He's murdered countless people. This is the only way.'

Nate nods and reaches into his belt, pulling out a curved hunting knife. He looks up for a second.

I grip his hand, so that we both hold the weapon's handle. 'We do it together.'

There's no time to debate the morality of murder. I think we both know what we are about to do is wrong. We hold the blade high above the President's chest. Instinctively, without agreeing to do so, we aim for his black, black heart.

'On the count of three,' Nate says.

We count together. 'One . . . two . . . three . . .'

It surprises me how easily we plunge that knife down, straight into his flesh.

ALICE

I close my eyes and brace myself for the click of the trigger, for the burst of sound and the nothingness which awaits me. But it never comes. Instead, I hear this low grunting sound. The pressure of the gun leaves my temple. I open my eyes. Stoneback is clutching his chest with both hands, blood spreading from beneath them as though he's stabbed himself with an invisible knife. At first, I think he shot himself by mistake, but that's impossible; the gun was still pressed to my temple only seconds ago and there was no blast. He looks down at his chest and then back to me. 'She found me,' he whispers.

'Who?' I shout. 'Who found you?'

He forces out her name, spraying my face with blood. 'Violet.'

The gun hits the ground only seconds before the President. A pool of blood creeps across the kitchen floor. I step out of the way. I'm wearing Jimmys after all.

'Stoneback?' I whisper, scared I may wake him. He doesn't reply. I use the toe of my shoe to prod at his face. It lolls to one side, lifeless. He's definitely dead. I've no idea how it happened, but somehow Violet has killed President Stoneback. She's killed Fanboy.

Maybe she managed to stop the virus being launched too.

And maybe, just maybe, there's a chance she can bring Nate home. My chest swells.

I glance at my watch. 11.30 a.m. Well, she doesn't stand a chance if his life support is turned off in thirty minutes.

I've got to stop them.

I dash to the computer. The last post was published over twenty minutes ago – it already has hundreds of views. I could sit down and write an epilogue, something where the serum is real, try and help my friends via the Fandom. But I don't have time. I have to focus on what I can do in *this* world. I have to trust that Violet is doing her bit in their world, and judging by the dead

President sprawled on the floor before me, she's doing something right.

I pause to put Danny into the recovery position. He groans and his eyes fix on me. 'Al? Are you OK?'

'Yeah, I've got to go do something really important, then we're going to get you some proper help, OK?'

He smiles weakly. 'Did you just save me?'

I can't help but laugh. 'I suppose I did.' I wipe the President's still warm blood from my face and lean over to kiss him on the lips. He tastes of apples and mint and home.

VIOLET

We just stare at the President, both of us taking shallow, quick breaths, our hands still clamped together and holding the knife. His blood pumps from around the blade and mixes with the fluid on the floor.

Loud crashing sounds from the room behind us, where Yan is performing his mind blend. The knife clatters to the ground and I run back into the lab, desperate to help my friends, desperate to keep Ash safe.

The source of the crashing soon becomes clear: Willow and Ash attempt to hold the door shut, the one which leads to the corridor. The lock has already buckled, and with every thud, the door rears open a little further. I rush to help them, leaning my weight against it.

Yan is now tapping wildly away on the computer – Oscar is unconscious at his feet. 'I'm nearly there. Just buy me a couple more minutes.'

The door bows; pain shoots up my arms into my chest.

'The serum is fake,' Yan explains as he waits for something to load. 'Oscar's mind was pretty well protected from telepathy, but I dug that out. It was a hoax, to convince Jeremy and the other Gems to go along with the virus.' And then another screen loads up and he's tapping again at the keyboard.

Nate grins. 'Good job that the serum wasn't the plan any more then.'

Gunfire erupts from behind the door. Ash and Willow pile on top of me, pressing me into the ground. The cold of the ground stings my cheek, my heart bangs wildly in my chest, and my muscles tighten with dread. We can't die, not now, not when we're so close to stopping the launch and going home.

The door flies open and four Taleters enter the room, heavily armed. They aim straight at Yan.

'No,' I scream.

Willow moves faster than I thought possible, his long legs carrying him into the path of the bullets. A series of red flowers bloom across his chest. My ears ring with the beat of gunfire and my heart fills with horror. Willow stumbles backwards, his face frozen with shock.

'NO!' A scream from outside the room. 'NO. GOD, NO!'

Willow slumps to the ground. Silence. Jeremy Harper races into the room and collapses on to his son. The sound of Jeremy's weeping combines with the sound of Willow's laboured breath. Sorrow squeezes at my chest. *Not Willow. He doesn't deserve this.*

Yan looks at me, his face drained. His voice sounds in my head. *It's done. The launch has failed. You have saved the Imps.*

Jeremy cradles his son's head.

Blood bubbles from Willow's lips. 'Dad?' he says.

'My son, my son, I'm so sorry, my son,' Jeremy whispers. 'I didn't know it was you, I didn't know . . .'

Willow begins to cough. He speaks again, this time weaker. 'Dad, this has to stop. Please.'

Jeremy buries his head in his son's chest and begins to weep. 'My son, my son, my son . . .' He murmurs it again and again like a prayer.

Willow manages to whisper, 'Violet.'

'I'm here,' I say. I glance anxiously at Ash, who's firm nod gives me strength. I cross to where Willow lies.

Willow gazes at me, but there's a faraway look in his eyes. 'You really do look like her,' he says.

And because I don't know what else to do, I lean down and kiss him on the forehead. When I sit back up, he's smiling. The light leaves his eyes and the smile leaves his lips, but he is still the most beautiful man I have ever seen.

The cry from Jeremy's mouth is almost inhuman, animal in its rawness, its intensity. I can hear the gentle sobs of Nate, the awkward shuffle of the other Taleters. Fury pulses through me, lending me power and chasing away the grief. I clasp Jeremy by the face, digging my fingers into his cheeks. He is a broken man, but he *will* listen to me. 'We have stopped the virus launch,' I say. 'Your President is dead. Howard is dead.' I pause, saying Willow's name is too hard, so instead, I say, '*Your son* is dead. The serum was a hoax. Stop with this evil before more blood is spilled.'

Jeremy looks at me. I think for a moment he's going to order the other Taleters to kill me — my heart locks mid-beat — but instead he says, 'Carry my son to the surface.'

The Gems hoist Willow as though carrying him in an invisible coffin, and exit the lab. Jeremy doesn't even look at me, he just walks away. But before he does, he calls over his shoulder, 'The chambers are rigged with explosives. Release Oscar and he will initiate the self-destruct sequence. The virus will be lost for ever.'

Yan looks down at Oscar and grins. 'It's OK, I got the self-destruct sequence from him too. He's officially dispensable.'

'You can't,' I say to Yan. 'You can't, there are hundreds of dupes through there. If you set off the explosives, they die too.'

Yan exhales slowly. 'Violet, the canisters imploded, killing the virus before it was released. But all of the plans for how to engineer it again are here. They're in this room in some form, in the computer, in Oscar's head. There are no backups, *Oscar* is the backup.'

'So you're going to kill Oscar too?' I shout, incensed. 'Murder is murder, Yan. That makes us as bad as them.'

'I believe you just killed the President,' Yan snipes back. 'Or doesn't it count when you do it?'

We stare at each other for a moment. He's right. And it's our only chance to go home. Once the virus is destroyed for ever, once I've saved the Imps, I can save my little brother.

'Besides,' Yan whispers, 'why do you think the Dupes called to you?'

I shake my head, confused.

'Stuck in those tubes,' Yan says. 'Experimented on. Treated worse than animals.'

My hand covers my mouth. 'They want to die?' I whisper, my breath heating my palm.

Yan nods. 'Wouldn't you?'

I pause. 'It's time to go home, isn't it?'

I catch those winter eyes. My breath shudders and my heart aches. Ash. I'm about to leave him behind; the least I can do is protect him from another viral attack.

'Do what you need to do,' I tell Yan.

Nate steps forward, a look of confusion gripping his face. 'Can anybody else hear that?'

He has a distant look in his eyes.

'What is it?' I ask.

'I can hear singing.' He crinkles up his nose, like he does when he's concentrating. 'Somebody's singing "Happy Birthday".'

31

ALICE

I glance at Danny's Corsa. Traffic will be heavy and the hospital isn't far . . . I always was a fast runner. I take a few wobbly steps in my Jimmys, mutter, 'Bollocks to this,' and chuck them in the gutter. Then, I run faster than I've ever run towards the hospital. The soles of my feet hurt and my chest burns, but I press on all the same, thanking the lord for my long legs. I pummel down a main road, bumping into several pedestrians and ignoring their cries of indignation. The hospital comes into view and I swing across the street, nearly getting knocked over by a taxi. The blare of the horn spurs me on.

I reach the hospital slicked with sweat, my hair sticking to my head and neck, my chest aching and sucking for air that isn't there. I don't even glance at the receptionist, taking the stairs two at a time. Today is not a day to take the lift. I worry if I stop moving for even a second, I will collapse from exhaustion.

I reach the corridor of Nate's ward just in time to hear Adam and Jane sing 'Happy Birthday'. Their voices crack and bend under the weight of emotion, drifting down the corridor, mingling with the scent of candles.

I've made it, just in time.

I burst in to the room. 'STOP!' I shriek.

Adam and Jane are holding a chocolate cake out

with sixteen candles on it, the flames lightly flickering, casting shadows across Nate's face. They stop as soon as they see me, tear-lined faces freezing mid-song.

I take a deep, painful breath. 'No, Adam, Jane, please don't do this.'

'Alice . . .' Jane begins.

But a security guard has already arrived. 'Is everything OK in here?'

'No,' I shout, 'Everything is not OK. They're about to kill Nate, they're about to switch off his life support when we're so close. I've already lost Katie, I can't lose Nate too. And I know Violet can do it, I know she can. She's already killed Fanboy, she just needs a bit more time.'

'Violet's in a coma,' Adam says, his face filled with sorrow and sympathy.

'But she's going to wake up, I know she is, and Nate. Just give them a while longer, please.'

A doctor steps forward, a look of concern pinching her features. 'Miss, are you feeling OK?'

'Yes, I feel bloody marvellous, what do you think?' I laugh hysterically. I can feel myself unravelling, the frustration and desperation of people not listening to me starting to pull at the tiny threads which barely hold me together.

The doctor takes another step towards me. 'I think you need to just take a deep breath . . .'

Before I can stop myself, I'm reaching for her. I don't know why. I think I just want to make her understand. I don't intend her any harm, at least, I don't think I do. But the security guard doesn't see it that way. I feel his hands close around my shoulders and within seconds I'm being marched back into the corridor.

'NO!' I scream. 'Adam, Jane, please don't do this.'

'I'm sorry,' I hear Adam say.

I begin to sob. I sob and sob until my body feels like it's going to rattle apart. The security guard and a couple of nurses try to scoop me up, telling me to calm down, telling me to breathe, asking if they can call someone.

That's when I hear the flatline.

VIOLET

It hits me full force in the chest. And suddenly none of it matters. The virus. Oscar. All that matters is that through layers of time and space, somewhere, my parents are only moments away from turning off Nate's life support.

'Quickly,' I scream at Yan. 'Destroy the virus. The story needs to end before it's too late.'

Nate steps back and looks at me. 'I can hear something. A long tone.'

'Oh, please, no,' I whisper. We're too late.

As Nate stares at me, the light goes out in his eyes and, very slowly, he begins to crumple to the ground.

I start to weep, hot angry tears pulsing from my eyes. My brother is dead. My real brother back home, and my new brother who I'd come to love here in this world. The grief rips me into tiny pieces.

I expect the hand on my shoulder to be Ash's. But when I turn to look, it's Yan.

He smiles kindly, but it isn't his voice which emerges, it's Baba's. 'You were right, Violet. The story had to end in order for you to return home. But you didn't need to save the Imps; forgive me, that was my own agenda. Though save them you have, Little Flower.'

'Baba?' I whisper.

'Yes, my child.'

'But you're . . .'

'Yes. I'm dead. And this is not a ghost you are hearing, but a telepathic fragment, implanted in the other precogs just before I died. Kind of like a tape recording.' Yan laughs, and the way his face lights up, all full of wonder at the world, I know for that moment, Baba lives in him.

'I didn't need to save the Imps?' I say. 'What was the end of the story then?'

Yan smiles. 'You've got the right idea, my child. You've just got the wrong story.'

'What do you mean?' I ask, my voice wavering.

'It was never the Imps' story which needed to end. It was yours.'

'My story?'

'What was the ending to your story, Violet? Just close your eyes, and it will come to you.'

I close my eyes and it arrives just as she said.

In less than a week, my brother will die.

'Nate's death?' I whisper. 'Nate's death is the end of my story?' I feel the weight of my brother in my arms. Hear the flatline still ringing in my ears. 'Nate *had* to die in order for us to go home?'

Yan cradles my face. 'That's right, my child. But don't lose heart. All the best stories are stories of rebirth, wouldn't you say?'

But I barely hear the words. All I can hear is that sentence beating in my ears: *In less than a week, my brother will die.*

And I know that Baba is right.

My story has ended.

It's time to go home.

I open my eyes just in time to see Ash, sitting beside Yan, an anxious expression on his face.

271

'Goodbye, my love,' I whisper to him.

Then I'm moving away, faster and faster, like a train shooting down a tunnel.

I'm looking down on myself, on Nate, on all of us: Oscar lying on the floor, Yan crouched beside me, looking into the sky like he can see me escaping. And I see Ash, my wonderful Ash lowering my body to the ground. Tears spill down his cheeks, questions pour from his lips, and the bluest eyes I've ever seen gradually slip from view.

And then, as though waking from a dream, I open my eyes.

I'm covered in wires, needles in my hands, a tube up my nose.

I sit up suddenly. 'NATE!' I scream.

I jump out of bed, pulling needles and tubes from my body and flinging them on the bed, swearing as the pain smarts. My legs quaver and my head spins, and I briefly notice the mess of letters carved into my arm, but I have to get to Nate. He's only in the next ward.

'Nate!'

I stagger into the corridor. Alice is slumped on the floor weeping, a concerned security guard and a gaggle of nurses around her.

She looks up and sees me. Her face bursts into the biggest smile I've ever see. 'Violet! You're awake.' But then her face falls suddenly. 'It's too late. It's too late. He's already gone.'

'No!' I scream, my legs crumpling beneath me. 'Mum, Dad. You can't. You can't.'

I hear Mum's voice first, followed by Dad's. 'Violet? Is that Violet?'

They run into the corridor, their faces a mix of every emotion possible. To lose one child only to gain the

272

other. What must they be feeling? But I don't have time for empathy.

'What have you done?' I shriek, that flatline still ringing through the corridor.

It stops.

They help me to my feet and I hobble into Nate's room, my heart pounding, my chest heaving.

The doctors look at one another. 'Time of death . . .'

'No,' I cry, falling on to his bed, grasping at his face with trembling hands. 'Please no, not after all that. We were so close. So close.'

But I hear something in my head, a voice which doesn't belong to me. It's Yan. *It's going to be OK, Violet. All of the best stories end with —*

But he never gets to finish his sentence, because at that moment, I hear a sound. A sound which makes my stomach flip, makes my heart burst, makes the grey hospital walls flood with colour. A sound which sends the hospital staff into overdrive, brings my parents and Alice to their knees with joy.

A sound which can only mean one thing.

Rebirth.

Pip.

6 MONTHS LATER

VIOLET

Walking beside Nate through London still fills me with joy. I expected by now it would feel normal, having him beside me, prattling on about his newest sci-fi discovery. But I still can't quite believe it. Every so often, I throw my arms around him and tell him I love him. And without fail, he wriggles from my grip and tells me I'm a twat. But like me, he remembers his second visit to the world of *The Gallows Dance*; he remembers his bleak backstory, he remembers the virus and Katie dying, and he remembers waking up amidst a sea of stunned doctors, smoking birthday candles, and weeping family members. So the word twat is always followed up with, 'Love you too, sis.'

The London wind cuts through my parka; I'm hugely grateful when we round the bend and Frank's café comes into view, spilling its golden light and coffee-bean scent on to the street. Through the windows, clouded with condensation and lined with snow, we see Alice and Danny. They sit side by side, snuggled around a laptop and two steaming cups. Ever since we sat Danny down and explained the whole fantastical, twisted story, they've gone from strength to strength. Admittedly, it took a few hours to convince him we weren't collectively losing it, or he wasn't a victim of an elaborate prank, but having seen the

President inexplicably spewing blood from his chest and knowing the mystery surrounding our comas, he eventually believed us. And as Alice so blithely pointed out, someone who frequently asserts the existence of UFOs is in no position to quibble over transdimensional tunnelling.

Fortunately, neither Alice or Danny were implicated in the strange happenings at Timothy's flat that day. They told the police that they went to check on Timothy, only to find his corpse stuffed in a cupboard, and an unknown man dead on the floor. The evidence supported the fact that President Stoneback murdered Timothy, and the coroner found that the unidentified male died a week after this from a heart attack. Thankfully, the cut inflicted by Violet, visible above Stoneback's heart, was too superficial to result in death or account for the amount of blood loss in our world. He remains a mystery to medics and the authorities alike.

Only the four of us know the truth.

'There's Dalice,' Nate says, sticking two fingers into his mouth and pretending to retch.

I jab him with my elbow. 'Come on, they're cute.'

He laughs. 'Still a hopeless romantic, hey?'

I nod. I am a hopeless romantic. Losing Ash has only strengthened that. I mean, finding true love in an alternate universe has a way of firming up your belief in fate and, sadly, 'the one'. I say sadly, because that's the thing with 'the one': by definition, they're irreplaceable. Even now, I miss him more than I thought possible. Every shadow bends into his shape, every distant laugh spins my head as I hopelessly seek him out, and every morning, just before I wake, I feel the press of his skin against mine. Sometimes I wish I couldn't remember him this time round, then at least I could look at that achingly blue, winter sky without my vision smudging with tears.

Nate must notice the sudden change in my demeanour, cos he rests a hand on my shoulder. 'Maybe this isn't the end for you and Ash, maybe one day you'll cross over again.'

'God, I hope not,' I say, as glibly as I'm able. 'I don't think my heart could survive another stint in that place.' And therein lies the tragedy: the thing my heart craves above all else can exist only in a place which will surely be the death of me.

I open the door to the café, enjoying the comfort of the warmth and chatter as it wraps around me. We slide into the booth opposite Dalice. Without even a hello, they spin the laptop to face us.

'Ta-dah,' they sing together.

'Oh my God,' I cry, grabbing the laptop. 'This is beautiful, guys.'

A flock of golden swallows circle the top of the screen, free from the silver loops of barbed wire which glint below. And in the middle of the screen are three simple words: The Fandom Rising.

It was Alice's idea. We were brainstorming how to maintain the freedom of the Imps, not just from the Gems, but from us. From the authors, the publishers, the film company, the rogue fanfic writers. And she simply said, 'Maybe we should just give it to the Fandom.'

After my infamous meltdown at Comic-Con, the fans were intrigued for months. *Why should there never be a third book?* Well, the answer is about to be revealed: the third book isn't ours to write, the story no longer belongs to Alice and me, it belongs to the Fandom. Alice managed to convince Sally King's estate to approve the concept, she even sweet talked some really high-profile celebrities into getting involved with publicity. And whilst we finish our degrees, we'll gate-keep the fansite and ensure no single voice becomes dominant, that no single narrative can influence their world. Perhaps then, the Imps and Gems can write their own future.

Danny and Nate click on the various pages, talking in really high, excited voices. There's space to load fanfic, fanart, and fanvids; it looks amazing. Danny really is gifted at web design.

Alice reaches over and clutches my hand. 'She would have been so proud of you, Vi.'

I take a swig of coffee, tears burning my eyes. 'Maybe.'

'Maybe, my arse,' she replies. 'One hundred per cent bursting with it. You saved the Imps, brought Nate home, and now you're about to launch the most ambitious fansite out there.'

'I just wish she was here to see it,' I say.

Alice smiles. 'She kind of is.'

Danny clicks on the dropdown menu and a new page opens. It makes my heart ache and swell in equal measure. Photos of Katie stare at me from the computer. Her beautiful smile shines from the screen; at parties, playing in orchestras, dressed as a helix and squeezed between me and Alice. And written at the top in gold font: *This site is dedicated to our best friend, Katie.*

I reach across the table and pull Alice into a hug, weeping into her cherry-blossom hair and whispering my thanks. She holds me tight, and I can tell she's crying too. After a few minutes, she gently unpeels me from the embrace and fixes me in her inky-blue gaze. 'I'm sorry I couldn't write you a happier ending.'

My hand automatically lands on Nate's shoulder. 'It was happy enough,' I reply.

Some endings are black. Some endings burst with

colour. My ending, like the city in which I lost my darling Katie and left my one true love, sits in shades of grey.

Nate rests his hand on my own. 'Come on. It's time to give the power to the Fandom for real. Who wants to do the honours?'

'We do it together,' I reply.

I position the arrow and look hopefully at my three friends. One by one, they place an index finger over mine.

'Go,' I say. Together, we hit the publish button.

Something — a shadow or a distant laugh — pulls my gaze beyond the window and across the street to a solitary figure. His head is lowered and the passing traffic causes his shape to flicker in and out of view, but I recognise him all the same.

My heart soars. Laughter pushes from my lips and my body starts to shake as it floods with joy. Of course. The President crossed into our world; the tunnelling process works both ways. How did I not think of this before?

Nate gasps, following my gaze. 'Is that . . . ?' he asks.

But only as the figure raises his head, allowing a glimpse of those bluer than blue eyes do I dare to whisper, 'Yes.'

ACKNOWLEDGEMENTS

I have so many wonderful, supportive people to thank. Until I was published, I never realized quite how many people it takes to get a book on a shelf – it really is a team effort. So, here goes . . .

My darling children, Elspeth and Charlie. You have filled my life with love, laughter and joy. You are the centre of my universe and I am blessed to be your mum.

Simon Rainbow. Words can't express how happy I am to have you back in my life. Every day you amaze me with your love, kindness and inner strength. I didn't even need to transdimensional tunnel to realize that 'the one' is not a thing of myths. Bonus! May we always be like peas and carrots, Sweetheart.

Mum and Dad. I really do have awesome parents. Dedicating this book to you seems like such a small gesture when compared to the love and support you have given me my entire life. Thanks, guys!

Before I thank this person, I feel I need full disclosure: her name should be on the front cover too! Kesia Lupo, you are a star. Thank you so much for helping shape my messy, amorphous ideas into a novel. You are always so lovely, helpful and supportive, and you always see things so clearly. I absolutely love writing with you, thank you.

Chicken House Publishers, you really are a little book family. Special thanks to Barry Cunningham, for always being so supportive and believing in me as a writer, and to Rachel Leyshon for her faith in Alice and my ability to do her justice on the page. Huge thanks to Jazz Bartlett for her amazing publicity ideas and her sheer Fandom-enthusiasm, and a big thank you to Fraser Crichton, who I think may have a small planet for a brain; respect for understanding this plot better than me! And finally, huge thanks to Elinor Bagenal, who I maintain is a magical book-selling wizard – thank you so much for all your hard work both with *The Fandom* and *The Fandom Rising*; my writing has been translated into more languages and sold in more countries than I ever dared dream. Helen Crawford-White and Rachel Hickman, your covers are just beautiful, thank you so much for creating not one, but two, stunning book jackets.

My lovely readers, not just for all your advice and support, but for being such fantastic people: Isobel Yates, Heather Thompson, Jenny Hargreaves, Helen Spencer, Shanna Hughes, Lucy Fisher, Gill and Len Waterworth (aka Mum and Dad). And to Liam Gormley, for reading an early draft and reassuring me it was worth persevering.

The Big idea and the Times/Chicken House Children's Fiction competitions. Both of these competitions have enabled me to fulfil my dream. And thank you to Angela McCann for coming up with such a great concept for *The Fandom*, without which this book would not exist — I really hope you enjoy this sequel.

Over the past couple of years I've made some lovely writer friends; the writing community has been so welcoming and supportive. Thank you to all the wonderful authors, librarians and booksellers who have supported me. An extra big shout out to Melinda Salisbury, who I like to think of as Fandom's godmother, and to Shanna and N. J. Simmonds for their constant support and enthusiasm.

I wish I could thank every blogger here who has supported *The Fandom*, please know that just because I haven't mentioned you by name doesn't mean you aren't hugely appreciated. Across the globe, you have given your time, enthusiasm and support for zero fee, and I am so extremely grateful to you all. Thank you so much. Special shout out to the Northern Book Bloggers – thank you so much for your general awesomeness!

The foreign publishing houses and all the lovely people I've worked with over the past couple of years. I wish I could thank you all by name – please know that you have all helped build my confidence and courage to continue the Fandom story.

My fantastic niblings – Isobel, James, George and Alice Yates. You never fail to put a smile on my face. And a big thank you to Dr Dave Yates and Dr Helen Yates (aka sis) for their consultation around hospital and medical issues, and to Len Waterworth (aka Dad) and Alan Gronner, my lovely uncle, for their computer know-how.

And a final big thank you for reading this far, you've definitely earned a cup of tea!